DOWN
THERE
by the
TRAIN

DOWN THERE

by the

TRAIN

a novel

Kate Sterns

Shaye Areheart Books
NEW YORK

Published by Shaye Areheart Books, New York, New York.
Member of the Crown Publishing Group, a division of Random House, Inc.
www.crownpublishing.com

SHAYE AREHEART BOOKS and colophon are
trademarks of Random House, Inc.

Originally published in Great Britain by
Bloombury Publishing, London, in 2001.

Printed in the United States of America

Design by Lynne Amft

Library of Congress Cataloging-in-Publication Data
Sterns, Kate.
Down there by the train : a novel / by Kate Sterns.—1st ed.
p. cm.
1. Ex-convicts—Fiction. 2. Mothers—Death—Fiction. 3. Single
women—Fiction. 4. Stepmothers—Fiction. 5. Islands—Fiction. I. Title.
PR9199.3 S785D6 2003
813'.54—dc22   2003059515

ISBN 0-609-61015-5

10   9   8   7   6   5   4   3   2   1

First U.S. Edition

For Eva

What man is it that liveth and shall not see death?
JOHN DONNE

I began to think whether there might not be a motion, as it were, in a circle.
WILLIAM HARVEY

DOWN
THERE
by the
TRAIN

1

FOR A FELON IN A JOYNT

Dry Bay Salt and beat it with powder, and mix it with the yolk of an
Egge, and apply it to the grieved place in the beginning before the
Felon be broken: but if it be first broken then take the juyce of
Groundswel, the yolk of an Egge, a little Honey and Rye flower, mix
them wel together, and so apply it.

EVON HAWKE stared at the reflection of himself in the
window of Sweeney's Diner. His left hand clutched a letter
concealed inside the pocket of his red nylon jacket. He extended
his right hand toward the glass. Another hand, the mirror-image
of his own, reached out to meet it, as if to pull him through the
ripple of fingerprints into a looking-glass world, where words ran
backward and, he hoped, time did too.

Across the street stood a row of dilapidated Victorian redbrick
houses. Snow had piled in drifts at the sides and on the roofs, as
if they were packed in Styrofoam and had just now been lifted
out of their box. Their reflection was displayed in Sweeney's window like a Christmas toy.

The houses had been converted into apartments at the heel-
spin of the century and crammed with immigrant families. Next
to each doorbell was posted a handwritten menu of names: the
rickety chairs of Chinese script, the consecutive cigar rings of

Irish O'Somethings, a flea-market jumble of Eastern European consonants. Steam rose from boiling pots of pasta to soften the bristles of the upstairs Polish neighbor as he shaved.

Levon watched in the window as a woman scurried out to retrieve a rolled-up newspaper from the pavement. She wore a parka thrown over her nightgown and galoshes on her feet. Pink curlers nested in her hair like newborn hamsters. Here was the commencement of a morning routine: an alarm clock buzzing, lights switched on, fumbling kisses, curlers unrolled, teeth and hair brushed. Ah! The bird's wing-flap of a newspaper being spread open. The hunt for the prize in the cereal box. Levon fantasized about following the woman inside, seating himself at her kitchen table and begging her, whoever she was, to make room for him; to pass him the jam or a section of the paper, to accept his presence without any questions asked. Preposterous, of course. He'd given up on all that. He'd had to. Life was behind him. Or was it in front? Since he couldn't walk through either brick or Sweeney's glass, it was out of reach to him whichever direction it lay in, forward or back.

It didn't matter. Like the dog in the fable, Levon preferred the reflection of that bone-hard, bone-white world he'd let go of to the reality of it.

Light from a street lamp dissolved like a lozenge on a tongue of sunrise. He glanced at his watch, an old-fashioned wind-up Timex hanging loose around his slender wrist. The time was 7:06; or 6:07, he supposed, according to the glass, the little hand sweeping counterclockwise.

He, too, was traveling in a counterclockwise direction. It was two years since he'd last been in this neighborhood. Two years, six months and three days according to the precise records of the prison, from which Levon had been released an hour ago with all due ceremony of a dog being let out to pee.

His outstretched fingers collapsed at the joints into a fist. His knuckles rested on the glass. Step too far to the left or right of the window frame and he'd be erased from the scene as though he didn't exist. Of course, he *had* been erased, Levon reminded himself. Despite having lived four years in this neighborhood not even a fingerprint of his remained. (The prison authorities kept his on permanent file, a memento of his visit.)

Leaning in, he pressed his fist harder against the window.

He glanced around. Sweeney's was still here, obviously, and next door, the same boarded-up driving school. On the other side of it, a corner shop that sold cigarettes and newspapers, a notice-board tacked up outside with grubby white index cards pinned to it, the ends curled up like soiled bandages, advertising cars for sale and available babysitters.

Levon shivered from the cold. So did his counterpart. That was the thing about a looking-glass world; unlike the real one, it was sympathetic to him. Here was Fergus Street: unchanged, uncaring, oblivious to all that had happened to him in the intervening years; whereas the glass he smashed the night of his arrest had fallen completely to pieces, just as *he* had done, it being so soon after Alice's death. Shards of shattered glass had lodged in his skin without his even being aware of it. Later, as the police surgeon sewed up his bloodied hand, Levon wondered, in a detached manner, how deep he'd have to be cut to find any real tenderness in himself. His wounds healed in time, except for a splinter of glass that had evaded the surgeon's tweezers and embedded itself in his skin, causing a callused bump, like a grave mound, to cover over the infected area. He smiled, recalling that the old word for an inflamed sore—*one who, or that which, is filled with bitterness or poison*—was *felon.*

Thinking of the splinter, Levon angled his injured hand toward the glass. Shen Nung, the ancient emperor and physician, father of Chinese pharmacopoeia, was rumored to have incised a hole in his abdomen and installed a window in it. Using a mirror, he was able to examine his internal organs and judge the efficacy of the various remedies he'd administered to himself. Superimposed on the chipped white paint advertising Sweeney's "daily" specials, Levon saw only himself, pale and delicate as a chicken bone sucked clean of meat. He saw a wound, but no cure for it.

He sniffed the air and caught the faint metallic whiff of an incipient snowfall. How odd it felt to care about the weather once again, to stand outside, unprotected from the elements. The wind plucked at his jacket, pinched his cheeks, tweaked his nose and flattened his hair, behaving like a demented photographer about to take Levon's portrait. He grinned toothily at the window.

—Cheese, he said.

Why hadn't Sweeney opened up yet? He sighed. The world operated in such lackadaisical fashion compared to prison.

Levon withdrew his hand and jammed it into his other pocket. He gazed balefully up at his old apartment, located above the diner, where, back in time, he would have been enjoying the warmth of his snug kitchen, his fingers laced around a mug of steaming coffee, a book propped up against the sugar canister in front of him. William Harvey's *De Motu Cordis.* The prison authorities had returned his wallet (nearly empty) and his watch (his time also empty) along with his key—Levon felt the serrated metal against his skin—but it opened no doors for him now. Following the trial, his parents had boxed up his meager possessions and shipped them off to be buried in their damp, earthen basement, gathering dust and mold, or disintegrating altogether, including Levon's abandoned Master's thesis, *William Harvey and His Use of Metaphor: Implied Narrative in Medical Histories.*

Perhaps that's the reason he was standing here outside Sweeney's Diner. Blood was impelled to move in a circle; Levon had merely surrendered to a similar compulsion.

An old-fashioned Coca-Cola sign hung above the door, creaking in the breeze. Red plastic letters that could be removed or scrambled to make new words were slotted into ledges, like a child's learn-to-read toy. The first line said: SWEENEY'S DINER. REPUTABLE SINCE 1955. Underneath that was an advertisement for the $2.99 BREAKFAST. SERVED ALL DAY. And then: GO D EATS HERE.

He blinked twice, speculating as to whether Sweeney had succumbed in his old age to an uncharacteristic bout of religious fervor. Levon's aunt, Anna-Lee, had switched from the Anglican church to the Pentecostal after her divorce (*More action!* she claimed), and now spoke in tongues. Without stopping, his father grumbled.

Levon soon identified the problem: there was a gap between the *o* and the *d.* A letter had slipped its mooring and sailed off on the wind. A missing, what, consonant? Gord eats here. No, of course not. A vowel, then. An *o.* That was it. The sign should have read: GOOD EATS HERE. God was meant to be good. How scandalized Anna-Lee would be at the notion that He was a mere typo: an error, an absence. Levon guffawed. Religion, Harvey's great discovery, grief—that's all it boiled down to in the end: a red *o.* A bloody circle with nothing at the center of it.

To occupy his time while waiting for Sweeney's to open, Levon decided to search for the letter. First, he looked about at his feet but saw no telltale splash of red.

He'd have to seek it farther afield.

The snow on the pavement was worn down and grubby as an old bar of soap. Ice, partially thawed, then frozen again, felt nubbly on the soles of his shoes. He trod accidentally on a patch of smoother ice and his feet shot forward while his upper body jerked back, as if a rug had been yanked out from under him. His arms windmilled in an undignified effort to right himself. He would have to watch his step. His shoes were prison-issue after all, designed to stick only to the straight and narrow.

Hunched over almost double, Levon investigated all the nooks and crannies into which the letter might have drifted. He spread out in an ever-increasing circle from Sweeney's doorstep. The street's detritus was primarily confined to cigarette butts, used bus tickets and smudged, inky receipts for groceries but here and there were items of more interest: a child's purple woolen glove with the thumb chewed off, a theater ticket for the following week's production of García Lorca's *Blood Wedding*, an unopened packet of violin strings, a crumpled page of the Personals with one advertisement circled in red. *(Short, balding middle-aged man seeks nineteen-year-old blonde for companionship and moonlit walks.)* Then, half a block down, in front of the corner shop, sticking out amid a small pile of discarded soft-drink cans and candy wrappers, he saw it: the errant, the lost, the desired *o*.

He returned, the letter pinched gingerly between his thumb and forefinger, to discover the CLOSED sign on Sweeney's door had been flipped over. Levon reached for the handle. He realized with a start that this would be the first door opened of his own volition in a long time. In prison, doors were controlled electronically, the mechanism emitting ominous clicks and clanks as they slid back and forth in front of the helpless inmates, like an army parading its weapons after a successful *coup d'état*.

Levon's reflected self watched with an amused smirk as he indulged in a vision of his triumphal entrance into Sweeney's. The prodigal returned. Eager to prove his musings true, Levon pulled confidently on the handle.

The door did not budge.

Sweeney must have forgotten to unlock it when he changed the sign. Levon tugged again to make sure, then rattled it in frustration. He was about to pound on the glass when he noticed a square of cardboard taped above the handle. On it was handwritten a single-word instruction: PUSH.

Sheepishly, Levon did so.

He entered the diner through a mist caused by his breath on the glass.

Time had not run backward in Sweeney's but marched on, and in muddy boots from the state of the floor. Dog-eared posters, distributed free by the Businessman's Association, advertised the city's main tourist sites: the university clock tower that ran fast, as if exhorting the students to run, run, run to keep up with it; the harbor; the fort, now maintained by the tourist dollars of a nation it had been built to keep out; and the Italianate villa of the country's first prime minister.

On the right side of the room were three stools and a counter. Behind that stood the grill, a large stainless-steel refrigerator and a revolving pastry cabinet. The shelves were stacked not with the usual wedges of coconut, apple and pumpkin pie but with well-thumbed Penguin Classics.

Two cramped rows of booths occupied the other side of the room, the seats stiff-backed as pews, upholstered in beige vinyl chapped with age. A miniature jukebox was installed at each table. For reasons no one dared to ask, Sweeney programmed them to play only heartbreak songs: "I'd Rather Go Blind," "I'm So Lonesome I Could Cry," "You're Right, I'm Left (She's Gone)." Each tune a tear-stained hankie left behind by the booth's previous occupant.

Here it was, seven-thirty and no one in the place except Levon and Frank Sinatra. Quite unlike the atmosphere Levon remembered when, even at 6 A.M., at least a couple of elderly Italian gentlemen would be here already, sipping coffee, griping about their wives *(those saints!)*, or, perhaps, a psychiatric outpatient mumbling over his plate in several different voices, Sweeney listening attentively to all of them.

A clock ticked its disapproval of this state of affairs—*tsk, tsk, tsk*—and Levon agreed. En route to the diner, he had passed a new fast-food restaurant, the kind that infantilized its customers by forcing them to use googly, babyish names to order a simple hamburger. Had Sweeney's customers all defected to it? The bleary-eyed students he allowed to sit hour after hour for the price of a coffee; the single mothers who ate on credit; Frank, the "Midnight Cowboy," all the other neighborhood crazies?

—Take a seat, said a voice. I don't mean that literally, of course.

A dappled cranium rose up from beneath the counter.

Sweeney at least had not altered. He was in his late seventies, tall and broad-shouldered. His rounded stomach, packed into a white T-shirt, melted like a scoop of vanilla ice cream over the rim of his apron. When still a young man, he tried his hand at acting in Hollywood. Preston Sturges even cast him in a bit part in *Sullivan's Travels*. He had directed Sweeney to say his single line over and over again, then cut it out in the final edit. The lingering disappointment of that experience left Sweeney with a habit in real life of speaking with conviction and of never repeating himself.

Levon pulled out a stool and sat down.

—What can I get you?

—Eggs, scrambled, toast, coffee and . . .

He stared at Sweeney's ears. They were pinkish and slightly wrinkled with white, fatty lobes.

—Bacon, he concluded.

Sweeney crossed his arms over his chest.

—Aren't you forgetting something?

—Uh, I don't think so.

—Think again.

—Hash browns? Levon ventured.

—Say *please*.

—Oh. Excuse me. Please.

Sweeney lifted a pot off the burner, slopped coffee into a cup and pushed it toward him. There was a lipstick stain on the rim. Levon considered asking for another but thought better of it. Sweeney had grown up during the Depression; in a service economy, he upheld economy over service.

Or leave a kiss but in the cup. Levon lifted it to his lips. Whoever the woman was, she had a generous mouth. He ran his tongue across the impression of her bottom lip, blew gently on it, then pressed his mouth flush against the white porcelain. A tongue of scalding coffee mingled with his own before sliding, not without a trace of bitterness, down his throat.

—You new here?

—What?

Sweeney's eyes were the iridescent green of a pond gilded by the sun. A glint now appeared in them, like a fish hook catching the sunlight, various thoughts swimming suspiciously around it.

—We got five prisons here, you know, Sweeney told him.

—Really?

—This city is founded on people's mistakes.

The *o*, which Levon had brought with him into the diner, was pinned underneath his saucer. He wriggled it free and, placing his forefinger in the hole, scooted it across the counter in Sweeney's direction.

—What's that?

Levon smiled at him.

—A red-letter day, he said. Don't you remember me, Sweeney?

—Should I?

—I'd like to think so.

The old man stroked his whiskery chin, his fingers stained the color of dried apricots from smoking. He scrutinized Levon's physiognomy.

—You look older, Sweeney said at last.

—Yeah, Levon shrugged. Well.

His prison file noted that he was twenty-five years old, stood five feet six inches in his stockinged feet, and weighed one hundred and thirty pounds. Blood type A positive. No distinguishing features apart from a front tooth he broke after a childhood tumble from a bike and never had capped. Shaped like a guillotine, the tooth had acted as one, chopping off the first syllable of his sentences. His file did *not* say that, for a time, only his sister, Alice, could understand what he said. He'd outgrown his impediment long ago, and Alice was dead, but he still felt the same.

—Jeez. Levon Hawke. How are you?

—Fine, thank you. And you?

—Fine, thanks.

Sweeney laid out strips of bacon on the grill.

—When did you get out? he said.

—Couple of hours ago.

—That so? How does it feel?

The bacon began to buckle in the intense heat.

—Feel? said Levon.

—Yeah. You know.

Did he? Levon drummed his fingers on the countertop as he pondered the question. Looking inward to his emotions did not come naturally to him; he wasn't convinced there remained any left to observe had he done so. Since Alice's death he had felt . . . well, numb. He experienced *physical* sensations: hunger, cold, exhaustion. For a short while after the accident, he had even sensed a phantom pressure in the crook of his arm where he'd cradled Alice's head, pressing her ear against his heart as if demonstrating the proper beat to a faltering musician. Hear, this is how it goes. Listen, *listen*. She, gasping for breath, was unable to speak while he, facing the loss of something so much greater than mere words, had cried out to her. His anguished howl had echoed in the chamber of his ear and then, like Alice herself, died slowly away.

Since then, though, he had not been able to manufacture in himself a credible, identifiable emotion apart from grief, which itself was no emotion but a guard against them; a pair of sharp scissors patrolling the garden, snipping off buds the minute they appeared. For his parents' sake, he learned to counterfeit feeling and in that, whisky had helped. For a time, until prison took over in keeping the real world at bay, Levon had preferred the taste of Famous Grouse to anything else. He carried a bottle concealed in his rucksack wherever he went, stealing fortifying nips throughout the day. His glassy eyes were then able to reflect back to his parents their own loving concern; to others—at least, those who did not avert their eyes altogether—his expression mirrored their kindness, or their contempt or their boredom. Levon became so proficient at it that, for a time, people marveled at how splendidly he was coping with the tragedy. It was a neat trick, an illusion. He had learned in a high-school geography class that a lake froze from the top down; ice never extended to the bottom, thus preserving marine life during the winter. Levon reversed the process. Deep down he was frozen while on top he was a watery mirror, waving merrily back to people who sensed, perhaps, that if they actually stopped to dip a toe in, they might find him too cold for their liking.

Curiosity, on the other hand, was trickier to forge. Especially with a canny old bird like Sweeney. Levon supposed he could, in turn, reflect back curiosity about *Sweeney*; but that wouldn't be accurate. Even if it was a mere courtesy, Sweeney's interest was in *him*, Levon.

What's more, Levon had to consider the possibility that offering a genuine response to Sweeney's question was something he very much wanted to do.

He gazed out the window at a group of gangly teenaged boys converging for an early-morning game of road hockey. Some wore the sweaters of their favorite team, the Toronto Maple Leafs or the Montreal Canadiens, but most were in hand-me-down ski jackets or bulky sweaters, unraveling at the wrist and neck, knitted in jaunty butterfly colors.

Nets were being positioned at either end of the street to catch them.

For his part, Sweeney didn't rush Levon. He had met enough prisoners in his lifetime to understand that being released was a gradual process. What had that poet said? *All men are sleeping prisoners.* Slow to wake up to the world. John Do. Did. Donne. That was it. John Donne. Third shelf down, where the banana cream pie used to go, back when he had customers. Who had lent him that book? Poor old Frank, must have been. Loopier than a roller coaster. Donne had clung on, however, through all the ups and downs of Frank's various medications. Frank said he preferred the sermons to the poems. Twisting a white paper napkin into a dog collar, he used to recite them in a booming voice that, Sweeney reckoned, *would* drive a man mad if he had it ricocheting off the confined space of his skull. Frank had recently returned to the psychiatric hospital for one of his periodic spells of incarceration. Sweeney missed the edification of his visits.

He cracked the pates of two eggs, dribbled the contents into a bowl, added salt and pepper and beat them together. That done, he poised the whisk in midair, golden ribbons dripping from it. For a moment, Sweeney resembled a down-at-heel general who had pinned his medals to his undershirt.

—How does it feel? Levon repeated dreamily.

He returned his attention to Sweeney.

—Like I've snatched a purse, a thing of value that's not mine to keep, and I've got to keep running or they'll catch me. It's not the relief I expected it to be.

—I never heard what you did. It wasn't murder, was it?

—Don't be ridiculous, said Levon.

The eggs spread in the grease, crinkling at the edges.

—Fraud?

Sweeney inserted two slices of bread into a toaster and depressed the lever. Shoulder to shoulder they descended, two miners down a shaft, still white at the start of their shift, but soon to be blackened and smelling faintly of carbon.

Levon motioned toward the letter on the counter.

—Are you aware, he said, that your sign out front claims God eats here?

—Really? It says that?

—Uh huh.

—Those damn kids.

—That's all it is then? A prank?

Sweeney chuckled.

—You don't believe in signs, do you?

—Yes, I do.

Levon took another sip of coffee.

—Beware of dog, he said.

BEWARE OF DOG. He ought to have noticed the sign taped to the window. Looking back on it, that night had been crowded with signs: burning bushes, locked doors, dogs. The works.

He was oblivious to them all.

Levon had flown back to the city for the autumn semester, a few weeks after Alice's funeral. His return was due to his grandfather's wishes, not Levon's. The old man was a carpenter, an immigrant whose Polish name, his last remaining link to his motherland, was snipped like an umbilical cord on his arrival in the New World. His surname had shriveled to Hawke and a little of his pride with it. He regarded the English language as he did fish forks and water bowls; the correct placement of verb and subject baffled him. *Turn to your mind other things,* he advised Levon, as though the mind was a lathe that could fashion for him thoughts other than of Alice's death. How could Levon explain to him that all the information he'd acquired during his studies meant nothing now? His grandfather saw in the old, square-cut limestone buildings a testament to learning; Levon saw headstones. Even his beloved medical-history textbooks, which he shelved nights at the library, were no longer tomes but tombs, enclosing dead men's dead ideas. *I have poor and unhappy brains for thinking,* he scrawled on a postcard to his grandfather.

He had emerged that night from the library at around nine o'clock—the books he'd shelved would remain untraceable, wildly out of order, for months and months—to find the air singed with smoke from various bonfires. The dwindling of Indian summer was being celebrated in parks and backyards all over the city. Crackling voices of hyper children up past their bedtime mingled with the snap of fed-up parents, and of branches and leaves being munched in the flames. A pall of smoke wound around the city, unseen in the darkness but woolen and scratchy on the throat. Too hot to be comfortable on that mild evening.

Levon was wary of fire. Any fire. Candles bothered him. *(Here comes a candle to light you to bed. Here comes a chopper to chop off your head.)* Matches, too. When lighting his cigarette he closed his eyes until he had shaken out the flame. Fires with their shiny Christmas colors boxed in a fireplace? He preferred not to open them. And now these bonfires! Jumping about in the open, reaching out to him, as eager to ensnare him as the Holy Rollers his aunt once invited to camp out in the field behind his parents' house. His skin prickled with sweat.

He whorled his last gulp of whisky around on his tongue before swallowing, then planted the empty bottle, neck down, in a flowerbed. He licked his dried lips at the prospect of this fiery netherworld the city had become, a Hell he'd have to navigate in order to find his way home.

The *refrigerated* blood returns to the heart, *the fountain, the dwelling-house,* where by *naturall heat, powerfull and vehement, it is melted and is dispens'd again through the body, being fraught with spirits.*

Levon's heart, his dwelling-house, was certainly haunted. Not by the vital spirits William Harvey believed resided in the blood, but by the spirit of his sister. He was fraught with grief, *powerfull* and *vehement* all right. It compelled his brain to circle back continuously to the glorious days of summer just a few short weeks before, when the watery tines of sprinklers had raked the grass; and the air, pulpy in its humidity, was redolent with the scent of overripe apples rotting in the orchards. Weather forecasters had predicted an early fall. Nobody had believed them, least of all Levon.

Until the accident.

Levon left the campus and drifted north up Carnegie Street, then along Newhouse and over to Jane Street, toward his apartment. City planners had nudged this unappetizing neighborhood to the side of the plate and, opting for a shortcut, he found himself meandering through a jumble of dimly lit, garbage-strewn streets until, after a wrong turn, he mistakenly entered a cul-de-sac. A dead end.

He was about to double back to Jane Street and continue home when the sight of a redbrick bungalow brought him to a halt. His breath caught in his throat and ripped on something sharp that lodged there. He could scarcely credit it but here—positively, incontrovertibly, undeniably—stood his parents' house. A modern, two-story brick at odds with the limestone the rest of the city was built of. Look, there was the green plastic awning over a cement porch on which a couple of garden chairs, for his grandparents, were placed companionably side by side. And while he couldn't see it, he knew a green snake of garden hose lay curled in the grass; that the kitchen smelled of cooked onions and that, taped to the wall, were prized examples of his and Alice's grade-school artwork; fading blotches of color on construction paper with each artist's name scripted neatly by the teacher next to a gold star or a frilled tissue-paper rosette.

His dwelling-house.

Levon wove eagerly, if drunkenly, up the path, then up the cement steps to the front door, which was half wood, half glass. He flattened his nose against it, searching for signs of Alice: her soccer shoes, the ladybug barrette *(Your house is on fire, your children have flown!)* that always clung to her hair, the bottle of pink calamine lotion that ended up as artistic daubs on her sturdy, tanned legs and arms.

Leave truth to the police, Auden wrote. However, neither the fact that Alice was eighteen when she died, no longer a child; nor that their parents' house was out west, a thousand miles from here; nor the police themselves, would impinge on Levon's consciousness until much later.

His parents had left the porch light on as usual but his key wouldn't fit in the lock. Odd. Perhaps he'd damaged it. Never mind. He bent down and rooted under the Welcome mat until his fingers enclosed the spare key. Levon was grateful his parents hadn't heeded his advice to hide it elsewhere. Lucky for them he wasn't a burglar. You couldn't be too careful these days.

Inserting the key into the lock, Levon opened the door and proceeded to wander back into his childhood.

A skewed version of it, as it happened.

The kitchen was not, as he believed, at the back and to the right but on the left side of the house. Swimsuits, adults' and children's, hung drying on door handles and chair backs, giving off a powerful odor of chlorine. Levon had grown up in the Prairies, where it was only tall grass that waved and a sweetheart's affection could drown you. He never learned to swim.

He opened the fridge, sprinkling the kitchen with a powdery blue light. Inside was a tub of potato salad, a six-pack of beer and the muddy remains of a chocolate birthday cake.

Taped to the wall next to the fridge was a Milk Board calendar. Idly, he glanced at that day's date.

Scrawled in the appropriate square was the word *Robbery*.

Well *that* was an odd thing to plan for. Come to think of it, though, he once opened his mother's personal diary to discover certain days marked with a red dot. *My period*, she explained briskly, without going into further detail. Levon had remained mystified for several years why anyone, even a teacher, would set aside days for punctuation.

He blinked once or twice, then looked again. Ah. Rob's *birthday*. That made more sense. Except it didn't. He knew of no Rob. No uncles, cousins, co-workers or neighbors of that name. Why, then, had his mother baked a birthday cake for him?

Levon might have spent longer examining this problem if another had not presented itself. There, open on the kitchen table, was a fourth-grader's math primer. Alice's homework. Sketched in the margins were calculations in her familiar hand, the numbers written in great loops, like a bird circling way over her head. Math was not her strong suit but Levon enjoyed it. His math teacher, a rotund man tightly casked in trousers belted under his armpits, often scribbled math equations that took up the entire length of the chalkboard. He then bounded ahead of his students, an enthusiastic scoutmaster pointing out exotic flora and fauna to his troops. While the rest of the class slumped miserably in their seats, doubled over as if suffering terribly, but in noble silence, from acute appendicitis, Levon's hand shot up, volunteering to solve the problem.

Not Alice. Storm clouds of rubbed-out pencil scudded across the page of her math book. Thinking to help his sister out, Levon picked up a pencil, wet the tip of it with his tongue, and began to write.

Addition, subtraction, multiplication and division.

Ambition, Distraction, Uglification and Derision, a pedantic, rather melancholy voice echoed in his head.

This was *simple*.

Suffused with noble purpose, Levon carried numbers over, through and under, like a soldier returning with wounded comrades across enemy lines.

He flipped the page.

Fractions. Harder but still manageable.

He was girding himself to tackle them when his elbow knocked against a glass of half-drunk milk. (Oh Alice, Alice.

Everything half finished. What *will* become of you?) It clattered
to the floor, splintering into a thousand pieces. A jagged prow of
glass protruded from a foamy winter sea, surrounded by flotsam
and jetsam. Levon got down on his knees and hurriedly began to
pick them up, anxious about what his mother would say to him
about this mess.

Just then, he heard a heavy tread on the porch surrounded by
lighter steps. The sound of voices. Whispers, giggles. Had his
family been at the bonfires all this time? He heard the door knob
being turned.

And another noise, at once unfamiliar and dreadful.

A howl, tossed like a bone down the corridor. This was followed
by a rapid clicking of sharp nails against wood as the dog raced to
fetch it. This startled Levon so much that he lost his balance and
fell onto the glass, cutting his hands. Something was wrong here.
Alice was allergic to . . . they'd never owned a . . . but . . . here it
was. The beast, a brindle terrier, seemed exceedingly pleased to
discover waiting for him in the kitchen a real bone, padded with
flesh, to deposit at the feet of its astonished masters.

Who were, needless to say, complete strangers to Levon.

—I got caught, said Levon, doing homework.

Sweeney regarded him, baffled.

—*Homework?*

—Not my own. The law was clear on that point.

—A real thief leaves nothing of himself behind. Not fingerprints. Acts of kindness neither.

—I'm not a thief, Levon protested.

—That was a harsh sentence you got.

—The judge's house was broken into the night before the trial. He wanted to send a message, I guess.

Levon swallowed his coffee. Bitter, stewed too long in the pot. He banged the sugar container on the counter to loosen the granules. The noise reminded him of prison guards patrolling the corridors, tapping their batons against the cell bars, testing for weakness in the iron and the men behind them.

Outside, the game was in full swing. Hockey sticks waggled like rudders, anticipating the ball's every shift in direction, testing whether it was to be luck, skill or brute force that would catapult the boys' goals beyond the parameters of their street. One of the goalies, his skin pocked and oily as an orange peel, white as the pith underneath, flipped the bird to a chunky kid on the opposing team who, seeing the net was undefended, spotted his chance and took it. He pulled back, dreaming of a career in the National Hockey League (the perfect arc of a slap-shot carried more hope of salvation than Noah's) and let loose. The ball careened off the goalpost's metal rim and bounced once, twice, three times . . . an ellipsis, trailing off down the street until another kid, a hanger-on, his boots too big for his feet, raced after it, scooping it up and tossing it back to the waiting players who pounced on the gray, furry tennis ball like ravenous wolves on a fieldmouse.

—My criminal days are over, Sweeney, said Levon.

He produced from his jacket pocket a letter folded in tight, even squares as though, from the letter's contents, he could fix for himself a latitude and longitude. He smoothed it open on the counter and read aloud:

Levon,

Come to the island. I will teach you how to make Finnish Pulla, Ka'kat and Leaf-Shaped Fougasse. Also, Couronnes, Croissants and Grape Cluster Pain de Campagne. You can learn how to bake blind, a silk handkerchief tied around your eyes, and poach apricots without getting caught. Which, from your recent incarceration, I judge you could use some help with. As I need yours.

> *Your cousin,*
> *Simon Tibeault*

Sweeney dumped an island of egg and a sprig of parsley onto Levon's plate, arranged the wavy bacon and two triangular sails of toast, well buttered, beside it, and set it down with a flourish on the counter.

—A tad whimsical, this cousin of yours, he observed.

—I was granted early parole on the condition that I accept the job. I'm supposed to start tomorrow.

—Ever been to that island? Sweeney quizzed him.

Levon shook his head. During the summers, his university pals used to hop on the ancient ferry that chugged between the city and the island, picnicking and swimming in the coves, while he went out west to be with Alice. The island had a Native name of about a dozen syllables that meant either Long Island Standing Up or Short Island Sitting Down, or something like that. He couldn't recall. At any rate, the Natives had been unceremoniously polished off centuries before and with them, the name, until it was simply referred to as "the island." Levon's mother was a Tibeault but her branch of the family had vacated the island two or three generations before. Simon's letter had come as a complete surprise, the formality of its invitation matched by the neat calligraphy of the letters.

—I'll tell you a story about it, said Sweeney.

He refilled Levon's cup and poured himself the syrupy dregs of the coffee pot.

—Around 1849, a wireless operator sent a telegraph from there to County Cork, Ireland. They wanted fifty tailor's needles. Lives more often than words were lost on those voyages but, in this case, the message, when it arrived, read: NEED FIFTY TAILORS. What my dad, a printer, used to call a *pie*, you know, when the text gets muddled up like that. Like in a pie where there's all different kinds of fruit in it. Or it might have been so-called from the print types used in the old pre-Reformation book of rules. The ordinal was referred to as a pica, or pie, due to the rules being printed in black type on white paper, *pica* being the Latin for *magpie*, or maggot-pie as Shakespeare . . .

—Sweeney, Levon groaned, what's this got to do with the island?

The old man pursed his lips in disapproval.

—Stories follow on from other stories. That's how they live on, just like people. You can't just knot them and break off any old where or they die out. There has to be (and here he drew an invisible needle through an invisible cloth from his palm up to his ear in one fluid motion) follow-through.

—In due course (he continued) fifty tailors arrived on the island. I expect the island was scarcely big enough to contain their disappointment. Despite the misunderstanding, they made the best of a bad job. The majority of the islanders are descendants of those tailors.

Levon considered this information as he chewed his toast. He hadn't found the idea of living on the island, working for his cousin the baker, all that appealing. But if what Sweeney told him was true, the island might in fact be the ideal place for him. He was a pie, too, in a manner of speaking. His prison sentence had left him with mixed-up thoughts he couldn't make sense of to himself let alone to anyone else.

In geographical terms, the island acted as a stepping-stone between this shore and the next. Levon would regard it as a resting place, a peaceful spot where he might replenish his low spirits before moving on to somewhere else.

—What's your cousin like? Sweeney asked him.

—Never met him before.

He was adding ketchup to his eggs when an energetic thwack sent a spurt of red sauce hurtling over the counter.

—Careful, Sweeney barked. Ketchup don't grow on trees.

He plopped a damp rag over the mess and swirled it around.

—So why's he helping you?

Levon shrugged.

—Blood is thicker than water, I guess.

—And messier when it spills, Sweeney commented darkly.

Cramming the remains of his breakfast into his mouth, Levon jerked down a final swallow of coffee and wiped his lips.

—I'd better get moving. They expect me today and the morning's already half over.

—And just how were you planning to get to the island?

—By water, Levon muttered. How else would I go?

—Can't. Cutbacks, repairs. Plus a contretemps over the issue of fares. Only one ferry a day running to the island at the minute and you've missed it.

Levon threw up his hands.

—I've missed the boat. Isn't that typical? What am I supposed to do now?

He ran his fingers through his unruly hair, wavy as slivered cabbage.

—Could I walk? he ventured. It doesn't look more than a few miles out.

The prison overlooked the lake. From his cell, Levon had been able to view the island: a strip of black felt appliquéd to the horizon and stitched in place with a row of waves.

Sweeney smiled indulgently.

—Do a cheating Jesus, you mean?

—Excuse me?

—Walk across the frozen water. Islanders do it. The ice is thick at this time of year but there's always a risk.

—Ah.

—Can you swim?

—No, he admitted.

He tapped Simon's letter with his index finger.

—Will you draw me a map?

—You're determined to go, then?

Levon nodded, planting his bony elbows on the counter like the points of a protractor.

—I'll be in trouble with my parole officer if I don't.

Using a stub of pencil normally reserved for writing down orders, Sweeney quickly sketched a diagram on the reverse of the letter.

—Here's what you do. Stay away from the ferry route. The boat breaks a path through the ice every day.

He placed a hand, nicked from knife cuts same as the counter was, on Levon's wrist.

—That territory is hazardous to you. Head east is my advice and when you get to the shore, double back to the village.

Levon was shaken by the seriousness of Sweeney's tone.

—How long will it take me?

—Barring unforeseen circumstances, you'll reach the island before dark.

Sweeney lifted the glass dome off a plate of donuts, wrapped two in a napkin and handed them to Levon.

—Thanks, Sweeney.

—You know, I loved a woman who lived on that island once.

—What happened?

—It was a long time ago, he said softly.

He held out his hand to Levon, who took it. On the back of Sweeney's wrist were sparse dark hairs, fine as the scratches on the wall prisoners used to mark their time.

2

TO SHARPEN A SICK MAN'S APPETITE, AND TO RESTORE HIS TASTE

Take Wood or Garden Sorrel one handful, boyl it in a pint of white wine Vinegar til it be very tender, strain it out, and put to it Sugar two ounces and boyl it to a syrup and let the patient take of it any time.

L EVON EXITED the diner at the exact moment a hockey player was being dragged off by his mother. The captain, square white teeth billowing out of his mouth like handkerchiefs on a clothesline, immediately press-ganged Levon into replacing the missing teammate. Levon demurred, joking that his muscle definition was to be found only in the *Oxford English Dictionary*. The boys cajoled him into it, though, and he quickly amazed himself, and his team, with his considerable skills in defense. His approach was to regard the net as the lungs of the game: skinless, exposed and vulnerable, a delicate interweaving of vein and artery, blood and oxygen pumping through them in a continuous circle (the manufacturer's stamp was even dyed in a red-and-blue pattern on the threads). All it took for a gaping hole to be made in it was a sixteen-year-old boy's attention to slip, and his foot with it. Levon understood the danger of that happening all too well.

He never knew what had gone wrong that afternoon. The weather was clear, no rain or fog. The intersection wasn't crowded; a goodbye kiss lasted longer than a stroll down the main thoroughfare of his small town. What had the boy been avoiding? A squirrel? A drifting leaf? His fate? He'd sworn his hand was firmly on the gearshift; he was alert and in control of the car, except for a brief moment when, for that unknown reason, he swerved. Levon recalled that he wore a snazzy pair of snakeskin boots; also, that he'd managed to walk away from the accident in them. The boy was sorry, of course he was *sorry*, but by then it was too late; Alice's lungs were punctured. She was bleeding internally.

There seemed to be a dispute about the scoring. Levon consulted with the player closest to him, a boy with sandy hair and black roots, like an oil slick on a beach.

—Overtime, he explained. Sudden death.

Levon glanced reflexively at his watch. Noon. The two hands clapped together reminded him to get going. The January sky was a pasty white veined with leafless treetops. There would be little enough light as it was. Ceremoniously, he proffered his stick to his captain. Levon was tempted to quote from Homer but knew he'd be asked what team Homer played on, and what position, and what his number was. His number was up. Now the Greats wore skates.

Warmed up after his unaccustomed exertions, it wasn't until Levon had strolled the ten or so blocks south to the lakeshore that he realized how chilly the air was, and how inadequately he was dressed for crossing the ice. A lake breeze caused his blue serge trousers to pulse against his leg like a vein. *In parts the blood is refrigerated, coagulated, and made as it were barren.*

The damp air seeped through the thin lining of his jacket. The fact that the island appeared to be much farther off than he'd calculated added to his worries. Furthermore, it was wrapped in a shroud of mist, sewn, no doubt, by the ghosts of those long-dead tailors.

He chose as his starting point a section of the waterfront where the land sloped gently down, merging with the frozen lake and presided over by a modern sculpture, two enormous inter-secting aluminium rectangles, which no one had liked at first. Waste of money! Too abstract! Why not a historical figure astride a horse? *That* had worked for centuries. People had grown used to it, though, and even proud of it. Familiarity breeds art, per-haps, and not contempt. He had forgotten the sculpture was called *Time* but so it was. An appropriate launching place for this new phase of his life.

The ice felt reassuringly firm underneath his shoes although he was intrigued to discover as he walked (tiptoed more like) that the ice close up was not white, which was how it looked from shore, but a mottled purple and black, like a bruise. Nature was as fragile as a human being. Indeed, Sweeney's final warning, issued in a sonorous voice, still resounded in Levon's ears:

—A woman don't melt as fast as the ice sometimes does.

Each winter, the local newspaper reported the death of an islander who, either inebriated or too impatient to get home, gunned his truck over the frozen lake and, midway across, hit a weak spot in the ice. Levon imagined the driver scrabbling fran-tically to unlock his door as frigid water bubbled up from below, perhaps assuming the shape of the Harpies: fierce-looking women, the curve of the waves their breasts, the stench of sea-weed and rotting fish clinging to the spume of their hair. Released from their dank cave, the hags would drape themselves over the sinking automobile, surround the hapless driver and drag him screaming down, down, down to the underworld. Hadn't there been three? *Aello*, storm. *Ocypete*, rapid, and a third. Who was the third? Ah, yes. *Celaino*. Darkness. A storm, and then, rapidly, darkness. That was death and also life lived in the shadow of a death.

Levon did not relish becoming an item in *The Gazette*, that grubby, gossipy rag. He pictured his obituary, a column the shape of a coffin, framed in mournful black ink. Levon Hawke, *troublesome* son of Mr. and Mrs. Thomas Hawke of Muckfoot, Alberta; devoted brother of Alice, *now deceased*. Drowned. Silly bugger tempted Fate. *Serves him right.*

He pressed on as speedily as he could.

No skaters were out but there remained on the ice strokes in the shape of apostrophes, commas and parentheses cut by blades earlier in the day. The blank surface of the ice was edited into paragraphs, sentences, subordinate clauses, fragments, words: lost, hypothermia, arctic, Shackleton, fool, no, hero, Scott, idiot, no, misguided, frostbite, amputation, slippery, perish, uncertain, frightened, heart, diastole, systole, shit, falling, falling, falling, *fuck*.

His knees bashed against the ice, his chin, his elbows too. Pain lurched through him, down this corridor and that, like a drunk who'd forgotten where his bed was until, at last, it came to rest, reeling and nauseated, in the pit of Levon's stomach.

Cautiously, he rolled over on his back. He expected to hear the jangle of coin-sized bones within the loose pocket of his skin. No. No bones broken. What about the ice? Had he detected a shift, a slight bobbing underneath his shoulder blades? He thought all at once of cartoons, of how one character in pursuit of another would be lured to a patch of thin ice and would then watch it crack in zigzagging lines around him until he was perched on an ice floe. Facing the screen, the cartoon figure sank slowly, resignedly, into the water only to emerge unscathed on shore in the next frame, calmly wringing out his entire body as though it were a dishrag; first his feet twisting around and around, then his legs followed by his torso, his neck, his head and even his ears. He squeezed out every drop of moisture apart from tears. The cartoon character never cried. His response to adversity was anger and a wily, although inevitably disastrous, revenge.

No again. He and the ice were both intact. Frozen solid, in fact.

The pain dulled to a thud in his patella and olecranon. Still he couldn't bring himself to shift. Levon watched in groggy fascination as a she-moon, hovering above him like the blade of a scythe, cut down the feeble winter sun, which tottered, scattering a few drops of blood on the horizon, before falling to the ground. *Celaino* and *Ocypete*. The hour couldn't have been much past three in the afternoon, if that. Night, snow, the world was falling about Levon's ears. Stretched out on that gurney of ice, growing stiffer by the second, Levon could almost feel the whistle of the moon's blade as it swung, preparing to open him up for dissection. He trusted it was William Harvey's hand that held the blade over him and not God's. The doctor, at least, had a practical use for his dead. Harvey had cut into the living, too; dogs, though, not humans. He had wanted to examine their still-beating hearts.

When I first applied my mind to observation from the many dissections of Living Creatures as they came to hand, that by that means I might find out the motion of the Heart and things conducible in Creatures; I straightways found it a thing hard to be attained, and full of difficulty, so with Fracastorus I did almost believe, that the motion of the Heart was known to God alone.

Not that Harvey was fazed by this. Not at all. He continued to poke and speculate, reason, experiment and sometimes kill in order to understand how the human organism worked. Autopsy meant "to see for oneself" and Levon wanted to. He wanted to know, for example, why he remembered that passage (learned by heart as it were) and yet had forgotten so much of what was truly important: the name of Alice's first boyfriend, the part she'd acted in the school play, her favorite fairy tale: the subject she and Levon were arguing about when she stepped, just ahead of him, into the street. He was curious about what this jumble inside him looked like. Oh, he'd examined all the anatomist's drawings: the medieval representations of a man split from neck to pubis, a bottle-shaped opening in which his organs resembled the glops and squiggles left by an ineptly squeezed tube of paint; the Renaissance skeleton posed in mid-gambol as though its skin had blown off in a fierce wind; William Hunter's gruesome detail of a pregnant woman's womb, the trunks of her legs cut off mid-thigh as a butcher would a joint of beef. Levon's anatomy was undoubtedly of the standard variety but he felt a close kinship with the eccentric renderings of earlier times, when humors and spirits were believed to be as essential a component of the body as were blood and bones and tendons. Laid out in a neat geometric pattern, a square within a tilted square, were the four humors—choleric, melancholic, sanguine and phlegmatic, their corresponding elements—fire, earth, air, and water—poised at the angles. Levon pictured his own insides as being less ordered than that; more a child's finger painting with chaotic streaks of black and yellow bile merging with his red blood.

Aello.

Enough, the wind hissed. Icy fingers slid underneath his back and pushed him into an upright position. Move, the sharp edge of the moon threatened him. Run, thundered his heart, run *now*. But in which direction? He had tripped while a little more than halfway across judging from the distance of the city, which he sat facing. It was dotted with rouge—an artificial, rosy light—and the cheeriness of it beckoned to him. Levon knew it was fake, knew it would be wiped off in the cold, creamy light of morning. For now, though, the city represented the land of the living. The island, on the other hand, was barely discernible. A cluster of lights shone from what he assumed was the ferry dock. The rest was pitch.

Cool, minted air cracked between his chattering teeth. A grating wind shred curls of snow all around him. He brushed them from his hair and shoulders as others melted, trickling down his neck and along his spine, cold as the anatomist's knife sectioning him off. His pace became quicker. He ought to have refused Simon's offer, or at least waited until morning. A new life requires labor but this stumbling about in the gloom, not knowing how far off he was from the shore, or in what condition he would arrive, *if* he did at all? That was more like death than birth.

For comfort, Levon touched the pocket in which he carried Sweeney's parting gift, the *o*, a talisman. Think of that, he commanded himself: a letter can change everything.

God became good.

Alice became alive.

What, he wondered, would Simon's letter change?

For an hour or more he walked. The snow grew progressively deeper; first cushioning his soles, then slopping over his shoe tips and, at last, swirling around his ankles. This meant there must be a barrier here from the bristling wind that, in the center of the lake, swept the surface clean of snow. His eyes played a game of tag with the island, dodging left and right, trying to catch sight of it and so, be able to shout *Home free!* He thought he spotted a vague outline of tall, ghost-white shapes looming ahead, their arms waving, teasing him, challenging him to approach. At the same time, his ears picked up a low-pitched moaning punctuated by shrieks and whistles.

He stumbled forward, arms outstretched. A few minutes later, he felt a vicious jab against his palms.

A pine branch? Spruce? Squinting into the darkness, he supposed the paler forms might be birch, or beech. In truth, Levon didn't know his ash from his elm tree. Sweeney hadn't mentioned trees at all. The map he'd drawn for Levon resembled nothing so much as a boot, the toe pointed in a well-aimed kick toward him as he crossed the ice. The blow connected, sharply, as he stepped on shore.

Unwilling to step back onto the ice, even to follow the shore around to a clearer spot, he decided to brave the woods. As a child, he'd been an avid reader of fairy tales and, to a degree, his work in medical history began as an extension of his childlike delight in narrative. History was part story, after all. Levon's imagination loosely transposed the physician as hero, ignorance for the woods and disease for the dragon. It didn't hurt, either, that damsels occasionally swooned in the doctors' arms. However. Faced with the prospect of an actual wood, in which actual wolves might roam, his nerve wavered. He did not want to be mistaken for a thing with feathers.

He had no choice, it seemed. Gritting his teeth, he grasped a low-hanging branch farther ahead, at the same time letting go of the first one, and pulled himself forward. He repeated this action, partnering himself off as though at a square dance, and in this manner made gradual, clumsy progress among the trees.

Snow muted his footfalls. Levon heard nothing but his hoarse breath and, once, the purr of wings in the distance. This silence was unheard of in prison. There, it was never quiet. An inmate shouted at his neighbor to quit talking, another raised the volume of his radio to drown out the shouting. The next man thumped on his bars to signal that the radio was too loud. A guard yelled. A door clanged shut. Toilets flushed. It was thuggish noise, noise that loitered at corners and bullied passers-by, battering them, robbing them of their wits. In contrast, the woods were filled with the purposeful, respectful silence Levon remembered from the library, enforced by a librarian's gentle *shhh* as branches stirred at his touch.

Blindly, he went on, his fingertips brushing over tree bark, a kind of braille, the meaning encoded in a text that was unfamiliar to him. What was he to learn here?

He grew intensely aware of the darkness without as well as within him. Would he ever see light again? For almost three years he'd lived with the continuous illumination from bulbs dotting the prison corridor, their sulfurous yellow glow encased in wire mesh, as if light, too, could be imprisoned. An inmate was not allowed even his own shadow for fear of what he might do under its protection. Daybreak was just that: a broken day, unfixable, worthless, indistinguishable from night.

Given the absence of a real, discernible shape on which to focus, a horrible idea began instead to take shape in Levon's mind. He tried to shake it off but it stuck nonetheless. His sense of geography was weak and, after all, there had been no signposts, no illumination of any sort.

What if he had landed on the wrong island?

Thousands of them littered the lake. Ancient relics of a giant crack-up of the earth's surface. Some were no bigger than a teacup while others, like this one, were more substantial. The majority of them, he thought, were farther east, or was it west? In which direction was he headed? On what side of a tree did moss grow? Did the north star really shine from the north or was it a trick, like the question about who lies in the tomb of the unknown soldier? And which way was north anyway? He couldn't start a fire from striking two rocks together, or construct a shelter from twigs or track an animal, let alone kill it. He had never enjoyed *Boy's Own* stories and, while fairy tales were chock-full of adventures as exciting as any schoolboy might wish, the advice offered in them was not exactly practical. Elves weren't likely to spring out at him from behind a tree bearing magic hawthorn branches or golden apples or a pair of seven-league boots.

No, what appeared to Levon at that moment was far more astonishing than that. He rubbed his eyes, almost scraping off the corneas with his knuckles, as if underneath the image reflected there was another, truer one if only he could get at it.

A house.

In the middle of the woods.

The sickle moon had been hard at work here, clearing trees to form a semicircle of land in which the house, tall and angular, stood brooding. As Levon stepped forward, half-expecting the house to dissolve in a whirl of snowflakes, a bony branch hooked his collar, yanking him back. He unsnagged himself, impatient to be free of the splintery wood. Whatever was ahead couldn't be nearly so frightening, or unfriendly, as what lay behind.

The house slept, its windows shuttered. There was a faint creaking sound, like an old woman shifting in her corset. Levon's fingers probed knotted strands of ivy, lifeless and unkempt, that spilled down the walls. Icicles dripped from a snowy gable, a deserted bride's tattered hat and veil. A gnarled oak tree, thick around the middle, rapped insistently—*tip, tap, tip*—on a shutter, a suitor in disgrace begging to be let in, to explain, and to be forgiven.

Dazed, Levon drifted with the snow up to the front door. He picked up the ornate brass dragon knocker. Determined to observe the proprieties, despite the silliness of announcing his arrival at a house which had been deserted, clearly, for months, if not years, Levon listened to the reverberations fade without hearing any answering footsteps from inside.

He did not notice the brief lick of candlelight along the slat of a shutter. He was unaware of the shadowy cameo of a girl pinned to the inside wall, her profile regarding him in blank surprise. He did not hear her sharp intake of breath, which, Levon might have convinced himself, was the wind threading itself through the iron filigree.

Levon leaned his forehead against the doorjamb, confused about what he ought to do. He had broken and entered once before. No. He'd been broken-hearted and *then* entered. Not that the law recognized such a distinction. Anyway, merciless Nature was both judge and jury here. Wearing its black robe and snowy wig, it was Nature who would pronounce sentence upon him: a minimum of frostbite, the maximum penalty, pneumonia or even death.

I had no choice, Your Honor.

His fingers trembled so badly he could scarcely grasp the door knob.

It turned easily.

On hearing the door creak open, Obdulia Limb scampered back to the sofa. She tried to hide, all six feet one inch of her, behind the battered copy of the *Encyclopaedia Britannica* she had been reading when the knocker sounded. To calm herself, she coughed out little puffs of white breath into the cold air. She surrounded herself with ghosts; the guardian spirits of her mother, grandmother and great-grandmother who now hovered about her.

No visitors had come to the house since her mother's death ten years before. The echo of the knocking seemed to Obdulia to be the thump of a heart beating against the breast bone. She felt the ribs of the house expand and contract with the excitement of it, as if her mother had come back to her. Soon, she would send Obdulia scurrying to replace her father's photo on the mantelpiece, a ruse to convince the visitor that he lived there with them still when, of course, the whole island knew where he slept at night. There would be ginger biscuits and tea out of the good china cups. Not this set that was broken, then mended, the liquid leaking out of the cracks. The visitors had usually leaked enough; dewy-eyed girls who came to discover who their husbands would be and tearful older wives who came to find out which young girls their husbands were with.

Obdulia cocked her ear, listening. Floorboards protested the man's weight like a father grown too old to piggyback his son. Entering the foyer, he had a choice of three directions. Up the stairs to the second floor, left to the kitchen or, she thought, right to me.

He chose right.

Obdulia pulled her legs up to her chest. Her white cotton nightdress bunched at her thighs, her two bare knees like grapefruits, the edge of the *Britannica* resting on them. The door to the parlor was opposite her. She pictured to herself what the man's first impression of her would be: a mass of coppery hair sprouting from the pages almost to the floor, her face a mask of cracked yellow and maroon leather with gilt lettering on it.

It never occurred to Obdulia that he would not notice her first.

Levon might have, too, if he'd pushed the door wide open all at once. Alert, however, to a shimmering around the bottom of the frame, he nudged the door just a smidgen. Enough, at first, to see only a row of stubby white candles lined up along the mantelpiece, like golden-haired choirboys in their surplices.

A draft circled the room, sweeping across the bare floor. It fanned the flames of the fireplace, skimmed the top of an uneven pile of books leaned up against the wall, caught itself on the nails where paintings or photographs once hung but no longer, then yanked the door open, inviting—no, commanding—Levon to enter.

He was now able to observe a fold-out table next to the fireplace on which a china service was laid. A lacy handkerchief of steam waved to him from the teapot's spout. A red velvet sofa, the only proper furniture in the room, was plunked down parallel to the fireplace.

Obdulia peeked over the parapet of her book just as Levon, belatedly, registered her presence. They each held their breath, squinting through the gloom at the other. Her face was in shadow, her expression hibernating. Slowly, she lowered her book and leaned forward into a shaft of firelight. She blinked at him, her brow furrowed, her stare a mixture of crossness and, Levon thought, intense hunger. A bear, awoken from its nap, bemused by this intrusion of the outside world into its cave and, for the moment, undecided as to the best approach to take. Levon had camped once, in a provincial park with his schoolmates. He had witnessed a black bear nuzzle honey from a boy's hand but he also knew that a bear could break you in half if it chose to.

Weren't you supposed to play dead if a bear attacked you? Let the animal bat you a little between its great paws. Don't breathe. Don't twitch. For God's sake, don't . . .

—*Gesundheit*, said Obdulia automatically.

—Thank you, he sniffled.

She wriggled back among the sofa cushions. Whatever he was planning to do, she reasoned to herself, at least he'd be polite about it.

—What do you want? she asked him.

Lacking a handkerchief, Levon mopped his dripping nose with his sleeve.

—Well, he said. Better luck for a start.

The fire dabbed ineffectually at the cold. Levon remained at a distance, waiting for a formal invitation to step into the room. His clothes were damp from his tumble on the ice, his shoes and socks soaking wet. An uncontrollable quaking set in, beginning at his knees and working upward. He hugged his elbows and clamped his legs together in a self-imposed straitjacket to control the spasms but his body refused to be confined.

— Are you all right?

She exhibited a genuine concern, which touched him.

—I . . . I appear to be thawing. Everything tingles and itches. Funny. I didn't enjoy being numb but now that I'm starting to feel again, it hurts.

He dragged his eyes around the room. They were like sacks of coal that had been left in the rain, a startling black, but also cold and damp. Obdulia speculated on what might spark them back to life. There were no more logs so she reached for the first thing to hand, tossing her *Encyclopaedia Britannica* on to the fire. The flames leapt around it like pagans after a sacrifice.

Levon let out a strangled cry and bounded over to the fireplace, frantically searching for tongs with which to salvage the book.

Would he try that hard to rescue *me*, Obdulia wondered sadly. Could he even? He wasn't her idea of a gallant knight. He was slight, for a start, and considerably shorter than she was. Her exasperated sigh might send him hurtling up the chimney with the cinders. She liked his chipped tooth, though. His wasn't a mouth shaped for polite company, perhaps. More a cozy, familiar kind of mouth that her lips might enjoy exploring the indentations of, both the sharp edges and the smooth.

—I've burned much weightier volumes than that, she said. That's only X–Z. The thinnest one. Aristotle was consigned to the flames ages ago. So was Austen, Bronzino, Copernicus, Dickens, Einstein, Keats, Manilius, Newton, Housman, Oppenheimer, Shakespeare. The whole lot of them.

He found a loose piece of skirting and with it, inched the half-devoured book out of the flames. The gilt letters had blistered; the leather was bubbled and charred, the name blackened past recognition.

—But why? he gasped.

—Because, she replied tartly, there's nothing in them that *matters*.

Levon stepped back from the fireplace, heat pressing like a thin flannel against his torso and legs.

His childhood fear of fire had ignited along with the book, the flames illuminating not this house but one three doors down from his parents'. The grass there was overgrown with Queen Anne's lace. Alice used to enjoy dawdling in front of it on their walk to school, examining the undersides of the flower for the pinprick of blood that, supposedly, Queen Anne had shed as she sewed. The house belonged to a middle-aged couple, members of an obscure Christian sect, who had one child: a little girl of eleven or twelve, two grades above Levon. The girl (he never knew her name) was never allowed to join in the neighborhood games. He didn't think she was read to at night either, or allowed to lick the bowl of chocolate-cake batter. Summer and winter, she wore dresses of gray wool, outgrowing the outfits faster than her mother could sew them. The girl's belly and budding, cone-shaped breasts strained against the cloth like a wayward priest. The neighborhood seldom caught a glimpse of her and never without one, or both, of her parents, their steely hands encircling the girl's wrists, preventing her escape. Once, she and Levon exchanged appraising looks as they passed on the street, he on his way back from school to his house, she to church. Her hair was cut, raggedly, in a bowl shape, several cowlicks adorning her crown, her sole rebellion. As she sidled past him, she looked back over her shoulder and poked out her tongue. Levon was astounded; it was as if a cowlick had sprung out of her mouth. Before he could react, her tongue had disappeared again, smoothed down, put in its place.

I know in my bones, his mother would mutter, *that something terrible is going to happen to her.*

The expression puzzled Levon and he tried, as always, to figure it out on his own. For instance, his mother kept in her head all sorts of fairy tales, in which terrible things happened with great regularity, and could recite them without recourse to any book. She simply *knew* them. (Periodically, she would announce "The End" but since, with concerted pleading, she could be induced to tell the story all over again, Levon had no real conception of what "The End" meant. The idea that something, or someone, could be gone forever, was alien to him.)

He also knew what bones were. He had dressed up as a skeleton the previous Halloween and carried a plastic skull for a bucket to collect the candy. The painted bones vaguely resembled the rolled-up scrolls from which kings in fairy tales read their proclamations. He'd seen illustrations of this in books at school.

Putting these two apparently disparate ideas together, he reasoned that bodies were composed of stories that could be unscrolled and read from. That is, once you'd figured out the trick of it.

He learned it the afternoon of the fire.

His mother was wiping her hands on a souvenir tea towel from Edinburgh, the centuries-old fortress crushed unthinkingly between her soapy palms. Alice was blowing bubbles in her lemonade through a straw. Levon studied a bumblebee as it thumped with lazy willfulness against the screen door, possibly mistaking the sunflowers on Alice's dress for the real thing. Levon tapped the screen door with his index finger, smug in the knowledge that he was safe from being stung, when he noticed a thick skein of smoke unwinding from their neighbors' chimney. Levon's grandfather wore a sweater on even the hottest days (he suffered from poor circulation) but a fire in August set off warning bells that were soon augmented by those of the fire department, the trucks a streak of blood running down the street.

A curious crowd gathered quickly outside, the mucky runoff of neighborly concern. Levon was reminded of the bee as burly firemen in yellow coats and black hats battered at his neighbors' front door, wielding their axes until the wood splintered.

That's when Levon knew, in his bones, what had happened.

The little girl was in the oven.

The story unfolded as the afternoon wore on. Believing their daughter to be possessed by the devil *(had she stuck her tongue out at them?)*, the lunatic couple had crammed her into the wood oven, wedging their shoulders against it. They burned her alive. Firemen later discovered the scratches on the inside of the oven where she had scrabbled at the unyielding door, the flesh melting into bone, the bone into ash, the ash into evidence against the couple at their trial.

That night, and every night thereafter, Levon's mother refused to tell her children the story of Hansel and Gretel. But that one, too, he knew in his bones. Except that Gretel had not been burned to death. She had lived. It was then Levon began to understand that the real world did not follow the dependable rules of the fairy tale. The implications of this were horrible! If a story could trespass into real life, couldn't real life trespass into stories? Where then, Levon worried, would he find a happy ending? For months, he dreamed of witches gleefully chopping up the words *happily ever after* into broomsticks, then hopping aboard them and circling over his bed. Or of a troll, erupting with warts, rough-skinned as a tuber, who climbed up through the *o* in *once upon a time*, pointed at his feet, the long hair combed neatly over his toes, winked, then scampered off into the shadows. Or . . .

The fire snapped its fingers like an imperious magician breaking a spell.

Levon shook his head to clear it.

—What's your name? he said to the girl.

—Obdulia Limb.

—Obdulia?

O. Sweeney's *o.*

—That's right. What's yours?

—Levon Hawke.

She clapped her hand to her forehead.

—Where are my manners! she exclaimed. Have some tea.

—You didn't make it specially, I hope.

—How could I?

Since there was only one cup, Obdulia picked up the sugar bowl. She shook it the way a gambler does his dice and rolled the cubes onto the tray. She poured the murky liquid into the bowl and offered it to Levon. He accepted it, perching on the edge of the sofa, knees pressed together, both hands gripping the bowl so as not to spill his tea. A pattern of pink rosebuds was painted on the side of the bowl. Held against the firelight, the thin porcelain appeared threaded with minute cracks.

—An heirloom, she said.

—I'm not planning to steal it, you know, he told her hurriedly.

—This was my great-grandmother's house. She had Chinese blood in her veins and courted her husband with Mandarin love songs.

Obdulia appeared to be in her early twenties. Her cheeks had the pale, veined translucence of a fruit whose skin had burst. Her eyes were hazel and her nose was spread out, more concerned with being comfortable than delicate. There were fine lines around her mouth like apostrophes, as though everything she said was in quotation marks, borrowed from someone else. Her legs, he noticed when she swung them off the seat to make room for him, were muscular. She didn't shave them either.

He sipped his tea and immediately had to suppress an urgent desire to spit it out. He pressed his lips together and ordered himself to swallow. The taste of it, dreadful as it was, wasn't so bad as the *sensation* of it sliding down his throat. It was as if deception and melancholy and a peppery anger had all been brewed together with a pinch of ear wax and toenails and a hair wrapped around the tongue added for good measure.

—This tea is . . .

He searched in vain for an appropriate adjective.

—It's herbal, she said weakly.

Obdulia groaned inwardly. Oh, it was too late, too late. What had she done? Her head was so *muzzy*; she hadn't even considered . . . Well, she'd plain forgotten all about it in fact, with the hullabaloo over his arrival. His fault really for barging in uninvited. Yes. *His* fault. No, that wasn't fair. Be *fair*. Life was a random series of occurrences and unforeseen consequences. Levon was an occurrence. Obdulia would be his consequence. There was nothing she could do about it now. An accident, all of it. Death alone was deliberate. That was the lesson twelve-year-old Obdulia had learned at her mother's knee.

Levon followed Obdulia's gaze upward. He hadn't noticed it before but an upside-down garden was suspended from the ceiling beams. Dried herbs and grasses hung in bunches, some with their blossoms still attached, like rows of women seen from the waist downward, with cinched belts and full-flowered skirts.

—What are those?

—That one above you is called Stinking Willie, she said.

—I appreciate nature but I'm not on a first-name basis with it.

—It causes impotence.

—Christ!

—Even Him, I expect.

Levon clapped his palm over his tea. Obdulia continued her recitation.

—The green and glabrous one next to it is Sour Grass. That causes abnormal breathing and convulsions. Then there's Bloodwort, a stout herb with basal leaves, as you probably know. Corn Cockle irritates the digestive tract while Moonseed is a twining vine. Mechanical injury to the intestines. Purplish Wahoo, over there, induces nausea, cold sweats and prostration.

Too overcome to speak, Levon pinioned his tea between his thighs to hide the fact that he was shaking. Obdulia realized she was being cruel to him but didn't care.

—My great-grandmother was a midwife and herbalist, she went on. My grandmother and mother, too. Locals whispered about them being witches but it wasn't true. Rumors circulate on an island—where else have they got to go? One was that my mother had turned a local woman into a bird. It was only her mind that got turned, of course, and she was bird-brained to start with. My mother was also supposed to be gifted with second sight but she was forever tripping over sleeping dogs and bumping into lampposts.

She gulped her tea. *Hurry, please hurry*, she begged.

—None of *that* mattered, of course, when a cure was needed. We'd hear a rap at the kitchen door and there Mrs. Porter would be. Or Nancy Harold, or Petra Fen. Oh, Hereword, they moaned, I've got the bellyache, I've got the warts, the wall-eye, nightmare, tone deafness. I'm mooning over a boy.

—No cure for that, said Levon decidedly.

—Showy Lady Slipper baked in a cake. Or a pinch of Pie Plant sprinkled over the love object's cereal.

—A weed never changed a man's mind about anything.

—That's not the part of him it works on.

Levon squirmed. To change the subject he asked Obdulia, although he couldn't imagine it, if her mother lived in the house too. Chunks of plaster littered the floor. There was no heat, no electricity, no furnishings. Bedouin tents of dust were pitched everywhere. Levon could see his footprints leading from the door to the sofa already half obliterated by the wind that blew through the fissures in the wall.

Obdulia didn't answer at first. Instead, she wrapped a strand of hair around her index finger. Tighter and tighter she wound it until the circulation was cut off, the tip of her finger the same blood color as her hair.

—She's dead. Sort of.

—How can she be "sort of" dead? he inquired testily.

—Break through skin, there's bone. Break through bone, there's spirit.

—What is that? said Levon. A spell?

Her eyebrows swooped down to the bridge of her nose and perched there, a delicate wing arching over each eye.

—Don't be ridiculous. Her spirit lives here. That's all I meant.

—Then you're not planning to conjure her up or anything.

—Don't you admire a woman with spirit? she asked indignantly.

—I like a woman with spirit. With. The two conjoined. A spirit all on its own is another matter.

—Well *exactly*, said Obdulia.

Both of them were at a loss for words after that. Levon, glancing at the encyclopedia at his feet, nudged it open with his toe. A flock of half-charred paper fragments flew up into the draft, circling their heads. Smiling, Obdulia reached out and captured one midair, cupping her palms around it.

—Can you guess what it says?

—Of course not.

She peeked through the tiny aperture between her thumbs and pretended to read there what she had, in fact, been studying when Levon interrupted her.

—Yggdrasil. In Norse mythology a giant ash, the World-tree, which supports the sky, holds the different realms of gods and men in its branches, and has its roots in the Underworld.

—That can't possibly be written there.

Levon reached for the paper with one hand, anchoring his teacup to his knees with the other. He brushed her skin as he retrieved the fragment.

—You're like ice!

—I am cold, she admitted.

Her bone-china teacup rattled against its saucer as she shivered.

—Unfreeze the cold! Pile plenty of logs in the fireplace!

—I've run out, she said.

—Horace. The poet.

—Oh. Are you a student?

—Was. But I also worked as a librarian.

—Really? she giggled.

Nettled, he responded:

—Casanova was a librarian.

—He wasn't.

—Was. *And* Philip Larkin.

He considered this.

—Of course, that comparison isn't nearly so flattering.

—No, she conceded. Are you still a librarian?

—No. I was . . . I was fired.

—You can be fired, she murmured, but not the books.

—It was a medical library. My job was to shelve the volumes. I came to love it, you know. Putting things back into their proper order. It pained me to see an empty space, an absent book, the books on either side caught off-balance without it. I began to resent the students checking them out.

—Is that why you were fired?

Levon had no wish to admit to her that he'd lost his job after being arrested. Mrs. Quinn, the head librarian, had been delighted to see him go. She was a stooped creature and her reptilian eyes, enclosed behind tortoiseshell glasses, used to roam slowly over him as he was called to task for one infraction or another.

—No, he lied. I spent too much time in the basement. The bowels, we used to call it. Medical librarian humor. That's where all the ancient volumes were stored. Books that no one read but me.

Arbuthnot's *Essay Concerning the Nature of Ailments*, Sir Astley Cooper's *Lectures on the Principles and Practice of Surgery*, Battie's *Treatise on Madness* and of course, Harvey's *De Motu Cordis*.

—Why would anyone object to your reading books?

—The bowel was a subterranean passage in every sense. There were articles down there on leeches, cannibalism, amulets, witch-finding. All of man's bungled attempts to just, well, feel *better*. But it wasn't science. Not according to the head librarian. She regarded my time spent in the bowels as time spent engaged in unnatural practices.

Obdulia set her teacup, rather shakily, on the table and drew her knees up to her chin.

—What were you trying to cure? she asked him softly.

—Nothing. What do you mean?

—Did you want to become a doctor?

—God no.

—Then it's obvious. You were searching for a cure for something. I think my mother was too.

Her earlier high spirits had vanished. Her shoulders slumped. Tears dripped down her cheekbones and were dashed off with the back of her hand. She reminded Levon of the prisoners who filed back to their cells after visiting day, exhausted by the effort of appearing cheerful in front of their children and spouses, their smiles like bow ties come undone.

—This tea is awful, she wept. I'm so sorry.

—No no, he assured her. It's not that bad.

She took hold of his hand, the width of a prayer book, and squeezed it.

—It's poisoned, she said.

3

TO KIL A FELON QUICKLY

Take a little Rue and Sage, stamp them smal, put to it Oyl of the
white of an Egge, and a little Honey, and lay it to therefore.

L EVON JUMPED to his feet in a puddle of tea.
— Then I'm dying too, he gasped.

—Pish, she said.

—*Pish?*

—You barely tasted it.

He teetered, collapsing onto the sofa. The walls of the room, draped in shadow, leaned toward him like mourners over a corpse. The plants whispered among themselves.

—Why on earth would you want to poison me?

—I wasn't expecting company, she said miserably. I forgot.

Which of the plants had she used? Levon had no idea what a mechanical injury was but he had an image of coils unspringing and screws coming loose inside him.

—What was in the tea? he demanded.

Obdulia ticked the ingredients off on her fingers:

—Peppermint Water, Burgundy Pitch, Spirits of Hartshorn, Gentian's Salts, Vinegar of Squills, Jesuit's Bark, Elixir of Vitriol, Sal Prunell, Ground Liverwort, Cream of Tartar, Wild Valerian

Root and Tamarind. Some others, too, but the labels had rubbed off the bottles. A recipe of my grandmother's. I found it in her notebook. I'm pretty certain I got it right. Her writing looked like flicks of water on a table, all dots and strings, you see. Difficult to read. So was she, come to think of it.

—No Purplish Wahoo? No Moonseed?

—No, she admitted. I was teasing about those.

—They don't make you sick?

—Oh yes. If you're a cow.

Levon fumbled in his jacket pocket for a leather pouch filled with tobacco and rolling papers.

—Do you mind? he asked her.

—Be my guest.

His hands shook. More tobacco sprinkled over Obdulia than on the paper. She relieved him of it and rolled the cigarette herself. He, distracted, plucked the littered tobacco flakes off her legs. When she finished, he stuck the cigarette between his lips and patted his pockets, searching in vain for a light. Obdulia pointed to a guttering candle on the mantelpiece.

—Thanks, he said.

Obdulia subsided to her corner of the sofa; a tide of white nightgown retreated with her. Her skin was flushed, her stomach knotted, her heart pounded. These symptoms were due to the tea, no doubt, but they were identical to ones described in a romance novel she'd just read, when the heroine first meets the hero. Oh honestly, she chided herself, that was *insane*. True, she'd never experienced either love or death firsthand, but she understood them to be entirely distinct from each other. As a matter of fact, when she first glimpsed Levon standing there, arms by his sides, the doorway framing him like a coffin, a velvety blackness behind him and his skin so pale, she thought he was a corpse come to haunt her.

A loose shutter banged against the outside wall. Not rhythmically but once, twice, very hard; then, a pause followed by several softer taps in rapid succession.

Levon was speaking to her.

—Have you ever heard of Mithradates? he said.

His voice sounded crumpled, the words tossed at her, thrown away as though nothing he said mattered anymore.

—No, she told him. I don't think so.

—He was King of Pontus in the first century B.C. Poison was the favored method of assassination in those days and Mithradates was *terrified* of being poisoned.

Levon dragged deeply on his cigarette before continuing.

—Luckily for him, there was a snake oil circulating at the time that promised to be an antidote. There was ground-up lizard in it, viper's flesh and about sixty other ingredients. Mithradates swallowed buckets as a prophylactic.

—Did the anecdote work?

—Antidote, Levon corrected her.

—Hah! she laughed. I meant antidote, of course.

—Against the poison, yes, it worked.

—Well then.

—He was stabbed to death. Mithradates was an idiot. There was no antidote against the unexpected. No cure for the inevitable. Think of poor old Charles II, administered with an enema every two hours in addition to being bled, blistered and plastered with pigeon dung, then given sneezing powder as well as forty drops of human skull.

He died soon afterward.

Levon sucked greedily on the teat of his cigarette; an udder of smoke hung above it. He recalled how, in the sixteenth century, tobacco was regarded as a miracle drug, a panacea for all ills. Monardes had recommended it in his *Joyfull Newes Out of the New Founde World* as a cure for any *grief of the body; griefes of the Brest, Venom & venomous woundes, old sores*. Levon, suffering from all of the above, knew better of course. Tobacco caused cancer, birth defects, emphysema and bad breath. He clung to his *precious stinke* all too aware of the damage it was doing to him, envious of those in past centuries who'd *believed* in tobacco. For Levon, *the new founde world* brought no *joyfull newes*.

A flake of tobacco stuck to his upper lip. Obdulia brushed it off in a lightning action so quick there was only the tingle of his skin to convince him that it had happened.

To hide his embarrassment, the red X he pictured on his lip where she had touched him, he bent over to pick up the broken pieces of the sugar bowl he'd dropped and stacked them on the tray. Obdulia fiddled with the lace collar of her nightdress. Neither spoke. They listened instead to the wind twirling around outside, a lariat preparing to descend, tighten, then drag the house off its foundation.

—Why, he said at last, did you do it?

Obdulia shrugged her shoulders. How could she explain it to him? She wasn't certain she understood it herself.

—You don't *know?*

—I'm . . . tired, she whispered. I'm tired.

When Obdulia was five years old, her mother had spent the summer teaching her how to swim. Even now she could see Hereword standing on a shelf of rock, the water a flounced petticoat spreading out from around her waist, her skin white as apple flesh with a paring of red where the sun had burned her shoulders. All of Hereword's ungainliness vanished in the water: she could balance the floating Obdulia, a big girl for her age, on the tip of her baby finger! She could perform somersaults and back flips and duck dives. Hereword wasn't afraid either, as Obdulia was, to put her face right in the water. Taking a deep breath, she pushed through her reflection, diving into her very self it seemed, until Obdulia, frightened of losing her altogether, tugged on Hereword's hair, pulling her mother back up and out into Obdulia's world.

The cove was too rocky to be a popular bathing spot so Obdulia and her mother usually had it to themselves. The lake, delighted to see them, kissed their cheeks and sent them tributes of hyacinth blossoms. Frogs launched themselves from their lily pads. A water snake slithered off a rock like a rope down a well.

That afternoon, Hereword, complaining of a headache, soon retreated to the shade of a weeping willow tree. Waves, collapsing like deck chairs, were dragged onto the shore after her.

She directed Obdulia to wade in the shallows while she dozed.

For a time, she did as she was told. But the sun, a wily jeweler, had laid out row upon row of golden necklaces against a velvety pillow of water. Each strand was more desirable, and farther from shore, than the one before. Obdulia, mesmerized, greedy for these glittering baubles, dog-paddled toward them, her chin held high; her neck elongated. A princess. She felt the cold clasp of each necklace around her throat as she swam into it and, almost immediately after, felt it slide off her shoulders. Soon, she was well past her usual spot, proud of herself but also fretful. Unable to sustain much of a kick, Obdulia's plump legs dipped too far below the surface, where the water was frigid. She learned then that the lake's warmth was a façade, like a witch's friendliness to stray children. The shock of that cold, slimy water closing around her ankles chased all thoughts out of her brain. In that instant, her arms forgot how to propel her, her lungs how to breathe. Without even knowing the words for it, Obdulia understood that she was sinking.

She was drowning.

Her fingers raked the water the way a cat might frantically claw its way up a green velvet curtain. She was too heavy, though, and continued to drop further and further into that dank, silent under-lake. Her muscles were soon exhausted. Her lungs ached to inhale a breath of oxygen. She began to wonder what the point was of kicking so hard.

Often at nights, Obdulia, despite her exhaustion, refused to go to bed, suspicious of the cage of unconsciousness her mother tossed her into each evening. What if, one morning, Hereword forgot to come to Obdulia's bedside and unlock it? She always resisted as long as she could the lull of bedtime stories, especially those involving sleep that lasted a hundred years. Bawling, she thrashed against Hereword's enfolding arms, all of her entreaties, her threats. Stubborn to the end, Obdulia propped open her eyelids with her fingers until weariness at last overtook her and she slept.

Her eyes now were on the point of closing when she saw her mother plunge into the lake, swimming fast toward where Obdulia had sunk. From below, it looked as if Hereword was flying through blue sky, among the clouds. She watched her mother's body stop and hang there above her, in another world far from this silent, airless one into which she'd descended. Hereword's head floated just above water, scanning the horizon for the likeliest place to dive. Her arms and legs jerked spasmodically to help keep her afloat.

After what seemed an eternity, through which Obdulia continued to fall, Hereword plunged bravely down to the cold depths, her expression panicked but determined. With firm strokes she elbowed the water aside as though she was merely in a crowded room and Obdulia, calling out to her, on the other side of it. As Hereword neared, her daughter's hand reached out for her.

She was at an age, still, when she was certain of being saved by her mother.

For ten years, Obdulia had been reaching out to Hereword who, she sensed, was suspended somewhere above her. To find her, Obdulia realized she would have to sink once again, not into water but into an unconsciousness colder, darker and deeper even than the lake's bed. She both desired it and feared it. The result was chronic insomnia. Each night, her goosefeather pillow gobbled in her ears and roused her. The goosedown quilt beat at her with its wings until she opened her eyes. Her horsehair mattress kicked, forcing her to get up.

Because of this, she'd thrown out all her clocks. Why did people say they could *tell* time? Time was as stubborn as she and did whatever it pleased: it crawled, dragged, flew, or stopped altogether. Having a clock beside the bed was like playing an interminable game of cards with an expert gambler; the clock's hand held a three or a four o'clock when what Obdulia desperately needed was a seven or eight. All she could do was stare the clock face down until it surrendered to the morning.

This time, it was Obdulia surrendering.

—Have you ever had a dream where you're aware that you're dreaming? she said. I mean, aware enough to be able to tell your dream self, *Don't open that door!* Or *He's not who he seems to be!* Or *That shoe will never fit!* Even as I was pouring the tea for you, I couldn't distinguish between what was real and what was a dream. I might have been imagining you for all I knew.

Levon's gaze took in the fire, the china tea set, Obdulia's pretty nightgown. There was a theatricality to this suicide, if that's indeed what it was, which niggled at him. She'd probably imagined herself being discovered in the morning, waxen and tragic, her arms decorously folded across her breasts. How thrilled she must have been to see him! An audience for her misery while she yet remained alive to revel in it.

He reached out and pinched her arm.

—Ouch!

She examined the two red crescent moons imprinted on her skin.

—Pain is real, he said. *I* am real.

Obdulia rubbed her arm to erase the marks.

—All right, all right.

—I don't suppose there's a hospital on the island?

—No.

—Doctor?

—There's a veterinarian.

—Ah.

She yawned prodigiously, not even bothering to cover her mouth.

—I'm sorry, said Levon frostily, is my imminent demise boring you?

—For pity's sake, she exploded, you only had a teaspoonful!

—Life, he pointed out, can be measured in coffee spoons.

—I didn't *ask* you to come . . .

She never finished the sentence. All of a sudden her back arched, her jaw dropped and a silken banner of yellow vomit unfurled from her mouth. A medieval declaration of war with Obdulia's body the battleground. The force of the opening shot propelled her upper body forward over her knees and, as she struggled to rise, another wave, and then another, forced her down again, the acrid fumes of her sick wafting up from the ground.

Levon was at a loss to know what to do. He blushed to recall his sentiments of moments ago. Even if she did irritate him, he had no desire to sit and watch her die. But, Obdulia was right, his knowledge of medicine was anecdotal. Oh, what Levon wouldn't give to have William Harvey—swarthy, choleric, brilliant Harvey—sitting beside him, instructing him. Levon clutched Obdulia's hand.

As likewise in tender and delicate people by griping of their fingers, I could easily perceive by the pulse of their fingers when the Feaver was at its strength.

—I'm here, he said feebly. I'm here.

Levon stared at her hand, now gripping his own, and another's came into focus; a man's hand, the nails chewed to the quick, his body a trap he was slowly gnawing his way out of.

His cell mate, Angus, had been imprisoned most of his life. His rib cage was made of vertical bars, his heart beating against them. He'd given up any hope of release long ago.

One morning, out of the blue, a letter arrived from Angus's ex-wife. Levon had never known Angus to receive so much as a postcard and he watched, curious, from his bunk as Angus removed from the envelope a fragile sheet of onion-skin paper on which a few quavering lines in pencil were written. For an hour or more, he studied the words intently. Then, the letter still in his hands, he asked to borrow Levon's pen. Angus could scarcely read or write but all that afternoon, he laboriously traced over the words in ink, keeping each letter exactly as his ex-wife had shaped it. Weeks later, he confided in Levon the contents of the note: Angus's ten-year-old son, his only child, had died of cancer.

He had hoped that, by preserving the letter in ink, he could prevent his son's memory from fading away too.

Levon pressed down hard on Obdulia's fingers.

For a long time, she rocked to and fro, one arm wrapped around her stomach, until the vomiting slowed to a trickle of clear bile running down her chin. She wiped it off daintily with the corner of her nightgown.

—You ought to be in bed, said Levon.

—I can't move.

—Right, then. I'll carry you.

Easier said than done. Lifting Obdulia was a bit like a child gathering the sheets off a giant's bed. When Levon had secured her shoulders, her legs were out of reach. Changing tactics, he got hold of her legs, but couldn't grasp her shoulders.

—Stop jostling me, she pleaded.

—I'm trying to help.

—Please don't.

Perspiring lightly, Levon resumed his seat. This, at least, could be said for prison—the system was armed against surprises such as this. Which suited most of the prisoners fine. Levon had shared his block with con men, robbers, forgers, drug runners. Most of them were meticulous, organizing their crimes down to the tiniest detail: escape routes, accountants, flight schedules. Shoes that didn't squeak. Their arrests had proved to be the one unforeseen occurrence in otherwise faultless plans. Resigned to their temporary setback, inmates used their time inside constructively, to improve their strategies for the next time.

Of course, it couldn't be done. Life stepped from the shadows, truncheon in hand, and collared you every time.

Levon placed his palm against her forehead.

—What are you doing? she croaked.

—Taking your temperature.

—Well?

—98.6, he lied.

He pushed a gloppy strand of hair off her cheekbone.

—That's normal, isn't it?

—You're hardly that, he said.

Worried, he laid his ear against her breast, which bucked at the shock of his touch, then snorted and shivered, the way a horse does after a fly has landed on it. Anyway, he wasn't certain what he should be listening for. He heard the beating of fists trapped inside the burning wall of Obdulia's chest. Or was it simply the echo of his childhood nightmares in which the little neighbor girl had cried out to him from the flames to let her out, let her out, let her out?

To this add, that the blood does easily joyn of its own accord to its beginning, as a part to the whole, or as a drop of water spilt upon the table to the whole mass, as it does very swiftly for slender causes, such as are cold, fear, horror, and the like.

Obdulia poked his neck with her finger.

—Am I dying? she said.

—Of course.

She placed her broad hands against his chest and pushed him roughly into a sitting position.

—But not today, he added. You appear to have given yourself an emetic.

—A what?

—A purgative.

Obdulia's eyes dipped into his until hers were buckets filled to the brim with tears.

—I don't feel purged, she said at last. I feel . . . sad.

—Sad? he repeated incredulously. You put us both through this because you're sad? *Sad* is a *puddle* of a word. There's no depth to it. Nothing tragic. *Sad* splashes your ankle and stains your trouser cuff. *Sad* is missing your bus, not being run over by it. Do you think Lear was sad? Or Hamlet? Christ Almighty! And don't tell me He was *sad*.

Obdulia sighed, rekindling the blaze in the fireplace as she did so. The embers changed from near black to blood red, like a skinned knee after a scab has been picked off.

—I think I'm owed an explanation, she said.

Baffled, he replied:

—For what?

—Why you're here.

—Oh.

—Yes. *Oh*.

—I . . . I . . . well . . .

—Yes?

Bright sparks leapt out from the fireplace. Levon hurriedly stomped on them.

—I was lost.

—On your way to where?

Her tone was surprisingly gentle. She placed a hand on his and without thinking he covered it, rubbing her palm gently, the

way he'd seen his grandmother roll rose petals to extract the oil.
Where to start? When he had let go of Alice's hand? When she'd
slipped away from him? Obdulia didn't mean that, of course,
but, to his astonishment, Levon heard himself telling her all
about his sister's death, his crime, his arrest and his job offer. The
tea seemed to work as an emetic on him as well, but instead of
vomit it was words he spewed forth.

—I was released from prison today, in fact, he concluded.

Her eyes widened.

—Are you wanted? she said.

—You're wanted before you go to prison, not after.

She patted his shoulder comfortingly.

—That doesn't seem fair. And who is it that's offered you a
job?

—My cousin, Simon Tibeault.

—Simon?

—You know him?

—Yes.

A line was drawn in the sandy expanse of her forehead. Levon
was not invited to cross it at the moment.

—Wait, he said. Where are you going?

She was struggling to sit up.

—Please, she said, holding out her arms to him. Help me
upstairs.

Obdulia's bedroom proved to be at the end of a long corridor on
the second floor. The house was much bigger than it appeared
from the outside. Levon counted four shut doors before reaching
her room. Flowered wallpaper slipped off the plaster like an

unzipped dress from a woman's shoulders. The ceiling slanted downward, skimming the top of an armoire. A single bed was shoved against the wall and a table beside it. A drop of moonlight splashed against the gable window pane.

Obdulia tumbled into bed. Candle in hand, Levon asked where he might find the bathroom.

—Down the hall. Third door on the left.

Pipes shrieked as he twisted the taps but no water poured out, not so much as a drip. The sink was rusted, ingrained with dirt, as was a clawfoot tub that stood in the center of the room.

Rubbing a spot clean on the mirror, Levon inspected himself. Not a prepossessing sight: a scratch on one cheek from his passage through the trees. Beard stubble coarse and dark as burned toast. His hair disheveled. He licked his palm and drew it across his errant locks in an attempt to restore order, without success. The candle, balanced at the edge of the sink, threw into relief his shadow, his darker self, which stalked the wall behind him. Perhaps that was the reason Obdulia's tea had no effect on him—he was already poisoned. What had she used? Vitriol? That was in him, certainly. He was like a man addicted to arsenic, at risk not so much from the poison itself as from the slow withdrawal of it from his blood. As he assisted Obdulia up the stairs, her hand like an epaulette on his shoulder, her breast pressed against his side, he had experienced an unaccustomed feverishness. Similar, maybe, to the sort physicians used to induce when cupping a patient. In order to draw out impurities in the blood, the doctor would heat a glass over a flame. Once it was piping hot, he applied it to the patient's skin, rim side down. Toxins rose to the surface along with the blisters and these were then lanced in order to release the poison from the body. What if, after all these years, the anguish, the *vitriol*, festering in Levon's blood were to come to the surface? A blistering grief that would soon break open and weep. He fingered the grave mound on the back of his hand: the rough, protective skin he'd worked so hard to develop. No, he was not about to allow a strange girl whom he might never see again to wriggle under it.

Prescribed, by way of blister a young belle . . .

—You're no Don Juan, Levon scolded his reflection.

He wasn't even hobble-footed Byron.

Opening the cabinet, he discovered a tube of toothpaste (squeezed from the middle, he noted with disapproval) and a ragged face cloth. Both of these he took back to Obdulia who was nestled under the quilt.

He smeared a bit of toothpaste onto her finger, which she swiped across her teeth.

—God Almighty, he said, your breath would knock a buzzard on its arse.

—Well you give me a pain in mine.

—Pray to Saint Fiacre then. He's the patron saint of sore arses.

A mist from their mingled breaths dissolved over the green pond of Obdulia's quilt.

—It's freezing up here, he said.

—I know, she agreed. What we ought to do is build a need-fire.

—A what? he asked.

He dampened the face cloth with his spit and rubbed it over her face.

—Create friction.

Noticing Levon's blushes, she added hurriedly:

—Rub two sticks of dried wood together. Need-fires were supposed to contain magical properties, good for curing disease. My grandmother was brilliant at making a need-fire.

Obdulia abruptly dragged the quilt over her head. From the undulations underneath, Levon guessed she was removing her soiled nightgown.

—There's a clean nightie in the armoire, she mumbled.

A jumble of stuffed animals, knit jumpers and books (hardbound editions of *Alice in Wonderland, The Secret Garden, Anne of Green Gables*) toppled out as he pulled open the door. He rescued *The Little Princess* from the pile and rifled the pages. Corners of it were nibbled on.

—Mice are eating your books, he said.

—No, that was me.

—You *eat* your books?

—Devour them.

Levon extracted a flannel nightie from the pile, tossed it to her, and scooped the rest of her things back into the cupboard. All except for a framed black-and-white photograph.

A couple posed at the altar of a modest, rural church. The man's black, brilliantined hair caught the photographer's flash like the moon on a rain-slicked country road. He was packed into a too-tight suit, his legs jammed into his trousers as though stomping trash into a bag. His blurred hand fumbled at his throat, wanting to untie the knot, convinced, it seemed, that he would never breathe easily again.

The woman beside him looked young, perhaps seventeen to his thirty years, although she stood taller than he did. Her face was bent slightly toward him, whispering to him. Her pale, delicate hand, spread open on her stomach, was etched against the dark material of her dress and reminded Levon of a fossil embedded in rock: a curious tentacled creature long dead yet still vaguely present in this world, simply waiting to be excavated.

The couple did not hold hands, or even touch each other. In fact, the man looked as though he was itching to cross the border of the photograph and escape.

—That's the only picture I have of me with my mother, said Obdulia.

Levon scrutinized the photo.

—Where are you?

Obdulia warmed her stiff fingers by passing them quickly over the candle flame, like a hypnotist testing a patient for consciousness.

—Inside her. Those are my parents on their wedding day. She was pregnant. That was that.

On the island a woman's reputation could tumble like a lock clicking into place. Marriage, and *then* children, was the only acceptable combination. Along with recipes for apple jelly and blueberry pie, women passed on to each other cures for unwanted babies: hot baths, dry gin; a straightened hanger that, afterward, would be bent back into shape for her father or husband to hang his coat on. Some girls knitted their babies out of the yarns old women spun them and buried the tangled mess in the back garden at night.

Obdulia's grandmother had often parceled out various herbs to girls in her teenage daughter's condition. Hereword, in her desperation, had probably sampled them, too. Rooting through her mother's possessions after the funeral, Obdulia came across a folded-over tissue. Tasting the residue left on it, she recognized some of the sourness of her mother's tongue.

—They don't seem very happy.

—No, they weren't.

Levon set the photograph on the table. His parents had hundreds of photos of Alice, of him, of both of them together. A photograph was almost like going through the looking-glass. Levon could step through the print into a world that was familiar—Alice in her sailor dress with red piping, her pre-braces teeth, winning second prize at the local fair for her unbaked cookie recipe—but backward. A world in which Alice still lived, held at an age she had in fact passed the second the picture was taken. Photographs fixed memories just as chemicals fixed photos, the image gliding silently through the mist until it docked. Without photos, Levon discovered, the chemicals in the brain tended to overdevelop memories, bleaching them until all that remained was the fog through which he peered constantly, his hand extended, shouting, *Come back, please, come back.*

Obdulia's eyes were closed.

—Get some sleep, he whispered.

—When I was a child, I was afraid a thief would come in the night and chop off all my hair.

—Not tonight he won't.

Balanced on the edge of Obdulia's bed, he gathered her long, rough hair into his lap and divided it into three even sections. He began to plait Obdulia's hair, alternating left and right over the middle. He hadn't done this since Alice was small, slapping the finished braids gently against her shoulder blades like a rein, crying, *Giddyup!* Right over left. Right. Left. Right. Left. Left. He'd been left. He was lost. He was *sad.*

Wind brushed over the island like a mother's hand smoothing a blanket.

Shadows crowded around him as his fingers nimbly descended the rope of Obdulia's hair, grazing her neck, her shoulder, her breasts. She wasn't beautiful. Not really. Her lips were too thin, her chin too square. She towered over him. He had to admit, though, that he felt himself trying to resist her, which meant, didn't it, that he must also feel an attraction. He frowned at the idea of it. He had been too long without female companionship, that was all. Prison had scrambled his judgment. The sooner he got out of this house the better.

Obdulia rolled over onto her side. She left a bruise in the center of her pillow.

The three roads of her braided hair joined together at her hipbone and he knotted the ends. It was a reminder to Levon that, no matter what path he took, the ultimate destination was the same. Whatever his fate might be, he couldn't avoid it.

He stood up. For a moment he paused over Obdulia's sleeping form, listening to her breathing, assuring himself that she had sustained no mechanical injury. Her breathing was regular: no rattles or wheezes. Nothing seemed amiss.

He picked up the candle, reasoning that she didn't need it but that he, without it, might trip on a loose floorboard, or tumble down the stairs and break his neck. As he shut the door behind him, he pulled a blanket of darkness over her.

With one eye open, she watched him go.

4

TO COMFORT THE HEART AND SPIRITS AND TO SUPPRESSE MELANCHOLLY

Take of the juyces of Borage and Bigloffe, of each one pint and a halfe, juyce of Pippins or Queen Apples one pint, juyce of Balm half a pint, clarifie them, then take Chochenel made into powder four drams, infuse it in the said juyces being cold in an earthen pan for two dayes, stirring it often, then strain it and with four pounds Sugar (or two pounds if you mean not to keep it long) boyl it to a syrup. Leave it and when it is almost cold, put to it Diamargaritum one dram and a half; Diambra four scruples.

Take a spoonful for many mornings together and when you awake in the night, if there be cause, you may add to some part of it Saffron to make it more cordial.

NEXT MORNING, Levon arose from the sofa, rumpled and out of temper. The fire had gone to bed long before he did, taking with it what little warmth it offered. Furthermore, a broken spring kept prodding him, forcing him into evermore contorted positions in a futile effort to avoid it. To make matters even worse, all night long the house produced strange whistles and *boings* and rumbles, like the ruminations of his grandfather's stomach, which had amplified over the years in apparent sympathy with the old man's deafness.

He was relieved, therefore, when a bone-pale finger of light at last poked through a slat in the shutters, pointing at him, indicating that now was the time to get up and out.

He planted his feet on the floor. In the semidarkness, he failed to notice a shard of broken teacup, stained brown as an old tooth, which sank deep into his stockinged heel. Cursing, he jammed his feet into his shoes—the cheap leather stiff and warped from having been soaked—and hobbled into the hall. The floorboards barked at each step.

When he reached the entrance hall, he breathed a sigh of relief, pausing at the foot of the stairs to look up toward where Obdulia was still sleeping. He hoped.

Silence.

Silence, that is, until he opened the front door. The rusted hinges whined loudly, plaintively, as if to warn Obdulia of his escape.

The house was as alert to Levon's furtive departure as a guard dog.

During the night, the temperature had dropped to below freezing although the wind had died. Levon couldn't help but wonder if Obdulia had taken a similar course. Or was she upstairs at this moment, alone, not dead but near death, gasping out his name?

He zipped up his jacket to underneath his chin. He wished he could steel his resolve to leave her so easily. Alice, he knew, would have been ashamed of him, sneaking off in this manner. Then again, what else could he do? Obdulia had already proved to him how impractical his education was; he couldn't take her pulse or measure her blood pressure, or even *lift* her, for God's sake.

To clear his head and loosen his clogged nasal passages, Levon inhaled deeply. The spiky scent of pine reminded him so forcefully of home that for a second he fell back against the door, disoriented. He could almost hear the clink of the metal bucket his mother carried from room to room as she cleaned, their household furniture eroding over the years from the constant polishing she inflicted on it; he saw his father, trying to read the Sunday paper, lifting his legs like a drawbridge as the Hoover, a roaring dragon, dashed under them. Nor were Levon and Alice spared. *Dirt sticks to what it's thrown at*, she told her children, pinching their chins to hold them still as she scrubbed. She meant: keep a laundered hankie in your pockets, clean thoughts and a clean tongue in your head. Encroaching dirt was a sign of abject failure. On several occasions Levon had overheard her say of so-and-so that *she kept a dirty house*, as though it was a vicious pet that might get loose and attack the neighborhood.

His eyes screwed tight, his cheeks tingling, not from the cold but from his mother's efforts to wash him clean, Levon had a sudden inkling of the added horror she must have felt watching the dirt descend on Alice's coffin. And yet, despite her aversion, his poor mother had not hesitated but had gone down on bended knees to press her palm against the damp earth, and then kiss it, as though it was her beloved daughter's forehead.

For weeks afterward, though, she had stormed through the house with mops and rags and ammonia. Levon and his father protested that it was no use. They urged her to stop, to rest herself. She didn't listen, didn't give in, despite the proof that stared back at her each night in the mirror as she brushed her graying hair: the grave remained, in her expression, too deeply ingrained for a spit on a handkerchief ever to remove.

For we do see, that by motion, heat and spirit is ingender'd and preserved in all things, and by want of it vanishes.

Doctor Harvey's prescription. Levon agreed with it; he had to start moving forward. He must think ahead to his future, where there was no Alice and never would be. After all, was hers the only spirit he had left in him? Had he none of his own to be ingender'd?

Limping slightly on his sore foot, he set off to search for a path, however faint, among the trees.

For half an hour or so, all questions about his future were shoved aside with the branches. Once more, Levon was reduced to a game of blind man's buff, his arms outstretched, his progress slow. His sole companion was a squirrel, inured to harsh winters, who hopped among the trees, chattering as it went. Levon reasoned that, since this was an island, the woods had to come to an end at some point although, soon after, he scared himself by positing the equally plausible theory that he might instead wander in circles forever, unable to recognize the clues that would tell him he'd been this way before.

Levon was teetering on the brink of panic when he spied a small opening up ahead, a widening between the trees. This broadened even further until, almost before he realized it, he had emerged from the thicket onto the side of a road.

After the shadowiness of the woods, the sky—a heap of gray ash under which a spark of daylight was still struggling to ignite—appeared brighter than it was. Nonetheless, it afforded Levon his first proper glimpse of the island. In the fields opposite, the new-fallen snow was a white canvas, with barbed-wire fences sketched in pencil against it and dark squiggles of trees at the edges; an ancient, weatherbeaten barn was propped, none too securely, against the sky. A herd of bony-flanked cows, with frosted muzzles and frosted breath, milled around, regarding Levon blankly. One of them cocked her tail and shat, then stepped backward into the pliant, waxy mound to imprint her hoof, her seal.

The main road was bound to lead to the village if he adhered to it, the only question being, which way was quickest? To Levon's right, the road curved while to his left the road ran straight. He opted for that direction and set off with renewed vigor, tracing the signature of telephone wire scrawled across the parchment island. En route, he passed a number of postboxes marking satellite roads that led to farms farther inland. Levon read off the names as he went: Chapman, Muirhead, Wardle, Smith, Bell, O'Shaughnessy, O'Neill, Malone, Walsh, Sloczinski-Kilpatrick, Koval, Ireland, Tobinsky, Hoek, Boaz, Carvallo and Wong.

He saw no postbox marked Limb.

His shoes on the Styrofoam snow squeaked as he walked. *Obdulia, Obdulia, Obdulia*, they seemed to say. He halted. Silence ensued, and common sense returned to him. He'd heard no such thing! He continued on. No, there it was again. *Obdulia, Obdulia, Obdulia*. The sound of her name caused his heart to flutter like a magician's fingers, conjuring up all sorts of images. In one, her arms were crossed over her chest in the chilly repose of the dead. Her feet were bare, the soles dirty and callused. In another, her features were scrunched into an accusatory scowl. In still another, she was alive, but barely, crawling after him on her hands and knees toward the front door, her hair like a stream of blood gushing out of her. *Obdul* . . . The final syllable hovered in the air, waiting to be squished beneath his heel as he considered whether he ought to turn around and go back to her.

He slipped a hand inside his jacket to massage his aching chest. He knew that attachment of sentiment to the heart was ludicrous and unscientific. Nothing good ever came of it. Think of Shelley's heart; of how his friend, Edward Trelawney, had supposedly rescued it, entire (while the delicate Byron cowered in his carriage) from the flames of the funeral pyre, even as Shelley's brains *literally seethed, bubbled and boiled as in a cauldron.* Gallantly, impossibly, Trelawney had presented the Romantic poet's heart to Mary Shelley, who, grief-crazed, enfolded it in her handkerchief and created a monster out of it. Or what about Louis de Buade, Count Frontenac, the French Governor of Canada. His passion for his wife, and hers for him, had disintegrated to the point that, in order to prevent scandal at the French court, he was dispatched, alone, to the Canadian wilderness. His heart retained a vestige of affection for his estranged wife, however, and on his deathbed, the Count requested that it be sent to her. Levon imagined her opening the leaden box in which the heart was shipped, her own skipping a beat perhaps in expectation of a gift of jewelry, or fine porcelain, and discovering instead an inert lump of muscle and moist tissue; like being serenaded by a novice bagpiper: no air, no beat, the valves limp. Useless. Distasteful. The Countess had spurned her husband's heart and returned it post-haste to Canada where it was buried with its owner in the Chapel of Recollets.

Levon pressed onward to the village.

Obdul . . . ia. Obdulia. Obdulia.

The heart was a *practical* organ: nothing romantic about it. A heart could be transplanted, after all, without the recipient receiving the previous owner's affections along with it. Alice's heart still beat, but in a stranger's breast and with a stranger's love. For that matter, Levon's own was, he was certain, shriveled from disuse; even so, it soldiered on, pumping blood, oxygenating him, sustaining him. *Damn* the heart.

—Damn it! he shouted.

A cluster of spruce trees, leaning tipsily against each other at the side of the road, boas of snow draped over their branches, quivered in the breeze, laughing at him.

He had gone a mile or so, encountering no one, when a far-off sound wrinkled the silence. A clanking, whirring, *put-putting* that did not diverge onto a side road and evaporate as Levon expected it to but, rather, grew louder and louder. Curious, he turned, shielding his eyes against the rising sun in order to catch a glimpse of whoever, or whatever, was approaching.

Through a cloud of fumes, he spied a ghost, an apparition of what, in its bygone days, might have been called a car. The exhaust coughed out matted clumps of smoke. Hundreds of assorted parts, each a different color (Levon counted pink, powder blue, red, gray, aubergine, maroon, yellow and rust before giving up), were welded together to form a single machine. Silver fins rose gracefully out of a sea-green trunk while a Mercedes logo, stolen from the genuine article, was duct-taped to the hood. The car hit a bump and all the various components seemed to disassemble, then reassemble, in defiance of both quantum mechanics and auto mechanics.

But its most astonishing feature was the old woman hanging out of the driver-side window.

—Get in! she screeched. Get in! I can't stop this automobile once it's started without divine intervention, which I don't believe in anyway. You'll have to hop in while it's rolling.

Her head withdrew into the car. Levon did not know how to refuse the invitation without appearing rude. Seizing the moment, he lunged for the door handle, stepping, as he did so, on a frozen puddle. It cracked beneath his heel like an enchanted mirror. This caused him to lose his balance and he was dragged a few feet before he righted himself. Extending his stride to its utmost length, he ran alongside the car until, at last, he managed to yank open the door. He uttered a short prayer, hopped in and slammed it after him. Only as he settled into his seat did Levon realize the old woman's hand was cupping his bottom.

—Lift up, she said. I was clearing the seat for you.

She retrieved a 78 recording and tossed it into the voluminous back seat.

—Carl Brisson singing "When the Lovebird Leaves the Nest." Do you know it?

—Afraid not.

The old woman's wrist bones were knitting needles, a slackened bit of wool slung between them; her fitted jumper outlined two breasts hung like Christmas stockings, an orange stuffed in each toe. Nonetheless, Levon continued to feel the burning imprint of her wizened hand on his buttocks, which she'd given a squeeze before releasing. He wriggled to erase the sensation. He'd have thought she was long past thinking of such things.

Her white, upswept hair, like a knob of garlic, gave a muchneeded illusion of height; in Levon's estimation, she couldn't have been much taller than five feet. This posed certain difficulties in that her feet *just* reached the pedals. When she pressed on the accelerator, she had to slide down a little on the seat, her eyes just above the dashboard. Her solution was to stomp hard on the pedal, forcing it almost to the floor, then to allow it to rise up halfway before scooting forward on the seat and pressing on it again. The old car, as far as Levon could tell, did not respond to this unorthodox method with any appreciable difference in speed.

—Tourist? she asked him.

—I'm here to visit my cousin.

She turned to him, her penciled brows raised questioningly.

—And who would that be?

—Simon Tibeault.

The old woman clutched at his arm with both hands.

—You don't say!

Levon seized the steering wheel with his free arm and jerked it hard to the right, narrowly avoiding a *corps de ballet* of beech trees dressed in frothy tutus of snow.

—You're the jailbird!

—Um . . . I . . .

—Honey, I'm your great-aunt by marriage, Berthe Tibeault, neé Humble. My my my.

A Scottish burr, worn almost smooth, stuck to the folds of her voice. Her trousers were tartan. His mother, a Tibeault, had sniffed at the Humbles' excessive pride in their Scottish roots. He noted that Berthe pronounced her name in the French manner, an inheritance from her in-laws, the Tibeaults, maybe. On an island, accents probably climbed the side of the bowl and then got scraped back into the mix.

—Do you mind? said Levon.

He indicated the steering wheel.

—Oh. Sure.

Berthe made a show of concentrating on the road ahead although she hated her profile. Her nose skidded to a halt right before the stop sign of her red, puckered mouth. She avoided calling attention to it whenever possible.

—I apologize for letting go, she said. I'm a bicyclist at heart, you see. Crazy for them. My whole family was. My great-aunt Olympia was one of the first women on this island to own a bicycle. When I turned six, she got me one too. Ordered it from the Sears, Roebuck catalog. Page 163, right next to the advertisements for Tombstones and Monuments. Third of June, 1930, it arrived. The Famous Red Head Elgin King Roadster model made of best quality Shelby seamless cold-drawn steel tubing, with rat-trap pedals, Hercules expanders fitted to the handlebars and a nicely form-fitting saddle.

To this day, Berthe pedaled around this island faster than any of the men thought she had a right to. *Running yer legs off to give yer arse a rest?* they used to shout out to her, loping alongside for a bit, trying to catch a corner of her dress to slow her down. Berthe had outpaced their wisecracks but not her parents' eventual insistence that at eighteen she get married and settle down. She chose Albert Tibeault, who clerked at his father's general store. He rode a Kenwood bike and the description of it in the Sears catalog matched Albert almost to a T: *It is the best bicycle we can turn out for the money. This bicycle will give satisfaction. It is well made and contains good material. Fitted with nickel-plated heavy square crown and is enameled jet black.*

Berthe was keener to get her hands on the bike than on Albert.

Since both of them were virgins on their wedding night, Berthe, anxious as ever to understand the mechanics of a thing, had snuck a dirty book out of her uncle's hidden stash to read up on it. She was disappointed to find her experience with Albert less elegant and sure-footed than the one detailed in the book. For a start, Albert's tongue did not probe delicately but, instead, swished around her lips as though licking the rim of a jam jar. She herself had needed to halt proceedings so she could visit the outhouse for a pee. Most disastrous of all, nerves and too much beer at the wedding had made Albert limp. At one point, Berthe had brazenly reached over and patted "it" on the head, both wary and eager that it would wake, but that didn't help either. At a complete loss as to how to proceed, husband and wife sat bolt upright next to each other on the bed. Apart from being naked, they might have been in their pew at church. Thinking of the hymnal, and to pass the time, Berthe reached under the bed and pulled out her uncle's book. Ignoring Albert's blushes, she opened it and began to read, at first to herself and then, as she became more excited, aloud to her husband. On a whim, she pressed the pages against his sweaty thigh; when she removed the book, the black hairs on his white skin looked like a mirror imprint of the words on the page. She then tossed the book aside and pretended to continue reading, not the book but Albert, tracing the words with her finger, peering near-sightedly at his chest, his stomach, his . . . her hot breath stirring him. Albert swooned against the pillow. His saddle wasn't as form-fitting as she was used to but she clamped it between her legs and rode him as fast as she could, pedaling hard up the hills and coasting down into the valleys.

After that night, Berthe always took the lead, sometimes pulling so far out in front of Albert that she overtook someone else along the road. She was discreet in her affairs, or tried to be, and her husband had died contented as far as she knew.

—That's the cemetery, she said.

To their right, a fringe of weeping willows. Beyond them, a large field sloped upward. Headstones were scattered throughout, possibly ordered from Sears, Roebuck too.

—We expected you yesterday, Berthe said to him.

—Er . . . I . . . I was . . .

Levon did not want to confide in Berthe. She might not believe him if he told her what had happened last night. And if, God forbid, Obdulia *was* dead, or even ill, Berthe might suspect him of having poisoned the girl himself. She had called him a jailbird, hadn't she? He knew from his cell mate Angus's experience that a prison record encapsulated all the mistakes a man had ever made but gave no hint of the good he might do in future. Employers looking over those forms peered at the black typescript as if through the iron bars of the inmate's cell, imprisoning his character as securely as the penitentiary had his body. This was supposed to be the beginning of Levon's new life. He wanted to be seen as unblemished. Innocent. That's what he intended to be here. To hell with Obdulia, then. Her problems were not his.

—You were . . . ? Berthe prompted.

—I was delayed.

Berthe's expression was wooden apart from her eyes: two slits through which she regarded him craftily, like a speakeasy bouncer appraising a new customer.

—You're here now and that's the main thing. I have a room all ready for you. What are you doing? What *is* that?

A newspaper aged the color of peanut brittle had stuck to the bottom of his shoe. For the last few minutes, he'd been attempting, quietly, to remove it. Finding that he couldn't, he crossed his right ankle over his left knee so the newsprint was visible to Berthe, who darted glances at it.

—Ah yes, she said. The obituary of a former lover of mine.

Levon tilted his head.

—Man Shot Dead by His Own Cow.

—Not *him*. The bank robber. Underneath. A good deal older than me, but so dashing! He outshot Jesse James and knew Bat Masterson. Robbed a train once in Oklahoma.

He scanned the article.

—And netted three bucks.

—You should talk. I met him after he got paroled. He became a chicken farmer for a while. Then a lawyer, a politician and an evangelist.

She winked at him.

—I have a soft spot for criminals.

—I never robbed a bank, Levon protested.

—No no. I meant evangelists. Here's the village.

He pressed his nose to the window.

—This is it?

Levon had a picture in his mind of quaint wooden storefronts painted in pastel colors. Oval wooden signs swinging from the awnings: *Ye Olde* this and *Ye Olde* that. A striped barbershop pole and a quartet to go along with it.

More cinema than *vérité*.

He doubted such a picturesque village had ever existed here but if so, all that remained of it were the scraggly threads after an embroidery has been picked apart. The road was cratered with pot holes, shop signs were peeling and lopsided. On one side was a ferry dock and paved parking lot. On the other, a cluster of squat buildings.

—No tall stories here, he murmured.

—People here made a living sewing sail cloths. Once steam put paid to that, lots of islanders packed their bags and moved to the city. A few game souls tried farming but when their crops didn't line up as neat as their stitches, they gave that up. One or two went back to proper tailoring like their grandfathers had done, except that customers complained about their outfits billowing in the breeze. They were rushed along the street at such a rate of knots per hour they landed headfirst in the bushes. And I remember the time . . .

Levon raised his hands.

—OK, OK. I rushed to judgment.

At the general store and bar, Berthe veered the car sharply toward the interior of the island. The road was narrow. Overgrown hedges scraped the side of the car like fingernails on a chalkboard.

—Where are we going? he winced.

—Simon's bakery, of course.

Levon slapped his leg, smothering another of the itchy sparks that were flaring up all over his body.

—It's a bit out of the way, isn't it? Levon commented.

—That depends on where you start from.

—Do you mean to tell me that customers trek all the way out here for a loaf of bread?

She shook her head.

—Customers aren't allowed at the bakery, Berthe said. Simon needs absolute privacy for his work. An order of bread gets shipped to the city every morning on a special boat fitted with ovens. The bread bakes en route and Simon's assistants toss out the fresh loaves to the crowd at the dock.

—If he already has assistants, why does he need me?

—Curiosity killed the cat, Berthe muttered. Or was that me? I felt a bump back there.

Five minutes later, Levon discerned the shape of an old-fashioned whitewashed chapel down the road; so white it might have been built of snow except for a door, painted forest green to match the surrounding pine trees, and two narrow stained-glass windows standing sentry beside it. Three ostrich feathers of smoke, stuck in the slate roof, waved jauntily in the breeze.

—There it is! said Berthe.

—There what is?

—The bakery.

—*That's* the bakery?

—The voice of one crying in this wilderness, Berthe recited. Prepare ye the way of the Lord, make his paths straight.

Levon sighed.

—Righty-ho, he said.

He had grown up in a Jesus-ridden town: a church on every corner but no libraries, no theaters, no art galleries. His parents, thank God, were not religious. His neighbors were, though, and his aunt Anna-Lee. At family gatherings, her reputation for righteousness preceded her as the iceberg had the *Titanic*.

—It's known as the Church of the Good Thief, Berthe told him. On the 10th of August 1862, one hundred and forty-eight inmates were ferried over the lake from the prison. It was a stunt planned by the warden. Organized religion wasn't enough for him, you see; he had to have a *better* organized religion. He informed all the papers that a church could be raised in a single day and he set about proving it.

By this time, they'd arrived at the chapel and were looping lazily around it.

—You see that steeple? she asked him.

Levon jutted his chin over the dashboard, craning his neck so that he could look up at it.

—It's quite tall, he observed.

—Tallest in four counties. The warden's doing. He wanted the steeple as high as the men's purpose in building it. Women wrapped the prisoners in scarves and mittens against the cold. Cups of tea were passed up hand over hand. By the time they reached the top, the liquid was frozen. Or so they say. When the steeple was finished, the warden was invited to take tea with the Prime Minister.

—And what were the prisoners invited to take? asked Levon sourly.

—The warden's gold watch. It's rumored to be buried in the foundation. What the prisoners should have been asked to take was *care*. That afternoon, late, a freak thunderstorm arose. A prisoner was fixing the metal cross to the top when a lightning bolt hit it. He was harnessed to the steeple and couldn't be brought down fast enough to save him. When they cut open his shirt, they discovered the shape of the cross seared onto his skin. Burned right through his clothes.

—That can't be true, said Levon.

—It's an *ipso facto*. Look it up.

—But that's horrible!

Berthe shrugged.

—We've all got our crosses to bear, she said philosophically. This church got used until about 1950. After that, congregations started to dwindle and each new minister blamed the location. There was crying in this wilderness until, finally, a new church was built, closer to the village. This one was allowed to crumble into ruin almost. Simon bought it when he came back to the island. A song he got it for. *Une chanson!*

—Came back? From where?

—Oh, she said vaguely, *away.*

They had concluded several perambulations at this point, each go-round giving Levon the opportunity to notice something new. The cross, for example, was no longer there, replaced by a weather-vane of a rotund man in a baker's hat, one leg thrust forward as if he was about to step off the roof. His toe pointed northwest at the moment. Levon had also seen a modern, windowless garage tacked on to the original building.

—Right, said Berthe, off you go.

Levon twisted around to face her.

—Now?

—What better time than the present?

—Aren't you going to stop at least? he asked.

—Told you, I can't. Now, when I say jump, tuck your head in and leap. Open the car door first, of course.

—But . . .

—No buts. Out! Shoo!

The speedometer read ten miles an hour.

—Couldn't I . . . ?

—No.

She reached across him and pulled on the car handle. The door swung open.

—By the way, she said, how did you like Obdulia?

—*What* did you say?

Berthe blew him a kiss.

—Now, she yelled. *Jump!*

With a firm shove Berthe sent Levon tumbling out onto the snow. He rolled for a foot or two, landing on his back, arms and feet akimbo, the wind knocked out of him. He lay there, gasping like a hooked flounder, until, gradually, he recovered his breath and began, cautiously, to flex his joints, testing his bones once again for breakages. Berthe was already gone. He heard the phlegmy cough of her ancient engine receding. Had she given him even a backward glance? No, he decided, self-pity burbling up inside him. This island was overrun with women for whom his good health and happiness were of no import.

A damp hand pressed into the small of his back, urging movement as a dance partner does. He closed his eyes and found himself drifting back to ninth grade. He was waltzing with Alice, practicing for his first formal dance.

The music was mapped territory and Levon stuck to it doggedly, afraid of getting lost. Alice was more adventurous. She pranced about in their mother's black velvet pumps, like hooves at the ends of her slender legs, squeezing through the bars of music, trespassing into a livelier step, a combination of her own devising: an Irish jig mixed with a polka. Levon hung back, far too serious (he was supposed to be *dancing*, for heaven's sake!), intent on learning to waltz properly. Alice gave up on him at last, breaking away. Grinning with delight, she twirled around the room by herself while Levon focused stupidly on his now empty arms, arms that remained held out to embrace her.

And still did. Swallowing a tear, he struggled to his feet, attentive to the slightest disorder among his spinal discs, the merest twinge in his ankle. Crankiness in his shoulder muscle. No, he was fine. Just fine. He stared down at where he had lain, intrigued to discover that he had inadvertently made a snow angel. Always, after the first snow of winter, he and Alice had raced outside, falling to the ground repeatedly, waving their arms and legs until they had created a mirror of an angel-strewn heaven in their own backyard.

He was out of practice. This angel was smudged, its wing dented where he'd dug his elbow in for leverage, as if it had fallen from a great height and landed unceremoniously in this snowdrift.

So much for guardian angels, he thought.

Levon straightened his clothes, bravely threw back his shoulders and headed toward the bakery.

5

AN EXCELLENT RECEIPT FOR SWOUNDING, AND BRINGING QUICKLY TO LIFE

Take of the common round black Pepper, and bruise it a little and take half a sheet of white Paper, and fold it up together, and between evry fold threw some of the same, and burn one end thereof in the fire, and hold it to the Nosthrils; 'tis very good.

I F LEVON had pressed his ear against the church wall, he might have detected a faint echo of religion, nothing more. Only the stained-glass windows, depicting the miracle of the loaves and fishes, had survived the church's transformation into a bakery. He squinted through a tulle of flour that hung in the air. Gone were the pews, the altar, the font. Instead, a wooden trough extended almost the entire length of the nave. A wooden platform had been built above it to support a large metal tank and from there, a pipe descended into the depression of the trough, blurting out flour at regular intervals. He could dimly make out two men in the center of the trough, their shirts off, trousers rolled to the knee. They were running in place, using their bare feet to incorporate the flour into an ever-increasing mass of dough. Sweat leaped from their brows like lemmings into the churning sea below.

—Their perspiration provides the perfect amount of salt, a voice whispered in his ear. A nineteenth-century technique I'm rather partial to.

Levon felt someone in that floury fog take his hand and knead it.

—Welcome, said the voice, welcome.

Flour tickled Levon's nose. Unable to stop himself, he let loose a roaring sneeze. The gauzy air parted to reveal his cousin.

Simon Tibeault was in his mid-thirties, the son of Levon's mother's brother. A cousin who had grown up distant to him in miles if not blood. Simon was over six feet tall, with a round face, ruddy cheeks and a second helping of chin. His two front teeth were sharp and turned against each other. This lent to Simon's benign expression an oddly feral quality. It was, Levon thought, as if a sheep had swallowed a wolf. Simon wore a baker's hat, cotton T-shirt and trousers, and an apron tied around his middle, all of them pristine.

Exuding an air of *bonhomie*, Simon flung a plump arm around Levon's shoulders. He peppered him with questions about his trip, his health, his parents, but left no time for Levon to respond, except to Simon's final question, which wasn't about Levon at all.

—Well? What do you think of our little operation?

Levon had been led, almost without noticing it, to a long oak refectory table positioned perpendicular to the trough, so that it formed a cross. Here, three more men were hand-shaping loaves of dough, weighing them on large brass scales and then wrapping them up in cloths and laying them tenderly in rush baskets, like rows of baby Moseses, on shelves built where the choir ought to have been. The rising bread gave off a rich wine odor.

Simon's mouth twitched like a neighbor's curtain, hinting at the presence of someone watching from the darkness, eager to know your business while keeping themselves hidden from view.

—Very . . . nice, Levon murmured.

He was distracted by the strange appearance of Simon's assistants. Including the two men kneading the dough, there were five altogether. They shared the same gangly limbs and shadowed, bony faces. Their piercing blue eyes were set too close together, knocking against each other like marbles.

—Quintuplets, Simon whispered. Oliver, Tango, Marmaduke, Isaac and Newton.

None of the men acknowledged Levon. Ranks closed with the firmness of a door against an arctic wind.

—Come, Simon said, let's get you started.

—Now?

Levon had hoped for an offer of breakfast and a bath. He'd begun to sweat in the intense heat of the bakery. He clamped his arms to his sides to diminish the reek of his armpits.

—No time like the present!

Simon picked up a spatula and, waving it like a baton, conducted a tour of the bakery. During the next half-hour, Levon inspected the bolting machine, a complicated mix of gears, levers and pulleys used to sift the flour. He handled cutters for separating the dough into smaller pieces and brushes for gilding the tops with butter or an egg wash before baking. He peered into large iron cauldrons of steaming water. Ovens were installed at the rear of the church in what must have been the sacristy. Splotches of communion wine stained the floor.

Levon stepped back to allow an assistant to light a hardwood fire in one of the ovens. Simon explained to him that it would be left to smoulder for hours and hours (*like a grievance*, he murmured) until the temperature was hot enough for the cinders to be shoveled out. Once that was accomplished, the floor would be swept clean and dusted with cornmeal to prevent the bread from sticking. The assistant's job was to brush the interior of the oven with a wet broom, to cool the temperature down a little, in addition to removing stray ashes. There were three ovens, all built of brick, all with a slightly flattened hemispheric shape. This, Simon told him, induced a more even distribution of heat. The dome measured about a foot and a half tall. Higher than that, heat was wasted, inhibiting the swelling of the loaves and drying out the crusts.

—These ovens must be fired up an hour before the loaves are put in. It is a baker's most anxious moment. A loaf that does not begin to rise at the summit of its exaltation is lost to us forever.

Levon noted with relief that the peels for inserting dough into the oven worked like the proverbial barge pole.

—How do you know when the oven is hot enough?

Simon scooped a pinch of flour from the floor and sprinkled it over the oven. The flour reddened immediately.

—Red is perfection. Black, the oven's too hot.

—I see.

—Come, come. You'll learn all of this soon enough.

—Perhaps, said Levon. But . . .

—But is for billy goats.

—Couldn't you have found a better building to locate in? More modern? More central? What I don't understand is, why a church?

—A *better* building? Simon gasped. How on earth do you mean? Baking *is* religion, you ignoramus. The Holy Sacrament.

Jesus took bread and blessed it, and broke it, and gave it to His disciples, and said, Take, eat; this is my body. Do you know what the roof of this oven is called? A chapel! We trace the sign of the cross into each loaf. We avoid placing a loaf bottom up, which is considered an act of desecration. Drop a loaf of bread on the ground, we kiss it as penitence. We mount the dough in the trough as Christ was mounted on the Cross. Voltaire and Rousseau considered it sacrilege—yes! Sacrilege!—to waste bread and wrote pamphlets condemning the use of flour in wig preparation and cosmetics. Need I go on?

In his agitated state, Simon's skin appeared to be lightly buttered. His large pores suggested he'd been pricked repeatedly by a fork to test whether or not he was done.

—No, said Levon. I take your point.

His cousin stomped back into the bakery proper, Levon trailing after.

—Don't you know *anything* about baking? he was asked.

—Yes, actually. I do.

An oversized, leather-bound cookbook lay spread open on a wooden stand. Levon peeled back the pages. Spilled grease made them transparent in spots; directions had transferred from one recipe to the recipe that preceded it. The future rewriting the past.

—I know that in France in the late 1660s there was a big kerfuffle over whether bakers ought to be using brewer's yeast to speed up fermentation. Barm it was called, right? The Paris Faculty of Medicine voted 45–30 to ban it. Gui Patin, a doctor, wrote that barm was the *écume*, the scum, of a doleful drink. Bread baked with barm was liable to cause damage to the nervous system, urological difficulties and leprosy.

Simon threw up his hands.

—Barmy! We use it of course.

—Hmm, Levon replied.

He was reading the asides, penned in a florid script, that embellished the edges of the recipes: passionate, indifferent, forgetful, playful.

—What are these words for? he asked.

—Father wooed Mother with recipes and recorded the effect on her of each.

Levon flipped the page.

—Flatulent?

—Obviously, Simon replied, some were less successful than others. Baking is both art *and* science. Abbé Pluche informs us that, in an ideal scenario, physics descends from the top of the celestial spheres *where it is pleased to reside some time in the bakery*. Science! No bakery can exist without it. At the establishment of the *École Gratuite de Boulangerie* in 1782, the students were told that chemistry can advantageously influence the most venerable of arts. Monsieur Cadet began his lectures—to a primarily female body of students—with a demonstration of how, under the new invention called a microscope, the genitalia of the male flea was, relatively speaking, almost as large as a man's.

He switched on the mixer, the beaters pirouetting like ballroom dancers, a skirt of batter swirling around them. He had to raise his voice to be heard over the humming.

—Love, too, is both art and science, is it not? A chemical reaction that induces two, otherwise sane, individuals to begin writing poetry and painting sunsets. The same applies, in a manner of speaking, to baking. Wheat contains proteins in its endosperm, for example. These proteins interact. This allows for an elastic structure to form that is durable enough for the dough to rise without breaking up. Like a marriage. All quantifiable stuff so far. But! A perfect croissant? Gilded, tender, with just a hint of sweetness. That is Art. A certain, indefinable . . . *je ne sais quoi* has been added. Who can explain it?

—Are you married, Simon?

He shook his head.

—Kissing don't last: cookery do.

For reasons he couldn't fathom, Levon suddenly pictured Obdulia's mouth. It turned up at the corners when she smiled, prow and stern; a ship that might transport him safely home or, more likely, capsize and drown him. He was reminded of Harvey's journal, in which the doctor had set for himself a series of questions he could not answer, such as *What kind of movement is scratching?* But the one Levon loved best was a fragment, so that it read more as a command than a query: *Leap out of the stern of a boat.*

He trained his eyes on the recipe in front of him.

—Batter, strain, coddle. Add thyme and sage. These terms could be applied to life, too.

—Yes, I suppose. We proof, we measure, we temper, we . . . I can't think of what else.

—Knead? Levon suggested.

—And what is it that *you* need? Simon snorted.

Levon scratched his head.

—A recipe for life, he decided.

—There is one more or less.

—No there isn't.

Simon bowed formally over a green ceramic bowl, adding a mound of flour that had collected in the folds of his baker's hat.

—What is a recipe but a series of measures taken to reach a known end? Let's say a . . . a loaf of Swedish Limpa! There is a finite amount of ingredients I may use and not much leeway in how I choose to combine them. I can, of course, make certain choices as to *degree* so long as I'm prepared to accept that my loaf may turn out to be too dry or too crisp or simply without flavor. But I will always end up with a Swedish Limpa, no matter what.

—Ah, said Levon glumly. Fate.

—Science is the recipe, art the creativity applied to following it. Plenty of scope there for amusement. Don't sulk.

Simon beckoned him over to the table. Two of the assistants (Oliver and Tango? Isaac and Newton?) flipped off the mixer and hoisted the bowl up as another (Marmaduke?) scraped the sticky dough onto the floured, wooden surface. Using a cutter, Simon separated a smaller piece from the mass and began, deftly, to roll it back and forth into an oblong shape. He then flipped it over like an animal he was about to vivisect and, with a stubby finger, pointed to a crease that split the underside of the spongy dough.

—The trick when kneading is to close this seam, he said. Otherwise, it cracks open during baking and the bread has to be thrown out. Try for yourself.

—I can't, Levon protested. I'll ruin it.

He clasped his hands behind his back: an uncomfortable reminder of his helplessness, and shame, the night of his arrest.

—We shall see.

Simon marshalled Levon's hands and forcibly laid them on

the cool, slick dough, as a piano teacher might to a reluctant student. He was painfully aware of the assistants looking down their collective noses at him. Simon focused on the bread.

Levon tried to manipulate the dough as he'd witnessed it being done but the puckered seam remained, much as the scar on his hand did, as a chastisement of his ineptitude.

—Never mind, Simon sighed.

—I'm sorry. I'm so hungry I can't think straight.

He clutched his stomach to emphasize the point.

—Hungry?

—I haven't eaten since yesterday. I was rather hoping that . . .

Simon held up his hand to indicate that he understood, no more need be said. He crossed to a shelf where a series of loaves, caramel-colored on top and pale underneath, like an Indian woman's hands, were cooling. *This* was what his customers wanted. Bread to make cheese sandwiches with or to sop up gravy. It was an insult to his gifts as a baker. Never mind, he consoled himself. All that was about to change. The act of eating his work, his labor, his *art* was soon to take on a greater significance. He would be recognized throughout the world for the artist he truly was. Simon glanced at a framed piece of embroidery hanging on the wall. *Art is not a handicraft, it is a transmission of feeling the artist has experienced.* How true! How perceptive!

Still, Simon had to acknowledge it: even Tolstoy must have been hungry now and again.

—Here.

He held out a thick slice to Levon.

—*Thank* you.

Levon bit into the bread. The crisp, buttery crust provided a perfect counterpoint to the slight tang of the warm dough, which was as airy as a compliment and, at the same time, completely satisfying. He'd never eaten anything so delicious in his life.

Simon clapped his hands.

—Come on. The tour isn't over.

—It isn't?

—The best is yet to come.

He turned to his assistants.

—Scat! he hissed at them. Get!

Five pairs of eyes swiveled toward him. None moved, as if calculating the risk of disobedience. It must have proved too great for, seconds later, with a twitch, a leap and a harsh, guttural laugh, the five men grabbed their jackets from pegs on the wall and shot out into the snow.

Once he was satisfied that they were truly alone, Simon crossed to a shelf crammed with pots and pans. He ran his fingers, like a plump spider, along the shelf. He inserted his hand in the space between a blue-and-white-striped earthenware bowl and a copper stock pot. Levon heard a faint click. Simon winked at Levon, who watched, amazed, as the shelf swung outward with an arthritic creak, revealing a plain wooden door.

—Wow!

—My partner built it. He's very clever at concealing things.

From a pocket in his apron, Simon produced an ornate brass key. To Levon's further astonishment, he popped it into his mouth, sucked on it for a moment, then spit it out again.

—I've been hiding it in a jar of raspberry jam.

He fitted the key into a lock and, with some effort, turned it.

—Sticks, he grunted.

—Why all the secrecy? Levon demanded.

Simon gave him a peculiar smile as he ushered Levon toward the portal.

—This, he said, is where I keep the bodies.

Hunched over his cello, the young man angled his bow downward to sustain the final note of Bach's Brandenburg Concerto No. 3. A sea-horse curl floated in the middle of his dewy forehead.

—Not very good, is he? Levon whispered to Simon.

The music had been performed with the frenetic verve of a housewife spring-cleaning her closet, throwing out notes no longer considered pretty or even useful.

—Break his finger, Simon urged him.

—Oh! Oh, I couldn't.

—Go on.

—Are you sure?

—Positive.

Levon sidled up to the cellist with an apologetic smile. Reaching out to the fret, he tore off the musician's index finger and stuffed it into his mouth.

—Good?

—Superb, mumbled Levon.

Simon primped the cellist's hair as if to discount his accomplishment by drawing attention to a flaw.

From even a foot away, the musician looked undeniably human. As if, at any second, he might rise up from his stool, stretch his aching limbs, brush the wrinkles from his tuxedo, scratch his cheek. Speak. Smile. Perform a tango. But up close,

Levon saw that the flush in the cellist's cheeks was due to apple skins baked into the dough. His hair was black liquorice shredded into strands almost as fine as the real thing; his skin was pimpled with strawberry pulp. His almond-shaped nails were, in fact, almonds. There was even a floury residue in the corner of his mouth where he might have forgotten to wipe off the toothpaste after brushing his teeth.

—Amazing, Levon breathed.

Simon giggled as he rubbed his hands together.

—Note the roundedness of his shoulders as he slumps over his instrument. That's to suggest a question mark: the boy's adolescent angst. I aim to re-create more than birth marks and hair color. A bit of their souls must be captured too.

—Trespassing on another's patch, aren't you?

—A baker, too, is accustomed to watching things fall and rise again, Simon replied.

—I see, said Levon in a tone that indicated the opposite.

—The whole enterprise began three years ago. I'd just withdrawn a baker's dozen of cinnamon rolls from the oven and was setting them out to cool when I realized that they bore a *remarkable* resemblance to Jesus and the Apostles. I mean, it was *uncanny*.

—Jesus? said Levon.

—Yes.

—And the Apostles?

—Yes.

—Do . . . do you still have them?

Simon waggled his hands in the air.

—And risk an influx of screaming hordes of religious maniacs? No, no. We ate them. But it got me thinking. What if I could re-create a human being using dough. I mean, *deliberately*. It was a whim that quickly became an obsession and, for a year, I closeted myself in here . . .

His arm wafted around the cramped quarters of the workshop. *Here* was the garage that Levon had seen earlier. A carpenter's workbench ran alongside one wall. Instead of saws and wrenches, the surface was littered with wigs of cooked spaghetti, pots of gelatinous substances, glass dishes heaped with pigment and paint brushes of various sizes. A large pot of something red bubbled furiously on a gas cooker. The air was scented with chocolate and nutmeg, petrol, paraffin, a snuffed candle, bitter almonds and dozens of other aromas Levon couldn't identify. He stepped into a cobweb only to find it was spun sugar. A man's torso was propped on a chair in the corner, a pair of willowy legs stretched out on the floor next to it. Three women's heads hung by their hair from the ceiling, their features coarse and unfinished, blank eyes staring into the distance, their mouths ajar in mid-scream.

—And so, I commenced to experiment. I added condensed milk and soured milk and the milk of human kindness. I gave a fig and then I didn't. I stirred the pot and watched the pot. Into it went snips and snails and puppy-dog tails, sour grapes and the grapes of wrath.

—That's fairy-tale stuff, Levon said. I thought baking was *science.*

—Oh all *right*, Simon snapped. I fiddled with the gluten content of the dough and with baking temperatures, plus the amounts of salt, baking powder, etcetera, that I used. Until, at last, I had concocted a dough that, with minor variations, might replicate any skin type.

Simon rose up on his toes, hugging himself with excitement.

—You and I, for instance, possess the same basic ingredients, but with minute, albeit crucial, differences. Why are your eyes brown and mine blue? Why is your physique weedy and mine robust? Genes! What I have done is not so radically different from our parents cooking us up with whatever is on the shelf gene-wise. I allow for nuances in form and texture, naturally, adding a pinch of this or that as needed. A hunk of blue cheese, perhaps, blue as the vein o'er the Madonna's breast.

—Browning? said Levon.

—Yes, for a darker complexion.

—Why, though? Who on earth, if I may be so bold, wants a replica of themselves made of bread?

—I'll admit the application of this formula eluded me at first. I felt like an alchemist who'd transformed lead into gold for a market that accepted only lead currency. I toyed with the idea of simply submitting the experiment as an article to the journal *Science*; or perhaps *Bon Appétit*. Something told me, however, that if I waited, if I was patient, I could make a much bigger splash. I was curious as to . . . you're looking a bit peaked, Levon. Why don't you sit?

Simon pulled out a stool. Levon removed a gingerbread hand that lay ghoulishly on top of it, and slumped down on the seat. Clinging to the gingerbread hand, he chewed ruminatively on the nails of it. Simon resumed his tale, pacing the room as he did so.

—One day, I happened to overhear this poor fellow complaining to a friend.

He placed a proprietorial hand on the cellist's shoulder.

—Despite his having a tin ear, his mother is determined that a great musician shall be wrought from it. To this end, she has booked a concert hall, displacing the Shriner's eagerly anticipated production of *Waiting for Godot*, and has advertised as far off as Toronto and Poughkeepsie. Listening to him speak about his horror of this event, a lightbulb went on in my head. What if, what if? So, I quietly suggested to him that I might, just *might*, be able to help. He came to me, I made a plaster cast of his features, snapped a few Polaroids and *voilà!* He will arrange to have his counterpart in place on the stage, while he sneaks out the back door.

Levon scraped off some gingerbread crumbs congealing at the corners of his mouth.

—What about the music? he said.

Simon pressed the hip of the cello, releasing a panel the size of a cigar box. Inside was a tape recorder.

—Your partner again?

—Isn't he marvelous? Simon whispered.

—You don't really believe that the audience will buy this, do you?

—You've heard his recording. By the middle of the first movement, the audience will have followed suit. No matter. The boy will be long gone by that time, on a train bound for Whitehorse. It will be his mother, if you'll pardon the expression, who has to face the music. Anyway, I'm sure she'll be much happier with my effort than she ever was with hers.

—A loaf of bread can never replace a son, Simon.

—Can't it? he asked slyly.

Levon gripped the gingerbread wrist so tightly that it crumbled.

—No!

—But why not? Simon persisted. She didn't want *that* son. Not at all. She wanted a musical boy, a neat boy, a boy without pimples or awkwardness or problems with girls. Never mind. If at first you don't succeed, try try again. Well, she can rip *this* boy's head off, devour *this* boy, swallow him whole, and what will she produce in the end? A shit. Another little shit. *That* is how the world *is*.

Levon was about to reply to this extraordinary theory when the workshop door flew open. The door ricocheted off the wall and back into the fist of a man who stood there as if waiting for it—no, daring it—to shut in his face. Instead, he bashed it again and stepped smartly over the threshold.

He was in his late fifties or early sixties. His hair, although flecked with flour, remained defiantly black and spiny as a bat's wing. Veins had burst on his nose and cheeks, blotches of purple bubbling up through a crust of dough stuck to his skin, like a pie whose contents have oozed out during baking. He wore a gray T-shirt, sneakers and black jeans.

The man did not speak but swung himself up on the counter. His movement was graceful, deliberate, as if protecting a flame inside him that might extinguish if he wasn't careful. Levon suspected that it was the fire's potential to burn, not the warmth of it, that he sought to preserve.

Levon had known a boy at school with that same build— square and muscular, like a jack-in-the-box—as well as this man's predatory gaze. Levon, being small for his age, was always leery of his schoolmate. The boy's temper was notoriously unpredictable; press his button, even inadvertently, and he would leap out at you, arms flailing, a joyless grin plastered on his face. He started hitting and wouldn't stop, having already decided that the best way to stand tall in the world was to flatten everybody around him.

—This is my partner, Simon explained. He suffered from high fevers as a child. All that heating up and cooling down has made him badly tempered. Levon Hawke, Elias Limb.

The man in the photograph. Obdulia's father! A seed of alarm sprouted in the pit of Levon's stomach, cold tendrils pushing up through his lungs and chest, wrapping around his throat.

—Limb? he said in a choked voice.

—You were supposed to be here yesterday, said Elias abruptly.

—Leave him be now, Simon purred. We don't want to start our relationship off on the wrong foot, *do* we?

—Have you told him? Elias said to Simon.

—Told me what?

Simon touched Elias lightly, it was almost a caress, on the wrist.

—Will you do it, or shall I? he asked softly.

Break through skin, there's bone. Obdulia's words came back to Levon as, without lifting his palm from the bench, Elias flicked a finger at Simon. Simon's eyes widened. Elias glanced into them cursorily, as if into a box that contained a trinket he might want to play with later. Simon's affection, Levon guessed. For now, Elias contented himself with deliberately removing his wrist from his partner's reach. Embarrassed at witnessing this odd exchange, Levon stared at the floor. It was covered with a silken carpet of flour, ripped in the spots where the men had stepped previously. There was the imprint of Elias's big foot treading on Simon's toes: Simon's heel digging into Elias's arch. A pattern of their dance.

—*I'll* tell him, said Elias.

—Goody, Simon whispered.

—Tell me what?

Crossing his muscular legs, Elias interlaced his knuckles and cracked them. Simon shuddered.

—I wish you wouldn't do that.

—Tell me *what*, Levon shouted.

Elias's black eyes were like ants swarming over a crumb.

—Why, he said. A story. What else?

6

TO MAKE SILVER LETTERS WITHOUT SILVER

Take tin an ounce, Quick silver two ounces, then beat them wel with Gin water, and so write with it.

IN THE SUMMER of 1910, a priest named Abiathar Babbitt arrived on this island. He was in his twenties and still wet behind the ears: thin, with a bulbous forehead, thick glasses, and auburn hair that struck out in all different directions, like young boys' after lighting a firecracker. He brought with him his diploma from Trinity College, Dublin, and also two shirts, both darned, two pairs of trousers, shiny at the knees, one pair of brogues, size twelve and a half, and six trunks filled with books. There was usually a slim volume of poetry sticking out of his pocket where his hankie ought to have been.

This habit was considered peculiar by the islanders given that almost none of them could read. News passed by word of mouth and, depending on the shape of the mouth that told it, the word might be accurate or distorted. It wasn't ever certain which.

Abiathar didn't mind. He liked to sit in kitchens, a piece of shortbread crumbling over his knees, a cup of tea in hand, and listen to their stories. Even the cookie tin had a tale attached to it, Oh, this belonged to Great-Aunt Hattie who, and this was a queer thing, sir, *could not* smile—or the chair he sat on, Carved out of an oak tree that shot up overnight, Mr. Babbitt, *overnight*.

God was their witness and Abiathar believed them as he believed in God. Which is to say, he wanted to, so he did.

That first winter he spent on the island was a raw one. The lake froze solid in November; snow drifts stood tall as a ten-year-old child. Icicle fangs hung from the roofs, turning the island into an open, snarling mouth that bit down to the bone. Hands and noses and feet were cold; the shoulder a woman offered to her husband at night was cold. The dead were whittled to a point at one end like a pencil and driven into the ground since it was too hard to break open for a grave.

Now, in those times, a stocked larder stretched so far, but never further than March, which islanders referred to as starve-month. By then, preserve jars were licked clean and all the root vegetables had been taken up from the cellar; people stole cheese out of the mouse traps and checked under the sofa cushions for stray crumbs. Abiathar, coming from Ireland, understood the crazed desperation hunger inspired and he fretted. The whole island grew quarrelsome—an argument will do to sink your teeth into when there's nothing else. Tailors swallowed pins, working them out of their system in needling comments to their customers. (A little *plumper* than last time, I think, Mrs. O'Shaughnessy.) Rumors were spread instead of jam. *That* person hoarded bacon. *This* one had a sack of flour. There was even grumbling in church when the communion wafers were finished off.

Abiathar didn't realize that starve-month was an annual occurrence, to be borne like childbirth or taxes or a pimply adolescence, with a good deal of complaint but also a sense of resignation. Just as a wound clock ticks forward, spring was sure to come at the proper time and with it, new crops. Nonetheless, Abiathar regarded the shepherding of his flock through this lean period as the first real test of his vocation.

Following Sunday service, he retired to his study where he remained for three days and nights. Abiathar instructed his housekeeper, Agnes Wyatt, not to clean the room until he emerged. She was in her seventies, her face lined so deep it looked as if she'd been wrapped in barbed wire when she was still young and impressionable. Agnes obeyed, of course, although she expended an unusual amount of elbow grease polishing the knob, her ear glued to the study door. People thought she'd gone doolally when she reported what she'd heard: a flock of frenzied pigeons trapped inside the room, with now and then a dull thud, as of a bird dropping lifeless to the ground.

Agnes barely had time to pick up her duster and pretend to be attending to the baseboards when the priest finally unlocked the door. He rushed out with a cheerful toodle-oo and a wave of his fingers. He *looked* the same. Thinner, maybe, and a bit whiffy after three days of no baths. Agnes poked her head around the door frame, expecting to see utter chaos, already griping about the hours of extra work for her in clearing up. Imagine, then, how perplexed she was to see that nothing in the room was displaced, except for a gap like a missing tooth in one row of books.

Meanwhile, the priest, his scarf trailing out behind him, flew through the village with the buzzing energy of a dragonfly. He distributed posters advertising a special church service for that evening. Since the islanders couldn't read, he'd drawn a church with a moon pasted on the background. He nailed the posters to trees, fences, the church door. He handed them to people in the street, stuck them in dogs' mouths to be trotted home to their masters. He slipped them under the beer glasses at Moses Visitor's bar. As the glasses drained, the drinkers couldn't help but see the notice, magnified.

Abiathar Babbitt was a man of the cloth on an island overrun with tailors. When he announced a church service, people came. The Catholics, the Baptists, the Presbyterians, the Protestants came. Even the Rosenbergs came.

That night, of all nights, there happened to be a storm. March was coming in like a lion but in the guise of a fleecy lamb. As people straggled into the church, masses of snow swirled in with them, flying up to the rafters and then descending thickly over the pews, the organ, the statue of Mary. The church resembled one of those glass globes that contains a winter scene. Shake the globe and snow begins to fall; falling, falling until it settles again and the glass becomes clear.

The congregation settled, too, but not until feet were stomped to regain circulation and fingers blown on. Children's coats had to be unbuttoned and scarves unwound. Hands were cupped to extinguish sparks at the tips of noses. Candles burning in the sconces caught snowflakes on their tongues, sizzled, went out, and had to be relit.

Finally, bottoms stopped wriggling and chins wagging. People hushed.

Abiathar appeared.

His dog collar, starched and cleaned, shone in the candlelight like a halo that had slipped a little. He'd tamed his runaway hair, cleaned his fingernails, polished his glasses. He was resplendent.

He mounted the podium, smiled weakly, licked his lips, opened the book and smoothed out the pages with both hands;

was about to begin, changed his mind and took a sip of water. The book submitted to being smoothed over again although he must have almost rubbed out the words along with the wrinkles.

Then he cleared his throat and commenced reading the lesson.

How Gargamelle, Bigswoln and Gargantua Ate an Abundance of Tripe.

No one recognized that it was Rabelais, naturally, although it wasn't the Bible: that much was clear. Backs stiffened, jaws dropped. Eyebrows raised like circus tents, various emotions being juggled underneath. Consternation. Curiosity. Prudishness. No one knew what to make of it. They whispered among themselves, finally concurring that Abiathar had his own fund of stories to tell, as they did. This Gargamelle and Gargantua must be relatives of his, poor man. Politeness demanded that they listen to him, as he did them. Soon, though, it wasn't just courtesy that kept them riveted. Abiathar had them in stitches over his outlandish tale. They were enchanted by it, head over heels in love with it, fascinated by it. More than that: about halfway through Abiathar's story, the congregation began to notice an odd sensation in their bellies. None of them could quite put their finger on the name for this feeling. It was vaguely familiar, on the tip of their tongues, and yet, and yet and yet . . . Then it dawned on them what it was: they were *full*. Satiated. Engorged. As though they themselves had been stuffed with an abundance of tripe. Men loosened their belts; women mentally unlaced their corsets.

After he finished the reading, Abiathar called on the congregation to take communion. A murmur of astonishment raced through the building like a naughty child escaped from her mother. There wasn't a wafer, a cracker or a cookie on the island. The priest knew that.

Abiathar urged them again and reluctantly a line formed. Thomas Legacy was at the head of it. He knelt down as Abiathar made the sign of the cross. Thomas had forgotten to put his teeth in that night; his mouth was as wrinkled as sheets fresh from the wash. He stuck out his tongue, nervous about what was to be placed there, and onto it, the priest laid . . . what? Thomas pretended to swallow but as soon as he'd peeled off the line, back to his pew, he spat it out.

A slip of paper! With something Thomas couldn't decipher printed on it.

Abiathar had cut up one of his beloved books. He'd scissored the pages into words, to be placed into the gawping mouths of his starving parishioners: carrot, help, lovership, hy-spy, enamoured, quintessence, nor'wester, adiaphorous, violin, acrobat, dinghy, forsooth, redeemable, guarantee, camstairy, cornucopia, language, death, malfeasance, cheese lip, grandiloquent, freckon, choir, pheasant, liquidity, juniper, Wales, beetroot, folly, columbine, contrariwise, doggerel, picicule, shench, Turneraceous, doodle, Hanafite, partake, and so, on, so, forth.

At the conclusion of the evening, the island had swallowed an entire novel. This though none had ever read a book before.

Back by popular demand, Abiathar read again the following night. This time from Dickens: the mutton scene in *David Copperfield*. Over the next few weeks, there were chapters from Anthelme Brillat-Savarin, *To a Haggis* by Robert Burns (calls for seconds on that one from the Scotsmen in the audience), Rimbaud's *At the Green Cabaret at 5 P.M.*, the bakery scenes from *Cyrano de Bergerac*, magic feasts from fairy tales and *The Arabian Nights*. Abiathar fed them stories each night. His cupboard was never bare.

Until one night, in late March, the unthinkable happened: Abiathar's voice gave out. He struggled to overcome it, to no avail. He coughed, he spluttered. His raspy throat filed words down to a mere whisper. Smack in the middle of *The Importance of Being Earnest*! The congregation grew frantic. Agnes Wyatt, who could practically taste those cucumber sandwiches, flung Abiathar into bed. She administered steam baths, gargles, mustard plasters and cod-liver oil. He was ordered to munch on garlic cloves and doused with oil of cloves. She attempted to cure the poor man within an inch of his life. Nothing worked.

For two whole weeks, the island went without his stories. Stomachs started grumbling again and so did their owners. An emergency council meeting was called. There was talk of specialists, witch doctors, medicine men; even a trip to Lourdes. All these were discarded as impractical. Then someone, they say it was Thomas Legacy, made one last suggestion.

The islanders must learn to read for themselves.

There was a unanimous vote in favor of it.

Abiathar, whose plan it was all along, leapt out of bed the second he heard this. He telegraphed the city's Board of Education with a request for a schoolteacher to come to the island on the next boat. The church was given over to men, women and children furrowing fields of paper with straight lines, copying out their letters, learning the rules of grammar.

Months later, at harvest time, Thomas Legacy, his hair also harvested, leaving behind neat rows of stubble, mounted the podium. In a ringing voice, he read out the lesson for all to hear:

He hath filled the hungry with good things.

—It's a moment no islander can recount without a tear in his eye, Elias finished off. Unless they're me.

—In the beginning was the Word, Simon intoned, and the Word was with God, and the Word was Good.

Levon, startled, stared at him. *And the word was God,* that's how it went. Sweeney's sign. A sign? How should he read it was the question. His cheeks reddened as he considered how often he had whispered to a girl *I love you,* or *You look beautiful.* Not because he meant them—usually quite the opposite—but because he knew she was starved for those words and would believe him and thank him in a manner pleasurable to himself. Perhaps it was this sense of guilt that caused him to see, where before he had dismissed it, a hint of Obdulia's high cheekbones in Elias's own; a dash of her feistiness in the way he held up his chin as he waited for Levon to respond.

—Abiathar Babbitt sounds like an honorable man, he said.

—Oh he was, exclaimed Simon. And the fact is, we *do* honor him. Every March the island hosts a cooking contest. Babbitt's Feast we call it. This year there are hundreds of entries from all over Canada. First prize is a trip to Paris. Think of that. Paris! My father dreamed I'd study there one day. He had a lisp and pronounced it "Parish." I grew up believing it was a city where bread and wine were worshiped. This year we, Elias and I, are going to enter.

—Oh? What with?

—You'll *never* guess.

—No, said Levon slowly. That's why I ask.

Simon glanced furtively around him. Elias and Levon unconsciously followed his example. Having ascertained that nobody was lurking in the shadows, Simon whispered:

—We plan to resurrect the dead.

Levon swiveled a finger in his ear hole to clear out the wax.

—Excuse me?

The windowless room shimmered in a dish of jellied light from a single lamp, the shade a red fez tipped forward drunkenly on its base. Simon straightened it before replying.

—Ten years ago, Elias's wife hanged herself. His daughter, Obdulia, has never really recovered from it and . . .

Elias interrupted him. His blunt tone might have effectively bludgeoned his wife into the ground if the rope hadn't got her first.

—Obdulia can't, no, *won't* move beyond her grief, he said. She's never left this island. Not once. She stands in the circle of it like it's a noose, not moving, afraid that if she jumped off, it would tighten and kill her like it did Hereword, my wife.

Levon couldn't speak. His tongue lay absolutely still in the grave of his mouth. He wondered whether Elias knew of last night's escapade, or if Levon ought to tell him. Better not. He doubted Elias would be either surprised or sympathetic. Obdulia had probably staged similar stunts before, setting herself up for failure because she wanted, deep down, to live, and all the while feeling guilty about it, as if hope was food she'd stolen off her mother's plate.

—She hungers for her dead mother, Simon went on. Our intention is to satisfy that hunger. I will re-create Hereword Limb. Her spirit will rise up with the dough, and we will then feed it to her daughter.

—I *beg* your pardon? Levon gasped.

Elias slapped his hands on his thighs. Lifting them again, he left behind two white palm prints.

—Look, he said, there's precedence for eating our dead. Cannibalism, for example. Think of Franklin's men. And warriors who ate the heart of their enemies for courage. In Mexico, the living eat sugar skeletons shaped like their dead relatives and picnic with them in the graveyard. Not to mention the Holy Sacrament.

—But that's *symbolic*.

—So? Money is too. Paper and ink is all it is, except that, collectively, we've invested meaning in these scraps. We could just as easily decide that this five-dollar bill . . .

Elias took a crumpled bill from the pocket of his T-shirt and ripped it in half.

—. . . is worthless. Religion is the same. We've *decided* that bread represents the body of Christ. Fine. Dandy. Simon and I can use that to our advantage.

He stuck the two halves of his five-dollar bill back in his pocket, intent on taping them together again later.

—How? said Levon.

—Have you ever seen Notre Dame? The Vatican? Westminster Abbey?

This apparent change of subject caught Levon off-guard.

—Pictures, yes. Of course.

—All that gold, those famous paintings, marble floors.

—Yes, yes.

—There's *money* in resurrection. Don't you see?

—No.

—Think of it, said Elias.

He spread his fingers as though framing a cinema marquee.

—Babbitt's Feast gets a lot of publicity. We unveil our re-creation of Hereword. A perfect likeness. Gasps of astonishment all around. After a ceremony of some kind, Obdulia eats her. Exactly like communion except that the wafer is bigger. We wait. We watch. A light returns to Obdulia's eyes. Her face is suffused with a rosy glow. She feels her mother's spirit moving inside her. We rent a couple of cute kids for photo ops. The mother in Obdulia coming out. That kind of thing. It's a miracle, folks! The crowds start arriving. Suffered a death in your own family? Mourning their loss? We'll bake to order. There's cash value in religion, Levon. In grief, too. Think of all the money that's literally sunk into the ground when a person dies. The casket, the burial clothes, the priest or whatever. The headstone. Thousands it can cost and what good does it do the living? None. We, on the other hand, can offer them something tangible in exchange for their money.

—And yummy, Simon added.

—But, Levon stammered, a mother is . . . is someone who tucks you in, not someone you tuck *into*.

—Why not? Elias said. Obdulia's never swallowed the fact of her mother's death. By Christ then, let her swallow her mother.

Simon dunked his finger into an open jar of blueberry jam. Slowly, he licked it clean, staining his mouth blue as a vein.

—For quite some time, he told Levon, I shared living quarters with four men, all of whom claimed to be Jesus Christ. Except for one of them, who tended to bite when he was cross, they tried remarkably hard to be *like* Jesus. Meek, gentle, platitudinous. Why the doctors wanted to disillusion them, I do not know. The fact remains, however, that no one, besides the men themselves, entertained for a second the idea that any of them truly was the Messiah. But then I commenced to think, why should anyone believe in the first Jesus? All he had going for Him, really, was a certain *originality* to His psychosis. We have no proof that He was the son of God, any more than we have proof that there is a God at all. And yet, this does not deter the millions who draw sustenance from their belief in Him, does it? Bread, on the other hand, *is* proofed. So why shouldn't Obdulia gain comfort from it? Why can't it be her mother's body she eats? Her mother's spirit, rather than His, who is resurrected?

Frightened, Levon had an urge to hold out his hand, muttering, *There there* as he backed slowly, without any sudden movements, out of the door. No wonder Berthe was so vague about where Simon had spent his years off the island. Many an evening, Levon had strolled along the lake shore, past the spacious grounds of the city's psychiatric hospital, a conglomeration of Victorian redbrick buildings. The hospital was situated next to a tawdry amusement park and, therefore, did not seem that far removed in essence from the asylums of earlier times, when charismatic Mesmerists staged fake trials to cure lunatics of their persecution complexes, or dropped patients into vats of live eels— a primitive version of electroshock therapy—or when Schiller, later to be a playwright, but then a doctor, set out to cure a patient who believed he had two heads. Schiller had constructed an artificial head out of cloth and stuffing and set it on the man's shoulder. Stepping back a few paces, he took aim and shot off the fake head so that the patient believed himself to be cured.

And then there was James Tilley Matthews. Levon had once written a paper on this eighteenth-century London tea merchant and student of Mesmerism, an early form of hypnotism. A distrust of Mesmerism *(demoniacal mummery)* was widespread at the time; there was even a fear voiced that Members of Parliament, each side in possession of Mesmeric powers, could send the other to sleep, or cause them to roll around in the aisles, frothing at the mouth. Matthews became convinced that the French, who were in the throes of the Revolution, were sending Mesmerists to

England in order to extract State secrets from government officials, as well as from himself.

Matthews's paranoia grew. He scribbled diagrams of a complicated device he called the Air-Loom Torture by which his enemies, a sinister quartet named Jack the Schoolmaster, Sir Archy, the Glove Woman and Charlotte, were able to manipulate his thoughts by magnetic fluid. In 1797, Matthews was committed to Bethlem Hospital, or Bedlam as it was commonly known. Despite his ravings, Matthews's family and two noted psychiatrists, Clutterbuck and Birkbeck, sued for his release, arguing that he was sane. In rebuttal, John Haslam, keeper of Bedlam, published Matthews's own writings in a volume in 1810, entitled *Exhibiting a Singular Case of Insanity, And a No Less Remarkable Difference in Medical Opinions: Developing the Nature of An Assailant, And the Manner of Working Events; With A Description of Tortures Experienced by Bomb-Bursting, Lobster-Cracking, and Lengthening of the Brain. Embellished with a Curious Plate.*

Damned by his own words, James Tilley Matthews spent several more years in Bedlam, after which he was released to Mr. Fox's Madhouse in Hackney, where he was given the task of supervising his fellow lunatics.

As was often the case, lunatics ran the asylum.

—You don't expect me to help you, surely, Levon asked nervously.

—Ah, said Simon. In fact, we do. We thought with your background in medical history, you might be able to give us a clue as to how to proceed. Hereword will rise. Of that I am confident. Obdulia is our concern. She, too, must come back to life, in a manner of speaking. The recipe, we feel, needs a little oomph. A little kick.

Elias scraped a scurf of dried dough off his cheek.

—That's right, he said. We want a secret ingredient.

—A secret ingredient?

—Know any?

Levon massaged his throbbing forehead.

—Back to life, you say?

A domino of black-and-white images nudged against one another inside Levon's brain, each collapsing against the next until all the pieces had fallen into place: the text of Galvani's *De viribus electricitatis in motu musculari.* Still smarting from his failure to knead the bread properly, and conscious of Elias's contempt for him, Levon wasn't averse to showing off a bit. How could it hurt to share an arcanum or two? It wasn't as if the information would be of any use to them. These were ancient ideas that had been laughed out of existence centuries ago.

He cleared his throat.

—Galvanism, he said. Luigi Galvani.

—Go on, Simon urged him. Enlighten us.

—That's it. The Enlightenment. Physicians weren't certain whether nerves were stimulated through mechanical, chemical or electrical impulses. Galvani believed that it was electrical and so, he experimented by introducing electrical currents into a frog's legs he'd skinned and hung from an iron rail. When he applied a current to them, the legs jerked.

—I don't see a connection here, Elias complained.

—Wait. I'm coming to that. Galvani's nephew, Giovanni Aldini, pushed the experiment a bit further. His interest was in whether Galvanism might be applied to humans in a state of suspended animation.

—Like Obdulia?

—Yes. No. Sort of. In 1803, Thomas Foster, a thief, was hanged at Newgate. Within half an hour of the execution, the fresh corpse was delivered to Mr. Wilson's Anatomical Theatre. There, Aldini proceeded to attach wires from a pile of copper and zinc plates to Foster's jaw, mouth, thumb, ear and rectum. The electrical jolt was powerful enough to cause the dead man to clench his hand and open his left eye.

—I'm not surprised, Elias said.

Simon's expression darkened.

—Electrocuted? he croaked.

—In a manner of speaking.

Simon wagged his finger.

—Oh no. No. No. No.

A similar experiment with electricity had once opened his eyes, too.

Simon had grown up, in the cramped quarters behind his father's bakery, with an invisible sibling: one who received all of his mother's attention, all of her tenderness. His father bestowed on this sibling various names, christening it: Exhaustion, Nerves, Depression. Simon called it by the names islanders gave it: Lunatic, Crazy, Madness. It was Madness his mother invited to her private tea parties. Madness she tucked in at night, and sang lullabies to. Madness she told nonsensical stories to. Simon could hear her on the other side of her locked bedroom door. He knew his older brother, Madness, was curled up beside her while Simon sat outside in the hall, his hands clasped around his dimpled knees, sobbing. Jealous and lonely, he would tug on his mother's dress and kiss her limp hand, begging her to notice him. Simon's father shushed him and warned him to *leave his mother in peace,* a word Simon mistook for "piece" so that he watched her anxiously, lest she come apart like his jigsaw puzzle and a bit of her fell behind the sofa cushion, or through a crack in the floor.

The morning she was to be committed to the psychiatric hospital, Simon's mother sat unresisting on the bed. His father dressed her in the green cotton skirt and white blouse he loved to see her wear while Simon, who'd recently learned to do this for himself, buttoned up her jumper, making certain that all the holes and buttons were aligned. He sat back on his heels, hoping for praise. None came. Deep lines had formed on either side of her mouth, like his parakeet's cage, imprisoning her words apart from an occasional meaningless flitter of her tongue. An anguished *peep*, *peep*.

Her husband, François Tibeault, his face damp with tears, gallantly extended the crook of his arm to her. A gentleman, and a thief, he stole Simon's mother away for good. For her own good, François assured him.

With his mother gone, Simon spent more time in the bakery, at that time still located in the village. He substituted silken flour for his mother's skirts, the heat of the ovens for a warm embrace. At night, François took down a loaf of rising dough from the shelf and laid it for a pillow on a bit of sacking. Simon fell asleep to the sound of dough being lifted, turned, caressed. Kneading, his father called it.

Another word Simon got wrong.

When he was too much underfoot, his taciturn father's hand closed on Simon's plump, rounded shoulder and tossed him outside to play. But with whom? The other children teased him about his lunatic mother, slapping and pinching him until blinded by the cloud of flour their beatings raised. He was never invited to birthday parties or to join in games of hide-and-seek.

Banished from the bakery, and from other children's company, he went instead to the woods near the witch Hereword O'Riley's house, where his classmates were afraid to go. Simon wasn't. The birch trees were as pale and slender as his mother in her hospital gown and, as he grew, the lower branches skimmed the top of his head, ruffling his blond hair with their knobbly fingers.

His mother had come here, too, during her worst fits. She hid in the woods as her namesake, Saint Dympna, had done, rubbing herself with dirt and weaving twigs into her hair. Her favorite spot was a giant oak tree. The base of it was a cave, the mouth of it a wizened old man's: the upper lip gnarled and scored with wrinkles. Inside, it was dank and foul-smelling. Simon would crawl inside the cramped space, his spine, like Narcissus, curved toward the reflecting pool of his buckled shoes. Throughout those afternoons, he witnessed the woods change from a sunny golden age to a copper age as the sun sank and, at last, to an iron age, when he crawled out of his hole and went home to his absent-minded father who, more often than not, hadn't even missed him.

Underneath the carpet of decaying leaves writhed maggots and centipedes and silverfish. Snakes had slithered in; a skunk sprayed him once. What of that? Simon hadn't crawled into the cave for protection. None existed in this world. Look at his mother! She had been dismantled from the inside out, unable to defend herself against the treacherous machinations of her own mind, or to run away from it. Neither could Simon, who feared that he'd inherited her same black impulses. If so, he was determined to master them. He reasoned that if he could sit at ease in this rank, shadowy cave, with its dangers both seen and unseen, then surely his mind, too, might learn to be at rest amid his increasingly shadowy thoughts. He wanted to transform *himself* into a cave. Nothing, he believed, would scare him then.

His plan seemed to be working until François, noting his son's increasing solitariness, his moroseness, panicked and whisked the now sixteen-year-old Simon off to the same hospital where Dympna had died the year before. Simon was not overly perturbed by this. It was a test. He excelled at tests. Doctors dropped words *(mother, guilt, loneliness)* like food at the mouth of his cave, hoping to lure him out, into their trap. He sniffed at them, then retreated, leaving the words to rot there until, defeated, the doctors dragged them back to their own lairs. Seeing that words didn't work, they grew bold, peering right into his cave, prodding him with sticks as if Simon were indeed an animal they wanted to force out into the open. He snarled at them, curling up tighter into himself, pressing against the wall of his cave, pleased at being able to elude them so easily.

He hadn't reckoned on the Demolition Experts.

One September afternoon, when leaves drifted about as lazily as a mind about to dream, when the air through the open windows pinched a little, Simon was wheeled into a small room. Not the usual doctor's office. Two men and a woman, all wearing lab coats, waited for him. He didn't realize that it was a disguise, a ruse to put him off his guard. Until then, he'd been impervious to all the doctors' tricks so, even when the woman trailed wires from Simon's brain to a big metal box, he remained calm. She had a pronounced mustache and a few scraggly hairs on her chinny-chin-chin. He counted them. Ten.

Her task completed, she stepped over to where the men stood, well back from him—for safety's sake—then pressed a button and detonated him.

Oh, the horror of seeing his cave destroyed! He trembled at the memory of it. It was like sitting in a cinema, watching the film on screen burn up. First, all the movement and color of the movie were replaced with a jolt of blackness, of stillness; then, the intense heat punched holes of white in the flickering dark, the holes increasing as the blackness contracted, shriveling, disappearing altogether, until the screen was entirely white, utterly blank. The *sound* still functioned, Simon could hear voices murmuring, a storyline continuing on, but oh, the blinding quality of that light after sitting so long in the dark! His eyes ached from it, his skin burned. He wanted to get up and walk out and he couldn't. He was strapped down, naked, vulnerable to *them:* his callous schoolmates, the sneering shopkeepers who'd ripped up in front of his mother the checks she signed Saint Dympna, the Demolition Experts.

Simon remembered screaming then. Screaming and screaming. And also that there were mirrors in the room. They were what saved him, those mirrors. It was when he saw his reflection, mid-scream, that he knew he'd be all right. That he'd won. He wasn't mistaken. There it was! His gaping mouth. Ridges on the roof of it like an old tree: a wet, yawning darkness. *There* was his cave. They hadn't destroyed it. He'd *swallowed* it! Swallowed it whole. He'd done it. He *was* a clever boy.

He shut up after that so the doctors wouldn't see it. He sealed up the entrance.

He fooled them all.

—I draw the line at plugging Obdulia in like a toaster, Simon said quietly.

Elias barked with laughter.

—Of *course* not, Levon replied indignantly. Anyway, Aldini concluded that the heart was different from other muscles. Those he could stimulate, but the heart remained impervious to Galvanism.

—What else? Elias demanded.

Levon's lip curled.

—There's Haller's Doctrine of Irritability.

—Jesus Christ, man, don't make us guess.

—Haller discovered that all muscle fibers were *irritable* while sensibility was the property of *nervous* fibers. Based on this, Aldini applied *volatile* to the corpse's nose and mouth to see what might happen. No *sensible* action resulted.

—That's no good either then, Simon muttered.

Levon didn't hear him. He had warmed to his task by this time.

—You could do what King Philip II's doctors recommended to shock the King's ailing son, Don Carlos, back into good health. They unearthed the skeleton of a holy man, Fra Diego, who'd been dead for a hundred years, and placed it next to the sleeping prince, to be discovered when he woke up. Come to think of it, why not use mummies? They were a popular cure during the Middle Ages and even into the Renaissance. Shakespeare mentions it in Othello. *And it was dy'd in mummy which the skilful conserv'd of maidens' hearts.* Embalming fluid. Or actual mummy, ground into powder. That was taken as a remedy for falls or bruises. Francis I always carried a little packet of it with him and Francis Bacon attributed to it great force in stanching the blood.

—Mummy, eh? Elias said.

He looked meaningfully at Simon, who responded:

—But of course!

Words scuttled madly under his breath like cockroaches suddenly exposed to light.

—Be she alive, or be she dead, I'll grind her *bones* to make my bread. I'll grind her bones to *make my bread*. That's it!

Elias chortled.

—Obdulia wants her mummy. She shall have her, eh?

—Well *done*, Levon. An excellent suggestion.

Simon clapped Levon on the back. The hairs on his neck prickled.

—What do you mean, *well done?*

—Why, your idea that we add mummy. I knew you'd be a tremendous help.

—No. *No!*

—I insist, Simon told him. Give credit where it is due. That's my motto.

Levon gaped at the two men.

—But you can't . . .

—Can't what?

—Can't mean . . .

—But we can! both men chorused.

Levon pressed his fists against his temples, too late to box his traitorous brain into submission. How could he have been so stupid, so careless?

—But none of those remedies worked, he said.

—Then why were they used at all?

—Well . . . I guess for a time people *believed* that they worked. But . . .

—There you are! Simon exclaimed. *I* believe this will work.

—Me too, Elias added.

—Those were stories, said Levon. I was telling you stories.

—Science, said Simon, means simply the aggregate of all the recipes that are always successful. The rest is literature. Paul Valéry. The hospital library consisted of only two volumes: *The Oxford Book of Quotations* and *An Introduction to French Cooking.*

—You're both mad.

Elias hopped off the bench. He prowled around the room as if shooting a game of pool, assessing his next shot. Levon regarded him warily. He felt uncomfortably like the eight ball.

—Mad? said Elias.

—What is a visionary, Simon said, but a man who sees clearly something that does not *yet* exist. The Wright brothers were mad. Isaac Newton was mad. Watson and Crick and Rosalind Franklin were mad. Wilhelm Reich was mad. Well, actually he *was*. But the point remains the same.

—You have no choice anyway. Help us or we talk to your parole officer. We'll explain how we tried to do the right thing by you, but you spurned our assistance. You're a rotten apple. Quite beyond rehabilitation.

—Don't be boorish, Elias, Simon pleaded. I am sure Levon is more than willing to aid us. After all, if we succeed . . .

—*When* we succeed.

Simon gazed at his partner adoringly.

—Such confidence! *When* we succeed, we'll have eradicated grief. Think of that. Not, We are *what* we eat but, We are *who* we eat! In which case, we need never grieve for loved ones again. We can simply incorporate them into our digestive systems.

What was this world Levon had entered? His head spun with the craziness of the last twenty-four hours. He'd almost frozen to death, been poisoned, run over, and now this: seconded into a lunatic scheme to serve up the dead *en croûte*.

The lamp was positioned so that Simon's and Elias's shadows loomed over him, their heads touching the ceiling. Levon wanted to smash the light, in the vain hope of extinguishing the two men with it.

—I don't know what you think you're playing at, he said.

—What are we playing?

Simon picked up a palette knife. His broad back was turned toward Levon, his shoulders rounded as he began to score tiny laugh lines around the cellist's eyes. Simon's voice when he spoke again, however, was entirely without humor.

—We're playing Simon Says.

7

TO MAKE THE FACE FAIR, AND FOR A STINKING BREATH

Take the flowers of Rosemary, and seeth them in white Wine, with which wash your face; if you drink therof it wil make you have a sweet breath.

T HE LATE AFTERNOON sky was a tipped rubbish bin. Out of it spilled crumpled, inky clouds and yards of shimmering fabric stained with pink dye. Seagulls rooted for their supper among the litter.

The moon was a fingernail paring.

Steam from the bath water had melted the frost on the window and through it, Levon could see winking at him the lights of the American shore across the bay. Berthe's house was situated on the southeastern tip of the island, in a cove called the False Ducks. A number of modern, understated cottages encroached upon it, the land parceled off when first Berthe's father, then her husband, died. Her house presided over them like the once-grand president of a Women's Auxiliary Club, faintly ridiculous but immovable. The newer members were apparently content to sit on the sidelines and await her timely demise.

Berthe had explained to him that the cove got its name from the smugglers who used to sink crates of liquor in the lake during prohibition, marking the spot with duck decoys and retrieving them later when the coast was clear. Berthe's father had been an accomplice to the smugglers' enterprise. He ran a "blind pig," an illegal bar, and was privy to a series of codes—special lanterns, handshakes and door knocks—that Berthe recalled as being more complicated, and more communicative, than the signals her parents used with each other. With his share of the loot, Mr. Humble belied his name. He proceeded to expand the original house, an ordinary two-story wood structure, adding an enclosed veranda, several wings and a third story with turrets. The effect was of a woman adorning a plain housecoat and slippers with an ornamental wrap, diamonds and a Paris hat. When prohibition was repealed and Mr. Humble's fortunes deteriorated, so did the house; her slip began to show; her wrap became tatty; her hat slanted at a rakish angle.

Earlier, as Berthe bustled around gathering towels for him and pointing out closet space, it struck him that this house was a rambling conversation between two old friends, the twists and turns of it familiar to Berthe, but not to him. He stuck close to her, afraid of getting lost.

They had entered through a vestibule in which hung an orderly bus-queue of coats, boots lined up underneath, hats above. Passing the living room, Levon noticed a stag's head that seemed to have crashed through the wall above the mantelpiece, and was then unable to back out again. Mahogany furniture with elaborately carved paws stood watch over their prey of animal-skin rug.

Stairs between the three floors were replaced with a ramp, enabling Berthe to bicycle indoors during winter.

—Just like Alfred Jarry, she said.

—The writer?

—Oh, was he?

Ancient bikes in various states of disrepair (various states of *repair*, she corrected him) leaned against walls, banisters, and sofas. Bicycle parts were spread like cuts of meat on butcher's paper over the kitchen counter. Levon trusted that Berthe would not confuse them with the chicken she was preparing for supper.

He reclined once more against the back of the tub, conscious of his bony knees and thin, pale arms. Levon consoled himself by rubbing his chest, which was reasonably sturdy. There was even a smattering of hair, although it was rather like what the family cat left behind on its pillow.

Now I am ready to tell how bodies are changed into different bodies.

He closed his eyes, willing his metamorphosis into a mythological creature: half man, half clawfoot tub. His chest was a foamy breastplate; he possessed powerful metal haunches, capable of launching him great distances, and fearsome talons. He was invincible. Immortal.

He swished the tepid water about, roaring under his breath.

His bubbles were dissolving.

At that moment the bathroom door blew open. There was no latch on it and Obdulia, jiggling on one foot, had pushed it open with only her frantic exhalations.

—I have to pee, she said.

Levon sat bolt upright, punctuating the floor with exclamation marks of water. She entered the room before he could stop her, her hair appearing ahead of the rest of her: a garden in May, untended and lush, tamped down in back, overgrown. Tendrils,

reacting to the moist heat of the bathroom, sprang from her forehead. Fragrances of camellia, rose, jasmine and sandalwood
seemed to burst forth from her and not from the oils Levon had
tippled liberally into his bath.

—What are you doing here? he whispered.

—I live here, she whispered back. My father is married to
Berthe. Didn't she tell you?

—Berthe is your stepmother?

Her mouth pursed as though swiped with lemons.

—Yes.

How, on such a small island, did events race so far ahead of
him? He would never catch up no matter how long he lived here.
How had Berthe phrased it? He was from *away;* the foreign word
in an otherwise plain-sounding sentence, skewing the meaning of
it.

Obdulia lurched toward the toilet.

—Permit me to . . .

He gripped the sides of the tub, his skinny arms bent at the
elbows like the frame of a kite. He was about to hoist himself out
of the water when she hiked up her skirt and dropped her underpants. A bouquet of red and purple veins lay on the marble table
of her thighs. She snuggled into the toilet seat, her bottom surrounded by a white porcelain ruff. After a second's hesitation,
out gushed a flood of urine.

—I'm desperate, she apologized.

He sank back into the tub, corraling a flock of bubbles over
his private parts, and politely stared out the window while waiting for her to finish.

He felt dizzy, confused. Not just by Obdulia's sudden presence
here in Berthe's house, in her *bathroom*, but by his reaction to her

arrival: trepidation, natural given the circumstances of their last meeting, laced with, and here he was at a loss to explain himself, *delight*. What did this *Get up, get up, it's Christmas morning* euphoria, this *Hooray! I've discovered gravity* sensation, have to do with Obdulia? Prying into Levon's chest cavity at that moment, what, he wondered, would William Harvey have discovered? In place of a heart, an addled cartographer overlapping continents and diverting the course of rivers, all the while attempting to convince the National Geographic Society assembled in his brain that, not only had Mount Kilimanjaro shifted to the Sahara Desert, and the Yukon Territories to Hawaii, but that this was as it should be.

Where on earth would he end up with this girl?

Eventually, her piss tapered off, a thick candle diminishing to the wick.

—I thought you lived in that other house, he said at last.

With her elbows resting on her knees, she fanned a clutch of hair in her hand and examined it with the seriousness of a poker player reviewing her cards.

—I go there, she said, when I'm feeling . . . when I want to be with my mother. Elias won't allow the house to be fixed up enough for me to live there. He wants to sell it to an off-islander who plans to tear down the woods and build a hotel or something. He can't do it without my permission, though, and he'll never have it. *Never.*

—Why not? It would fetch a good price and as it stands, which is barely, that house isn't fit to live in. Or die in for that matter.

—My great-grandmother died in that house! My grandmother was born there and died there, and my mother, too. *I* was born there. There are roots to that house, and seasons.

He bowed his head.

—I'm sorry if I offended you, he said.

—Oh, she said breathlessly, you ought to see it in the summer. Honeysuckle grows inside and grapevines too. Deer wander through the halls and nibble on the flowered wallpaper. When it rains, the basement floods into a pool and I swim there, looking up through holes in the floorboards, straight through the roof to the stars.

Levon added a gush of hot water to his bath, adding more steam to the tiny room.

Obdulia hiked up her underpants and smoothed her skirt. She flushed the toilet, dropping the lid to muffle the tide of water.

—Where is the soap, please?

He groped around in the water for the bar and handed it to her.

—Thank you, she murmured.

She had seen a naked man once before—Charles Dodge's son, Freddie. He'd been dead at the time. Drowned in a boating accident. Freddie was crooked as a dog's hind leg and a devil with the girls, so she'd heard. She had helped Berthe prepare his body for the burial. Perhaps it was his lack of . . . *animation* but she hadn't seen what all the fuss was about. She *had* admired the envelope flap of his narrow hip bones, that elegant V, until she reached what appeared to be a gray wad of chewed gum stuck to the tip of it. Berthe assured her that she'd understand in time but here she was, twenty-two years old, and she'd never had a lover. Boys on the island liked her well enough, she supposed; they called her clever at least—a second-best compliment pulled from the back of the closet—but they sensed she was often bored by them, and she was. Whenever she was in a passion about a book she'd read, or an idea she had, they instructed her to *calm down*, eyeing her as nervously as a glass being waved too enthusiastically at a party, the contents of it threatening to spill over them. She *hated* that. Somehow, she didn't think Levon would tell her to calm down, but perhaps she expected too much of him. Her mother had warned her against that. *Better to keep to your tower; reel in your hair.* Once, she remembered, she caught her mother holding a blood-soaked towel. When Obdulia asked, in a terrified voice, what was wrong, she'd been assured that it was just "the curse." *Like in a fairy tale?* she said. *Sort of,* her mother responded, *except that you don't get to sleep through it and then wake up next to a prince.* But hadn't Levon, in effect, roused Obdulia last night from her stupor? Didn't her heart, right now, skip a beat at the sight of him, sending out shock waves of blood to her cheeks and throat? Why, she was in more of a lather than the soap. Which, she noticed, he'd reduced to a sliver, fragile as a child's wrist. Obdulia stroked it gently; afraid that if she rubbed too hard it might disappear altogether.

She replaced the soap in the dish, then plunged her hands into the bath water, and twirled them around. To dry them, she ran her hands up and down the strands of her hair as if playing a harp.

—I'm sorry I ran out on you this morning, she told him. That wasn't kind.

Levon gaped at her.

—Wait a minute! You ran out on *me?*

—I couldn't sleep. I slipped out before the sun was up.

This, as his grandfather might have said, was *for the books a turnip.* To have run out on her was one thing; it was quite another for her to have done it to *him.*

—You ought to have left me a note, he said prissily.

—Sorry, she shrugged.

Staring into his bath, he saw in the bubbles the tight, permed curls of his second cousin, Cynthia. For a time, she had corresponded with an inmate, a forger, at the local work farm. When he proposed marriage to her, she had waved the letter around, delirious, as though it was she, fifty-three years old, her ankles like flowerpots, who'd been reprieved—from a life sentence as a spinster. On the appointed day, she wore the only white dress she owned, her nurse's uniform, minus the name tag, and a veil. *And surgical hose!* his mother exclaimed on the drive home. *It had a ladder in it. Did you notice?* Levon's father had grunted, *No man will want to climb up it now. She's had her chance.* The groom, granted a special dispensation by the prison authorities, was liberated from his handcuffs for the ceremony. When the minister said, *Do you?* he did, bolting out the back door of the church: quick, but not as quick as Aunt Anna-Lee's *I told you so.*

Imagine being abandoned at the altar, Mrs. Hawke kept repeating. *A place that signifies a man dying for love.*

—You were dreaming when I left, Obdulia said. I bent over the sofa to see that you were OK; your hand shot out, grabbed at my skirt and then you called out Alice's name.

—Alice?

Had he dreamed of her? He seldom did, almost never. Right after the accident, yes, but in those dreams Alice was still a little girl, her childhood a loss that he'd long ago reconciled himself to. That made the dreams bearable.

—I whispered in your ear *It's all right, it's all right* until your fingers loosened and you let me go. Don't you remember?

That no creature having blood does want a heart, by the impulsion of which it is made stronger and more robust and . . . is not only stirr'd up and down by the ear, but likewise is thrust out further and more swiftly.

Levon's flock of bubbles had dispersed. He speedily regathered them.

—I feel like an eccentric load, he muttered.

—A what?

—A load applied to a column that's parallel to, but out of alignment with, its axis.

—Oh.

—My grandfather's true religion was medieval architecture, you see. Gothic churches. Depending on the circumstances, Alice and I were either an eccentric load, a clerestory, or a radiating chapel. In my grandparents' room at home, he had drawings of all the great cathedrals. York Minster, Notre Dame, Saint Denis and his favorite, Canterbury. *Awesome is this place. Truly this is the house of God and the gate of Heaven, and it will be called the court of the Lord.* The cathedrals were supposed to be evocations of the heavenly Jerusalem here on earth.

Obdulia spun the toilet-paper roll like a roulette wheel, stopping it mid-revolution with her finger.

—Do you believe in heaven?

—No. I believe in circles, though. Revelation, Chapter 21. *I am Alpha and Omega, the Beginning and the End.* The circle. Eternal life. Heaven. That's why Gothic churches were built with arches and vaults. They're part circular, at least—you wouldn't want to worship God inside a giant beach ball, I guess—and the ceilings were designed to rise high above the congregation, to represent heaven. I think Grandpa's the reason I chose to study William Harvey. His treatise on circulation of the blood reminded me of the circles in Gothic churches. Harvey's religion was the architecture of the human body. A different kind of church but for him, God was present in it.

—I'd like to believe in a heaven, Obdulia sighed, but I can't seem to. I can't picture Hereword anywhere but here . . .

She waved her arms in the steamy air.

—. . . with me. Sometimes I feel like an anchor she's tugging and tugging at to get loose and drift away. Where do you think Alice is?

—I know exactly where she is. Plot 92 in our local cemetery.

—I mean her spirit.

—I don't think about it, he lied. There's no point.

—Well, where does your grandfather think Alice has gone?

—I can't say. He's with her, though, wherever she is.

Her hand went to her heart.

—Dead? she whispered.

—While I was in prison. A stroke. It makes me think of him being crossed off with a fountain pen.

Levon squeezed a daub of shampoo onto his wet hair. The bottle promised him manageability and luster.

—What was he like, your grandfather?

A shiny cellophane strip of sweat appeared taped to her upper lip.

—Do you really want to know?

She nodded.

—I've read about Gothic churches, too. Under *G* in my encyclopedia. An image wasn't an illusion but a revelation. *Splendor veritatis.* A radiance of truth. Reveal him to me. I want to see him. Please.

—All right, he said happily.

Levon transferred lather from his head to his chin and worked it into a creamy beard.

—Like this. White hair since he was twenty. Brown eyes the same as mine but a stockier build. He was accustomed to planting himself firmly on the ground as if to say, *I belong here.* He was an immigrant, though, from Poland, and rarely did belong anywhere, except with his wife.

Levon held up his hand before Obdulia could ask. He wiped off the beard and twirled his hair into platinum Shirley Temple curls. Two blobs of shampoo served for earrings.

—They arrived in New York in the late twenties, penniless. In 1931, Grandpa was hired to help construct the Empire State Building. One hundred and two stories high—one story a day, the Scheherazade of builders. He was a riveter and he worked with a team of four men, the same four always. If one man got sick, the others were laid off until he got better.

—Why? Couldn't the boss find someone else?

—Trust. What they did was like a juggling and high-wire act combined. Like a marriage, come to think of it. A good one. Work ground to a halt if one of them left.

—I see.

—Each had a different job: heater, catcher, gunman and bucker-up.

—That sounds cheerful.

—That was Grandpa's job but first, the heater had to forge the rivets in flaming coke. He was always one story behind the others. Using a pair of tongs, he tossed the rivets up to the catcher who sometimes used nothing bigger or fancier than a paint can. Imagine that. The bucker-up supported the beam while the gunman smashed (Levon slapped the water for emphasis) the rivets in with a hammer. Crowds used to gather to watch them at work. The best show in town during the Depression, and free. Those men straddled the top of the world. Kings of all they surveyed. I think it was hard for them to climb down at the end of the day and go home to Queens and their wives.

Red sparks flew upward as Obdulia piled her hair on top of her head.

—Grandma hated the building, he went on. She couldn't comprehend her husband's love of heights. For her, happiness was blending in with the other immigrants. The women didn't hold themselves above her. The men overlooked her.

—Not her husband.

—No. Not him. But each day she waited for news of his death. After all, she stumbled over English words. Tripped on her own tongue. She believed her husband could easily step out of a story into thin air and vanish.

Soap stung his eyes; Levon dunked his head in the water to rinse them.

—After months of seeing her so miserable, Grandpa at last agreed to quit his job.

Obdulia clapped her hands.

—A love story!

—When the Empire State Building was almost complete— one final rivet was due to go in—my grandparents joined the rest of the spectators gathered in the street. The rivet was solid gold and, as the hammer struck, Grandma put her hand in his. He felt her wedding ring against his skin. That night, they went to the library, opened up an atlas and searched for a perfectly flat place to move to. The Prairies. My father was born nine months later.

—Do you speak Polish?

—No, he said. I never learned my grandparents' language.

Obdulia jumped up from the toilet seat. She felt left out in some inexplicable fashion. Levon's life was all connected: Gothic architecture, William Harvey, Levon's grandfather, Levon himself. A circle. That's how it appeared to Obdulia, anyway. She envied him. Her life was a straight line, a braided rope, frayed at the ends where it had been cut to release her mother from this life, and from Obdulia's. Nothing to hang on to, nothing to pull her through.

She ran cold water from the taps into the sink, splashing her temples, her wrists. The mirror had steamed over and she stared into it, searching in that fog for someone whose features used to be as familiar to her as her own but were now hazy and distant.

—What are you goggling at? Levon asked her.

—Not what, she sighed, who.

He rolled his eyes.

—All right then, *who?*

Facing the mirror, Obdulia drew two circles, a vertical line between them, a horizontal line underneath. Her features superimposed themselves onto the glass, blurred around the edges from the steam. She looked as if she'd been conjured like a jinn from a bottle. A pair of troubled eyes stared back at her through the fog.

—My mother, she said.

8

TO BREAK THE STONE AND BRING AWAY GRAVEL

Take the inner bark of a red filberd tree, and have a good handful of it, and take as much Sanifrage and steep them in a quart of Ale or White Wine and drink a good draught thereof nine mornings together fasting.

BERTHE SURVEYED the dining room, shepherding her glances so that no detail would escape her. She'd assigned the task of setting the table to Obdulia and Berthe was pleased to note that, for once, the girl had followed instructions. An Irish linen cloth, thick and white as clotted cream, spilled over the table. The best china was laid out; the scrolled silver flatware caught the candlelight and winked at Berthe like a prospective lover, asking to be picked up.

This had been her father's favorite room. He had never traveled far from the island and his choice of furnishings was meant to project a worldliness, a sophistication, that he did not possess, but that he had purchased, on credit, from the Hudson's Bay Company in Toronto: the Dutch sideboard, its shelves adorned with pewter goblets and plates; the carved mahogany table with matching chairs and, beneath them, an oriental carpet; red velvet curtains that hung to the floor. She had drawn them earlier but felt on her cheek a draft, an airy kiss being blown to her, and to the photographs of her father, her mother and of all her relatives, hanging on the walls.

Satisfied that all was well, she bent over a polished knife to check her makeup. Excess mascara dotted her eyelids like crows on a wire.

Hastily, she licked her thumb and rubbed each lid clean. Berthe did not understand this modern trend towards *déshabillé*, as her late husband, Mr. Tibeault, would have referred to it. Her hair, wound into a neat *chignon*, was tipped with honeysuckle pink highlights after a recent trip to the beauty salon; the color complemented the lavender hue of her dress, a sprig of lilac embroidered across her bosom. She looked critically at Obdulia, skulking around the room in that misshapen yellow cardigan. Like a half-sucked lemon drop, the sourpuss. Obdulia cradled in her arms an earthenware pot planted with marigolds she'd taken from the greenhouse; the blossoms far outshone the girl that held them in Berthe's opinion, with that tent of hair and her long face stuck up in the middle of it. No powder, no lipstick. Berthe bit her tongue, a rough one where her stepdaughter was concerned, she admitted, her teeth forever chewing on bones of contention between them. But wait! Could that be a faint smear of blush on Obdulia's cheeks? Berthe thought it must be. Gone was the girl's habitual pinched countenance. It was as if a cloth had been lifted off a table that was still clean underneath. Perhaps there was hope for the girl after all.

—How do I look?

Berthe whirled around.

—Dear dear, she gasped.

Levon had materialized in the room without her noticing. Spreading his arms, he spun for her. His orange polyester shirt blazed forth from underneath his plaid jacket just as Simon, dozing in front of the fireplace, roused himself to pile another log on the flames. The combined brightness was too much for Berthe. She shielded her eyes.

The outfit was on loan from Mr. Tibeault's closet until Levon's parents could ship him clothes of his own. Mr. Tibeault had died in 1976 but his fashion sense was laid to rest long before that. The cheap fabric caused Levon to itch in the most embarrassing spots. Worse than that, the trousers were far too big for him: a child masquerading in grown-up's clothing. He had wrapped the belt twice around his waist, then cinched it at the furthermost hole. Obdulia cast sidelong glances at him, scrutinizing him, stifling her laughter. Simon remained silent, unnecessarily preoccupied with the task of poking the fire.

Berthe pinched a fold of excess material flapping at Levon's thigh.

—That's what widowhood was for me, she sighed. Roominess. I didn't know what to do with all that extra space I had.

Drawn to the bright colors, her white hands, powdered with talcum, flittered around his shoulders, lapels and collar, but did not land, repelled perhaps by the persistent odor of mothballs.

—All right, said Levon peevishly, I admit I appear preposterous in this get-up, no offense, but no more than . . . than *she* does.

He pointed to a picture hanging crooked on the wall. Berthe flew to it, tut-tutting. She swung the photograph delicately to the right, then to the left, soliciting Levon's opinion after each shift.

Obdulia scowled at her.

—You could ask me.

—You can't see straight when it comes to my relatives.

—Who is she? Levon asked.

—Oh Camel of the Occident! Berthe trilled.

—Camel?

—The bike, not her. My Great-Aunt Olympia on her Peerless Velocipede.

The texture of the photograph was grainy and Olympia's insolent expression hinted that she enjoyed going against it. A finger of smoke extended rudely from the tip of her lit cigarette, her hand draped over the handlebars of an ungainly three-wheeled contraption with a humped spine that did resemble, vaguely, a camel. Her other hand rested suggestively on the fastenings of a velvet jacket with puffed sleeves. She wore gourd-shaped bloomers that showed off her calves to great advantage. Her right leg was bent, her foot resting on the pedal of her bicycle; her shoulder was almost level with the seat.

—It was taken in 1869, moments before she pedaled off to the velocipedarium.

—She was insane?

Berthe bridled at the suggestion.

—No, she was *not*. A velocipedarium was a gymnasium designed for velocipedes. Bicycles to you and me. You weren't allowed to ride them on the roads so special arenas were built called velocinasiums. Or gymnacycliums or amphicyclotheatrons.

—You need a bicycle to get from one end of those words to another, Simon said languidly.

He yawned and stretched out his toes toward the fire.

—Olympia's dream was to become an instructor.

—A centipede? Levon ventured.

—A velocipedagogue. She was a pioneer, I tell you.

—What happened to her?

Berthe mumbled a response. Levon, cupping his ear, leaned toward her.

—Sorry, I didn't catch that.

Obdulia smiled spitefully at Berthe.

—She fell off her bike at Punkeydoodle's Corner. Sprained her ankle.

—And never rode again, Berthe fumed. She married the fool doctor who tended her injuries. He scared her into believing if she didn't quit, her facial muscles would contort into a grimace and freeze up, like she was forever bicycling into a high wind. Her husband's hot air, that's what *I* think.

A feather of ash floated lazily out from the grate and drifted toward Levon's foot. He kicked at it and it disintegrated onto the carpet.

—Bicycle Face, he said dreamily. I've read about it, but never hoped to hear of an actual case.

Simon examined his linen shirt, removing an invisible piece of lint from it.

—There is a terminology for this preposterous diagnosis? he said.

Levon averted his eyes from Obdulia as he spoke.

—Love was considered a disease in the Renaissance, promoting all kinds of mad behavior, why not bicycles? They offered women unheard of independence. Mobility. This frightened men. You can see why. One moment the little woman's at your side, the next she's miles away, a speck on the horizon, pedaling for all she's worth. Which probably wasn't much in the man's estimation.

Anyway, the men didn't enjoy looking foolish, hanging about curbsides, waiting for their wives to return. So, doctors, who were also men of course, invented a, not a disease . . . more a *condition*. Let's put the wind up the women's bloomers, they thought. A spanner in the works. Convince them to park their bikes.

—Oh, I *agree*, said Berthe. Men were always trying to latch onto my coattails as I rode past. To slow me down, you know. They never succeeded.

—Didn't they? sneered Obdulia. How far did you actually get?

—And what would you know of the price of eggs, miss!

Obdulia caressed a marigold blossom, the raggedy orange head like a comic book orphan's.

—What good is a bicycle on an island anyway? she continued. All it does is return you to where you started from that little bit quicker.

Berthe dug her fists into her bony hips.

—I'm so *tired* of your petty . . .

—*Petty!*

—Stop this.

Simon did not raise his voice, only a plump white finger. That was enough. The two women turned to it as ships in a storm, about to crash on the rocks, turn to a lighthouse, diverting their course.

—Aunt Olympia lived to be a hundred, Simon said. Quite content in her marriage. Died calling for her dessert as I recall. Speaking of which, where is Elias? I am famished.

At that instant a loud crack reverberated through the house, accompanied by a slight tremor. Berthe lunged to prevent a model of a bicycle seat from wobbling off its perch on the sideboard. Candle flames caught the breeze from the corridor and flattened themselves out, straining for an invisible finish line. Obdulia jammed her hair into a fist at the back of her neck. She produced a supply of bobby pins from the sagging pocket of her jumper and began stabbing at her hair with them.

> *Oh, it's rubber, rubber, rubber,*
> *There's rubber in your suspenders,*
> *Rubber hoods and rubber goods,*
> *That's sold by all the vendors.*
> *For it's rubber in the male sex*
> *When a lady goes by, with her skirts held high*
> *The boys will stretch their rubber . . . necks.*

Elias lurched in irregular measures down the passage. He was a clock that no longer maintained proper time; his internal mechanism was all gummed up, slowing him down. He paused, wheezing, lurched forward again, stopped, clanked as he dropped his keys, clinked as he retrieved them, then stuffed them back into his pocket with his spare change and his penknife.

He had passed the afternoon, and very agreeably too, at Moses Visitor's. His bar was located in the village, in a wood-frame house that listed considerably to the side. This quirk went unnoticed by Moses's customers, since most of them exited in the same condition.

—We waited supper for you, Obdulia scolded.

Ah, his loving daughter! She acted so damned upright, Elias felt queasy.

—Boo hoo hoo, he said.

Elias puffed out his chest, swaggering a little. He had learned long ago to claim as much space for himself as he could, so that no hand would have room to be lifted against him. Suck up all the air, so that others were left too breathless to yell at him. And if that failed, he would put his best foot forward, as if to kick aside whatever was in its path.

Staring at Obdulia, he pulled up the end of his scarf like a noose, then unwound it with exaggerated ceremony. His daughter blanched at the inference. He didn't care. Hadn't he been the one to cut down Hereword that morning? What a pain she was even dead. Not for her the mudslide of consciousness after a handful of pills, or the bloody derailment into the bath as the tracks of her wrist-veins were severed. No, that bitch had deliberately chosen a means of killing herself that raised her above him, which was how she'd always thought of herself.

Hereword had been an infant when Elias left the island as a young man; first, out east to work down the mines, then out west shimmying up hydro poles. Down and up, up and down. And at both the heights and depths there was the haunting specter of Berthe Tibeault's face. The gossip of their affair had circled the island faster than a dog chasing its tail. Even her dolt of a husband had been bound to find out and, in tears, she'd urged Elias to leave. He was twenty, she was almost fifty. *I could be your mother*, she said. *Find a girl your own age*. That's not what he wanted, he argued with her. He couldn't recall from science class ever producing a chemical reaction by mixing two elements that were the *same*. Berthe was adamant, though.

Out to sea he was, and out to sea he'd gone, loving no one but her. That love was in his bones and over the years proved vulnerable to the same aches, pains and breakages that his shin bone or shoulder blade was. Simply *there*, so that when at age thirty he'd returned to the island, he believed his feelings were calcified enough to withstand seeing Berthe again.

That first summer he was back, he worked as a caretaker for the church, pulling weeds, tending the graves. Hereword O'Riley visited the churchyard each afternoon to pluck dandelions for her mother to brew teas and remedies with. She was a tall, pale, serious girl. Her big feet slapped the ground as she walked. Her hair was braided fire. He imagined her in the mornings, half naked, her ice-white fingers handling those glowing curls, taming them, oblivious to the pain. Obdulia had inherited a darker version of her mother's hair. That was Elias's influence.

Hereword never said hello or goodbye to him but she was aware of his presence, he knew that, always choosing a spot closest to where he happened to be working. He would wait until she arrived before ostentatiously removing his shirt. His chest was a thunderstorm: a black cloud of hair with a single bolt of lightning streaking down his belly. His skin slick with sweat. The sight of him intrigued her. Hereword was at an age when a storm meant excitement, not indiscriminate damage; it meant the romance of seeking shelter. Elias had none to offer her.

There came, in late August, an intensely hot, humid afternoon. The sky simmered; a real thunder shower threatened to bubble over after weeks of drought. Elias didn't expect to see Hereword but she came after all, with her basket, her trowel and her shears, the blades slender as her teenage legs, snip snip snip, scissoring through the tall grass. Elias was hunkered down in the farthest corner of the graveyard: the woods behind him, the main road a mile off. Humped gray headstones stood in rows, like chairs set out in a school auditorium, facing the stage. Waiting for something to happen.

He looked over at her. Studied her. She was kneeling, her back to him, under the shade of a weeping willow, the branches like a young girl's hair being combed out after a bath. The realization of what he wanted to do to Hereword hit him unexpectedly, and hard, the way his father used to. Elias wiped his forehead with his forearm. Beads of sweat were sewed to his skin. He was jumpy, breathing fast.

Hereword's yellow sundress was cut low in the back, the straps sliding off her narrow shoulders. He observed the outline of her spine and ribs: a xylophone of bones. She was to be played with, then.

It was an invitation, a dress like that.

And it wasn't like she didn't want it. She had a crush on him, that was obvious. He savored the word. *Crush.* Her feelings delicate as the wispy spores of these dead dandelions he was raking. So tempting to pull off. So *easily* done. Not like Berthe, who still resisted him, for her ailing husband's sake. Every day, she biked past him in the village, her chin up, while Elias spun his wheels, pining for her.

He was tired of being left behind.

A sultry breeze, laden with moisture, stirred up the trees.

He thought Hereword would have heard the swish of grass as he approached her. She didn't turn around, however. Finding that he still carried his rake, he lightly, *playfully*, dragged the tines down her back. She screamed. It wasn't his fault her skin was so sensitive. He hadn't meant to scratch her.

She shouted *no* but it was weak, quickly knocked to the

ground, as she was. Placing his palm against the back of her neck, he pushed her forward into the earth. She smelled of ginger. Berthe's scent was lavender. The difference confused him. He was thinking so much of Berthe.

A gravestone bobbed up and down in front of his eyes, mocking him. *Dearly beloved. Dearly beloved.* This girl wasn't that at all. She was a mistake. A terrible mistake.

His ear was close to her mouth as Hereword, her cheek pressed to the ground, whispered, *Please.*

Afterward, she lay still on the green grass, her yellow dress as rumpled as the reflection of sun on water. That's how he wanted to think of her. Not as someone real but an image, so that if he dipped his fingers into her, she'd trickle off him and disappear. Elias buckled his trousers. She didn't move. He pulled up her underpants, smoothing her dress down over her rump. She rolled over at that point and sat up. That's when he noticed the blood.

The stain was the shape of a key.

He told her to spit on it, that her saliva would wash it out. She did, spitting again and again, vigorously rubbing the folds of the fabric together. Thunder rumbled above them.

The whip-snap of lightning.

—We'd better hurry, he said, if we're going to beat the rain.

Hereword looked at him then for the first time. Strands of hair like flames licked her flushed cheeks. A hissing breath emerged from between her lips as her tears dribbled over them. He felt as though he'd been the bellows and now Hereword was forging herself anew—into cold tempered steel.

At their wedding, when the minister asked Elias if he took this woman, she shuddered and said, *He already did.* She was three months pregnant, not showing anything yet except her disdain. The wedding ring she'd bought for him turned out to be too small. She clucked her tongue as she forced it, hard, over his knuckle. *And I took your measure, too,* she whispered to him.

But he saw her satisfied smile as he winced.

Elias scratched his neck and rotated his head to get rid of the kinks. He licked the fingers of both hands and plastered his hair to his forehead until it resembled gravy sliding off a plate.

Berthe's husband had died two years after Obdulia was born. On hearing the news, he'd raced to Berthe's house, unable to stop himself. There she stood in the door, waiting, sensing he'd be back, her thin, wrinkled arms like crêpe streamers, celebrating his return.

Now, he embraced her, his bride of ten years, kissing the top of her white head.

—Miss me? he said.

—You can kiss my Plaster-Cast Self-Adjusting Nature-Fitting Saddle.

Berthe's wiry arms rested on his love handles. She nuzzled her cheek against his chest.

—Bicycle face, bicycle face, Simon taunted her.

Reluctantly, Berthe pulled away from Elias and reached, in one fluid motion, for her great-grandson's hand.

—You know, Simon, when you were born we heard you had no fingers. Your father shaped some out of dough, stuck them on you and baked you in the oven.

Sweetly, she kissed the tips of his fingers, biting down hard on the baby finger, drawing blood.

—Julia Child! he screamed.

—Aw, she said, that story wasn't true after all.

Elias windmilled his arms as though shepherding a herd of recalcitrant cows to pasture.

—I'm starving.

—Chase me Charlie, I got barley up the leg of my drawers, Berthe sang out.

Obdulia breezed in and out of the kitchen, bearing platters, until the table was quilted with colorful, homemade dishes. Platters of warm poppyseed rolls, spinach, mashed potatoes, pickled beets, peas, squash spiked with nutmeg, homemade apple jelly in a cut-glass dish, roast chicken and gravy thickened with flour brushed from Simon's collar.

Elias sat at the head of the table with Berthe opposite him. The others squeezed in between them, except for Obdulia, who remained standing to pour the wine. She began with Elias, holding the bottle far down the neck. By candlelight, it looked as if she'd slit her wrist and was calmly emptying her veins into her father's glass.

Flourishing the carving knife, Elias clashed it against the sharpening steel, engaging in an energetic duel with himself. Light refracted off the knife blade into Obdulia's eyes.

—What's the matter with you? Elias challenged her.

—Nothing.

Simon tucked his napkin under his chin.

—If she wants to sulk, let her.

—Shut up, she snapped.

—Won't.

—Baby.

Elias waved the knife around.

—Cut it out, he said.

The stiff petticoat of skin protecting the tender meat underneath crackled as Elias pierced it, slicing the chicken into breasts, legs and thighs. Whoever sat closest to a particular side dish acted as server and after a few minutes of ascertaining who wanted what and how much, each of the plates was heaped with food. Obdulia refused nothing, slathering her potato with butter and drowning the chicken in a succulent gravy. Levon watched with approval. His own metabolism was an overeager waiter who whisked the food from his system almost before he'd tasted it.

Simon clinked his wine glass for attention.

—I'd like to make a toast.

—And who better?

Elias roared with laughter at his own joke.

—To Levon. Welcome.

Obdulia smiled at him. He gulped his wine and the blush transferred to his cheeks.

Knives clopped and clattered on the plates. Wine was slurped. Belches erupted. Apart from this, the meal was eaten in virtual silence. The four of them seemed to have run out of things to say to each other long ago. Conversation was as stilted as an old cat prowling from one familiar spot to another, encountering the usual irritants: a flea in its ear, a kick, a cross word flung at it. Mindful of her duties as hostess, Berthe picked up the slack in the conversation and with a few neat twists, a fold here and there, constructed an elegant tale of the 1904 Tour de France, a contest characterized by sabotage: itching powder in a rider's shirt, emery in another's trousers, fouled drinking water and nails distributed by desperate competitors along the route.

—Elias has promised to take me to it, said Berthe. I was born in July 1924, the exact day and moment that year's Tour de

France began. As the very first cyclist propelled himself into the race, so did I. I've waited a lifetime to witness that blurry parade of sinewy thighs and firm buttocks.

Levon dotted an amber necklace of apple jelly onto his breast of chicken.

—I've never been a big fan of contests, he said. I don't care that much about winning.

—What's wrong with wanting to win, I ask you? Elias demanded. Against your religion or something?

—No, only . . .

Obdulia pushed some peas around on her plate.

—Simon wants to win the Babbitt's Feast cooking contest, she said. That's all he thinks about. I believe he'd kill to do it. Wouldn't you?

—Not exactly *kill*, he giggled.

—What are you going to enter with? she asked him.

His smile was so oily it almost slid off his chin.

—Wouldn't you like to know!

—*Hardly*, she sniffed.

—Suit yourself then.

She speared a piece of chicken with her fork. Simon had hated her from the moment she came to live at Berthe's house: a knock-kneed girl whose dreams at night were of stumbling on her dead mother. She saw Hereword's tongue sticking out, as if her hanging was nothing more than a childish trick she'd played on Obdulia. She heard (were there sounds in dreams?) the scrape of Elias's penknife as he sawed the rope, strands of it loosening one at a time, like fingers letting go.

Her room was next to Simon's. Some nights when she woke, screaming, she sensed him standing over her before she saw his shadowy outline. Obdulia would fumble for the bedside lamp until he stopped her, five caterpillar fingers clinging to the skinny branch of her arm, weighing it down. *Let's remain in the dark, shall we? Much safer. Oh, much, much safer.*

He was jealous of her. He loved Elias. Obdulia had sussed that out long ago. Her father was a cliff that people were drawn to the edge of: even her mother, who had claimed to hate him. His craggy, impassive face dared you to put a toe over, to experience the dizzying sensation of flinging yourself off, somehow believing, against the odds, that you would be the one person to survive the fall. Simple Simon. A rock never took responsibility for people's foolish designs, nor did Elias. He was aware of Simon's feelings—it was because of them that Elias, who couldn't boil an egg, was now a partner in the bakery—but if Simon expected a fairy-tale ending, a reward for all the tests he'd been given, all the curses and the ogreish behavior, then he was a cretin. How could stories so laden with misery (a mother's death, wicked stepmothers, enchanted gingerbread houses where children were gobbled up) end happily ever after?

She glanced over at Levon, who was picking at his food, his appetite gone. The dash of *joie de vivre* thrown into the pan at the start of the evening had sizzled for a moment, then evaporated, leaving an aftertaste of *vivre* and none of the *joie*.

His chair faced the fireplace, in front of which the chair Simon had been using for his pre-prandial snooze remained, since it was surplus to their needs. Levon's mind was brought back to the family dinners at his parents' following Alice's death. There, too, sat an empty chair, its skeletal back a grisly reminder of their recent bereavement. For weeks, kindly neighbors had delivered casseroles, carefully wrapped in gingham cloths, with notes of instructions for baking attached. They were left secretly on the Hawkes' doorstep, like abandoned babies in a Victorian melodrama screaming, *Take me in! Take me in!* Forcing the food into his mouth, Levon had felt a grotesque kinship with those stranded explorers in the frozen north, forced into cannibalism to survive. But for what? To live on as someone who had eaten his dead friends and relatives? Who had been nourished by his loss. What sort of existence was that?

He shuddered as he thought of what it was Simon and Elias wanted him to do. A grave was a cupboard in which skeletons, best kept hidden, rattled. What would they resurrect along with Hereword's body? Instead of dirty plates and crumpled napkins, he saw her corpse laid out on the table in front of him. He saw Simon breaking off stalactites of meat from the cavern of her carcass and Berthe chewing, not on a poppyseed roll, but on a hunk of tender white flesh. He saw Elias gaily slicing meat from the tendon of Hereword's leg as Obdulia dug a grave for her mother in a mound of mashed potatoes.

A wave of nausea rolled over Levon's tongue, crashed against his teeth and rolled back down his throat. He clamped his napkin to his mouth and prayed he wouldn't vomit.

Using a splintered chicken bone, Elias gouged a filament of spinach from his teeth.

—Not hungry? he said to Levon.

—He's saving room for dessert, said Berthe. Noggin pie.

Elias banged the table.

—Let's be having it then!

The two women leaped from their seats to clear the table. Levon scraped back his chair to rise and help them. Simon stopped him.

—We need to talk, he whispered.

Reluctantly, Levon sat down again. He handed Obdulia his plate, his fingertips brushing hers underneath it, hers cool as the porcelain, before she vanished, with Berthe, into the kitchen. Elias sang as he doled out cigarettes from a lacquered box:

> *Here are we met, THREE merry boys,*
> *Three merry boys I trow are we,*
> *And mony a night we've merry been,*
> *And mony mae we hope to be.*

He tipped a candle forward. The flame lolled from side to side as he lit his cigarette.

—When is it to be? Simon asked him.

—Tonight.

—*Tonight!* Levon hissed. Impossible.

—Perhaps you're right, Simon agreed. Best get it over with.

The red flocked wallpaper throbbed in rhythm with Levon's pounding heart. He had trouble breathing.

—You *cannot* rob your wife's grave, he said.

Elias expelled two streams of smoke from his nostrils.

—If I'm not sentimental about digging her up, why should you be?

—I'm not sentimental, Levon said. I object on religious grounds.

—Hereword isn't buried on any. She was a suicide, remember.

—Then I object on legal grounds, moral grounds, *coffee* grounds.

Simon picked up a fork and pressed it hard against his palm.

—Why not think of it as anthropology?

—Anthropology?

After admiring the neat imprint of tines in his flesh, Simon set the fork aside.

—Lucy, he said.

—My God, Levon hissed, who else have you dug up?

—Lucy is our ancestor. Yours and mine. She was unearthed after 3.2 million years spent comfortably underground. Were people horrified? Was there an outcry? Of course not. Lucy was celebrated as a scientific discovery of unparalleled excellence. Champagne all around. According to you, however, we should have left her down below to disintegrate completely. Our history is in those bones. We know ourselves through them. Where is the shame in that?

I knew in my bones.

Levon had transferred Sweeney's *o* from his own jacket to the breast pocket of Mr. Tibeault's when he changed clothes. He touched it now, a target at which both Elias and Simon were taking aim.

—I don't see the sense of it, said Levon. You think a loaf of bread will make Obdulia forget that her mother hanged herself? That she's *dead.*

—God preserve us, Simon sighed, which He patently doesn't. Try thinking of it *this* way. You have a mother, as everyone does. Her hair is the color of an overdone loaf. She has an arch of gold over one tooth. Her skin is flecked with pores the size of fennel seeds. She also has an illness, an incurable illness. She has to leave you. Not her fault, of course, but off she goes to the hospital. It's not far away. On a clear day you can see the glint of its windows in the sun. Still, you're a small child. Over the lake might as well be over the sea. Years go by without seeing her.

Communication between you is sporadic at best. A postcard at Christmas. A phone call on your birthday. You are content, however, because you can *imagine* her in her life: spearing the melon on her breakfast plate, folding the corners of her bed sheets precisely so, clipping her toenails.

Simon blew his cigarette smoke out of his nose and sucked it back in again at his mouth.

—And then, one afternoon, the news comes. Your mother slipped in the bath and banged her head against the tile. Her skull was crushed. Poof! She's dead. Gone forever. To spare your feelings, no one even tells you she's dead until after she's buried. There is gnashing of teeth and rending of garments at the news, but then you stop and think to yourself *why?* By this time, she has been, for all intents and purposes, absent from your life for years and years. The difference now is, you can no longer imagine her performing those quotidian tasks. Instead, the best you can do is picture her underground, rotting away. Like a mime who pretends that there is a wall in front of him, your imagination, too, sees a wall where none exists. Break through it and your mother lives once again, as she did before, in your *mind*. Listen. The brain dwells on objects analogous to its needs; the memory recalls things that have been pleasant to the taste; the imagination pictures them, as it were in a dream. Brillat-Savarin said that and Abiathar Babbitt drew on those sentiments to satisfy the islanders' appetites when there was no food with which to do it. We merely propose to take this idea a step further.

A tear-shaped dollop of hot wax trickled down the candlestick. Levon intercepted it, rolling it between his fingers until it hardened.

—Then why, Levon asked, do we need Hereword's bones?

—That was your idea, Elias reminded him.

—All right then, why bake her at all?

—Why have the sacrament? Because, said Elias, we're a consumer society. We *consume*. Imagination is all right for some, but most of us crave something we can touch, smell, taste. We don't hanker after contentment so much as the things we believe will bring us contentment: a bigger house, a new stereo, a lover. Whatever. Grief is a kind of appetite. There's an emptiness that needs filling. Right?

—Perhaps. But I still don't see . . .

—That's it, said Elias. Seeing is believing! Think of how the mere sight of a person we love can be enough to set our hearts pounding. Now, what if you could smell them and taste them, too?

In the manner of a child who wards off unwelcome news by chanting loudly, Levon insisted that:

—Obdulia's mother is dead. Dead dead dead.

—Shhh, Simon whispered. She'll hear you.

Levon snorted.

—It will hardly come as a surprise to her, will it?

Elias leaned in close.

—Tell me, haven't you ever walked down a crowded street and for a second, a *split* second, been convinced, absolutely certain, that you've just seen someone you knew was dead, suddenly alive and well, sipping coffee in a sidewalk café, or peering at hats in a shop window? And weren't you, for that one deluded moment, deliriously happy?

Levon heard plates being scraped of debris in the kitchen, the low murmur of information being exchanged.

—Answer the question, said Simon.

—Once, he admitted.

It had happened not long after he returned to school, after Alice's funeral. He was downstairs in the bowels of the medical library, already drunk and intent on getting drunker. The basement was L-shaped: shortened rows of shelving with a wall at one end and then more shelves along the upstroke of the L. Levon was huddled in the junction of the long and short corridor. He had been sent down to dust the books and was reading them instead. *The Queen's Closet Opened: Incomparable Secrets in Physick, Chirurgery, Preserving, Candying and Cookery*. Thumbing through the pages, he'd uncovered a recipe for *Spirits of Pearmains good against Melancholly* and was attempting to memorize it.

He was repeating to himself *Take one pound of the juyce of pearmain And boyl it with a soft fire until half consumed* when he heard it. That voice. Her voice. Soft but unmistakable: honey with a piece of gravel hidden in it. She was murmuring, *Where are you?*

Alice!

She was on the other side of this shelf. A folio away from him. *Where on earth are you?* she whispered. She was searching for him. Of course she was. *Here*, he cried, *here I am*.

A joy such as he had never known exploded inside him, and a *want*, a desire to return to the world as it used to be, before the accident. He craved, more than anything else, to see Alice again. To hug her and dance with her (he'd get it right this time) and *talk* to her in the old way. He had got it all muddled. Her death was a dream, that's all, a nightmare, and now he was awake. *It didn't happen, it never happened, it didn't happen, it never happened.* These words repeated over and over in his brain as he raced along the aisle, tapping frantically at the books wedged in the shelf, pressing his ear against them, listening for a voice, a heartbeat, a scent. *I found you!* her ecstatic voice cried out at the exact same moment he shouted, *Alice!* She was so near to him! Their hands reached for the identical book, only she withdrew it before he could, forming a keyhole in the shelf.

Looking through it, he saw that it was not Alice (of *course* not) but a stranger in a lab coat three times her age, an age Alice would never see. Levon felt a vicious pain in his heart as, once again, it broke; as, once again, his sister died in front of him. He saw the basketball she was bouncing moments before, stilled: a planet at rest. He felt Alice being prised gently from his arms, so much of her blood on him that the paramedics hadn't known which of them was the more injured. He heard the frenzied wail of the siren, saw the red lights swirling around him, felt himself breaking down, then apart.

He burst into tears.

Hence it is that it may come to pass, that the heart being untouch'd, life may be restor'd to the rest of the parts, and soundness recover'd; but the heart being refrigerated or affected with some heavy disease, the whole animal must needs suffer, and fall to corruption. When the beginning is corrupted, there is nothing which can afford help to it, or those things which do depend on it.

Levon cleared his throat to rid it of the tremor he knew lodged there.

—During the time I spent in prison, he told his dinner companions, I saw more than one inmate paroled. Set free. Oh, their happiness was absolute at the instant of their being told, but within seconds a real panic set in. And with it, doubt. Prison was horrible but it was *familiar.* The world outside was very different from the one they'd known when they were sent away from it. Beyond the prison wall—a real wall, not invisible—they would be vulnerable to a thousand things they never had to think about on the inside. Perhaps the prisoner's wife had deserted him. Or his kids wouldn't know him, or even want to. You say grief is an appetite. I say it's a prison. Some people prefer living inside it to being hurt all over again.

Elias's hot breath blew across Levon's ashen features causing his cheeks to flush.

—What are *you* afraid of?

Levon listened to Obdulia asking Berthe where the sugar was, Berthe answering.

—Chemistry, he said.

Simon's eyebrows sprang upward, a telephone wire released from the weight of a bird sitting on it.

—*Chemistry?*

—Not the kind that makes things go boom, Levon explained. I mean, if that happens, you know you've made a mistake, don't you? I'm worried about the sort of chemistry that quietly changes the color of things. So you feel entranced but disoriented at the same time.

A tinkling of piled-up coffee cups next to their ears caused all three men to jump.

—Jesus, Mary and Joseph, Elias bellowed.

Obdulia stood before them, carrying a tray.

—What are you all muttering about?

—None of your business, said Elias.

—Levon?

—Um . . . well . . .

Before he could answer, Elias reached over and stubbed out his cigarette on Levon's napkin. It left an acrid smell of scorched cloth and a neat hole about the size of a bullet.

Levon's lips pressed together. He lowered his eyes.

—Coffee's getting cold, girlie, said Berthe, nudging her.

Obdulia, with a reproachful glance at Levon, poured while Berthe sliced the Noggin pie, a glutinous concoction of condensed milk, gelatine and cherries. Levon refused his slice. Simon added it to his helping.

Suddenly, a draft of cold air rushed into the room, with a force that suggested it had waited all night for the fire's red velvet barricade to be unhooked and let it pass in. Berthe rose from her seat to check the windows. They were fastened tight. She shrugged in answer to Elias's querying expression and sat down again. Meanwhile, the breeze had unsettled everyone else. Elias barked at Simon not to be greedy. Obdulia splashed Berthe with scalding coffee as she filled her cup. Simon pretended not to hear Elias's request to pass the cream. Levon hit his shinbone against the table and yelped in pain.

The family's ability to remain cordial to each other was being strained to the limit.

Obdulia, returning to her seat, rounded Elias's chair. His arm shot out and his broad, flat hand clamped down on his daughter like an oyster on a grain of sand: an irritant, which is all it is, or ever will be, to the oyster. Scowling, she jerked away from him.

Sniggering, he held out his palm.

—Button, button, who's got the button?

He'd torn off one of the fake pearl buttons on her cardigan. Obdulia poked her finger through the hole.

—My mother made me this sweater, she gasped.

—Hell, she made you and you got holes.

—Elias, said Berthe primly, don't be vulgar.

She pinched the edge of the pie server with her fingers, collected the gooey pink residue and popped it into her mouth. Simon watched the proceedings as he would a favorite movie he'd seen a million times, almost mouthing the lines along with the actors.

Obdulia flung herself into her chair.

—You did it on purpose, she accused Elias.

—It was an accident.

He honked into his napkin.

—Say sorry then, Elias, Simon goaded him, and be done with it.

Elias peeked at the nasal contents he'd discharged.

—Accidents happen, he said.

Obdulia's hair fell around her face. Bobby pins were strewn about her chair like railroad ties after a train wreck. She picked up her fork with trembling fingers and attacked her slice of pie.

—You should have been more careful, she retorted. You should have been more careful of *her.*

—I've taken care of *you* all these years, haven't I?

—Haven't *we?* Berthe interjected.

—Berthe and I. That's right. And what thanks have we ever got? You wished I was dead instead of her. I know that.

—You should have seen the look he gave her after he cut my mother down, Obdulia said to Levon. Like she was a stray dog he couldn't remember inviting into the house.

Elias plucked a marigold from the pot. The blossom drooped over his hand. He had a vivid, unwelcome impression of a woman with Obdulia's red hair, her neck snapped, the rope curled around a hook like a comma, a quiet pause.

He began to tear the petals off one by one.

—She loves me, she loves me not.

—Stop this, Levon begged him. Please.

—She loves me.

Hereword had left more than herself hanging between father and daughter. Guilt, anger, sadness, loss were twisted together; a cat's cradle of emotions, each one tauter and more complicated than the last. Whoever pulled the first string, forced the other to respond. The result was a tangled mess that neither of them could unravel.

—She loves me not. She loves me.

Simon, utterly relaxed, blew on his coffee to cool it. Berthe helped herself to another slice of pie.

When Elias spoke again, it was so softly that his breath did not disturb the last petal cradled in his palm.

—She loves me . . . ?

His eyes met Obdulia's. Father's and daughter's. Black eyes and green eyes; a storm blowing across a lake. She shook her head almost imperceptibly.

—Not, she whispered.

He nodded, as if satisfied with her response.

—Not.

These two motions, one of the ventricles, another of the auricles, take place in such a manner that the movements in question are rapid . . . where the trigger being touched, down comes the flint, strikes the steel, elicits a spark, which falling among the powder, it is ignited, upon which the flame extends, enters the barrel, causes the explosion, propels the ball and the mark is attained—all of which incidents, by reason of the celerity with which they happen, seem to take place in the twinkling of an eye.

Elias swung his fist at the marigold pot, knocking it over, sending clumps of dirt flying every which way. Levon flinched. Berthe cried out for her flowerpot and Simon, with an irritated *tsk*, flicked earth off his shirt. Obdulia jumped up from her seat to rescue the remaining flowers that lay half-buried in the earth. This seemed only to exacerbate Elias's anger. He grabbed for her, catching hold of her hair. In one hand, he scrunched a handful of marigold blossoms; with the other, he began rolling the ends of her hair around his fist, yanking her head down and to the side, closer to him, closer, until her cheek was flush with the table. Levon raced over to Elias, winding his skinny arms around Elias's muscular neck in an attempt to pull him off. But it was no good. Elias was Lustucru, the Skull Doctor, placing Obdulia's head upon his anvil so that he could beat out of her, as he beat out of all women, her obstinacy, her disobedience, her disapproval of him.

Levon shouted at Simon to help him, at Berthe to talk sense to Elias. His pleas went unanswered.

Obdulia batted at Elias wildly with her free arm, grunting with rage and pain.

—Let me go, she shouted. Let me *go*.

She's just like her mother, Elias thought as he stuffed marigold petals into Obdulia's mouth. *Just like her mother*.

And all the while he was whispering in her ear, Say you love me, say you love me, say you love me.

9

FOR THE PRICKING OF A NEEDLE

Take boulted Wheat flower, and temper it with red Wine, boyl them together to the thickness of a Salve and lay it on so hot as you can suffer it. This wil open the hole, draw out the filth and ease the pain.

THE SKY was a glass of bitter black tea, a thin peel of lemon floating in it. No streetlights illuminated the country darkness. No stars either. There was only the brisk sweep of a car's headlights, poking into corners, dusting off a farmhouse here, a fencepost there. Elias needed no signs to tell him where he was. He knew these roads like the back of his hand.

The grooves of the steering wheel dug into his palms as he struggled against the old car's tendency to pull to the right. Something in the automobile's plodding insistence on going its own way, despite Elias's wishes, made him think of Hereword and a well-spring of sparkling, cold anger, ever-present in him, bubbled up. She, too, had known the back of his hand. Not often. And there was that time when she'd launched a pair of garden shears at *him*, also a frying pan. Still. Elias wasn't a man for imagining things but he saw her now, dangling from his clenched fists like a grotesque marionette, tied to the end of his ever dwindling lifeline, her arms and legs jerking in a macabre dance, her head bobbing knowingly. The vision startled him so much that he lifted his hands from the steering wheel as if to fling her away.

—Levon's head snapped against the glass.

—Ow!

—Shut up, Elias snarled.

The car fishtailed on the icy road. Squinting through a windshield rimed with frost, Elias felt himself pitch forward momentarily, poised to sail through the glass into that dizzily spinning world: a flicker of trees, then road, then trees again. Shadows and gleaming, bony fingers reaching greedily for him. Here were all his childhood monsters, but grown up now, along with Elias. They had long ago abandoned that small boy's closet, the coat hooks like talons, and lurked instead in any situation that he could not control: in an unhappy wife and her equally miserable daughter; in an aging body whose muscles were deflating, the joints becoming increasingly arthritic; in death, coming closer, unavoidable.

He fought the instinct to brake hard and wrench the wheel in the opposite direction to the skid. The remedy was to steer *into* it: toward the woods, toward the ditch, toward disaster. So, instead, Elias shifted into neutral and pumped, gently, on the brakes, relishing the sensation of nature gradually ceding the upper hand to him, of the car surrendering to his authority. Crawling now. Obedient to his lightest touch. He exhaled, unaware until that second that he'd been holding his breath. This would be his lesson for the night. Concentrate on the mechanics of the job at hand. Don't think of Hereword as *Hereword*. That was a slippery slope of another kind. She was a heap of bones, nothing more. Nothing to him, anyway.

—See, he said to Levon. No problem.

Levon rubbed his sore temple and scowled. Groggily, he rested his cheek once more against the upholstery, wishing he were still in bed.

Instead, he drifted back into the dream Elias had roused him from a short time ago.

He was once again at Alice's funeral. Rain threatened and above him was a circle of black clouds that mirrored perfectly the mourners in their black clothes and fluttering veils huddled around the grave: Levon's father, mother. Aunt Anna-Lee. Cousin Cynthia. Sweeney.

The priest, ready to perform the service, cleared his throat. All eyes turned to him. He was a lanky young man, barely older than Alice, the girl they'd come to bury. Auburn hair stuck up in flames around his bulgy forehead like a lit matchstick. His glasses were as thick as ice in January, moist, protuberant gray eyes swimming under the surface. Size twelve-and-a-half brogues peeked out from beneath his cassock.

With a swish of his elegant fingers, Abiathar Babbitt made a circle in the air over the coffin. As if by magic, there appeared in his sleight-of-hand the red *o* from Sweeney's sign.

—God eats here, he mumbled.

—Amen, Sweeney murmured.

—Amen, echoed the others.

Levon cocked his head, certain he must have misunderstood the priest's words. He glanced at his parents. They were holding hands. Not parents who had lost a child but children themselves, lost and frightened, standing at the edge of a forest that went much deeper than six feet. What crumbs, Levon wondered snidely, would the priest toss them to help them find their way home? As Abiathar Babbitt opened his book, Levon braced himself for a litany of turgid, comfortless homilies. Genesis. Revelation. Corinthians, perhaps. *O Death, where is thy sting? O grave, where is thy victory?* Instead, he heard:

> *When Levin first returned from Moscow, and while he still started and grew red every time he remembered the ignominy of being refused, he had said to himself: "I blushed and started like this, and thought the world had come to an end when I was ploughed in physics and did not get my remove; and it was the same when I bungled that affair my sister entrusted to me. And what happened? Now that years have gone by I recall it and wonder that I could have grieved so much."*

Anna Karenina! It was the novel, to the very page, that Alice was reading the day she died. The book was a summer-school assignment and she had struggled with it, never quite sorting out the Russian nomenclature: last names first, the first shall be last. After his parents banished him from the hospital, Levon had raced home, up the stairs to Alice's bedroom, unable to countenance that she was not there waiting for him, wrapped in her quilted bathrobe, hunched over the book, a frown of concentration on her normally smiling face. But there was only the novel, abandoned at her bedside, the covers shut: unfinished, as Alice was. The last page she'd read was marked, the remainder of the story a promise that, for her, would never be fulfilled. For a time, Levon entertained the romantic notion of finishing the book—he hadn't yet read it and so he packed it among his belongings—for Alice's sake. Every so often, he plucked it from the shelf by his prison bed, always opening it to page 197, the bookmarked page, the page the priest was reading.

So it will be with this grief.

The others evinced no astonishment at the unorthodoxy of Abiathar's sermon. Even Aunt Anna-Lee raised no objection. Was it Levon alone who heard:

Time will go by and I shall not mind about this either.

He made a beeline to Sweeney, who stood apart from the others, his hands clasped in front of him.

—Draw me a map, Sweeney.

—Say please.

—Please.

The old man tugged at his collar, uncomfortable in the snug black coffin of his suit.

—You're determined to go then?

—I'll be in trouble if I don't.

—That territory is hazardous to you, Sweeney said.

A breeze wafted behind it the sickly perfumes of all the various flower arrangements, most of them wilting, dying, planted throughout the cemetery.

—I loved a girl who once lived.

—What happened? Sweeney asked him.

—It was a long time ago, said Levon.

Sweeney gripped his shoulder and began shaking him roughly.

—Wake up! Wake up!

Levon sat up, yawning and rubbing sleep out of his eyes. The car swerved into a circular drive and he registered blurrily a modern church, a dunce's cap perched on top, and a frozen fountain of weeping willows. Elias killed the engine and the lights went out.

—We're here.

—Thanks for pointing that out, Levon replied. I'd never have guessed.

Elias kicked viciously at his door, twice, until it creaked open, and he hopped out.

What little heat there was seeped fast out of the car. Despite the insulation of a pair of longjohns, a turtleneck, a fisherman's sweater and a parka, Levon's teeth began to chatter.

First seeing death is a corruption which befalls by reason the defect of heat, and all things which are hot being alive, are cold when they die . . .

The passenger door was yanked open.

—You plan to sit there all night?

Levon buried his chin in the collar of his borrowed parka.

—If there's any chance you'll let me, yes.

—I'm losing patience.

—Where's Simon anyway? Levon demanded. Why isn't he here?

—He doesn't want to get his hands dirty.

—So, you admit what we're doing is wrong.

—No, I'm saying that he doesn't like getting his hands dirty.

—Do you know what the definition of a felony is? said Levon. A *grave* crime.

—Dogs dig up bones every day of the week, for Chrissakes.

Defeated, Levon leaned his head against the dashboard. There was little point in arguing with a man of Elias's temperament. Even if Levon managed to push a rock-solid argument up the hill, Elias would send it hurtling back down, squashing Levon flat.

—You're a bully, Elias. Do you know that?

Elias stamped his feet, from cold or irritation or both.

—I wouldn't get my way nearly so often if I wasn't.

Willow branches, beaded with ice, clicked a rosary, a breezy prayer. For whom, though? Hereword? Alice? For all of them, the living and the dead? Levon's warm breath had disturbed the pattern of frost on the window until only fragments of it remained, disjointed as the memory of his dream.

Nothing got buried deep enough, it seemed, so what did it matter in the end?

—Lead on, he sighed. I will follow you to the grave.

Not a man to shed more light on a situation than he needed to, Elias shaded the lantern with his gloved hand. Levon stumbled after him, lugging a canvas sack that clanked ominously every time he bumped into a headstone. After slinking around to the rear of the church and unlatching a wrought-iron gate, they had quickly found themselves in the oldest section of the cemetery. Here, graves sprouted higgledy-piggledy, like teeth, mossy and decayed, crammed in a too-small mouth.

Again, a muffled but audible clink, clank.

Elias put a finger to his lips.

—I'm not doing it on purpose, Levon whined.

—I believe you. I doubt purpose has figured much in your life. Now, keep quiet and stick close to me.

—Oh *there's* a recipe for success.

With a sigh, he shouldered the sack again, afraid of losing sight of Elias altogether.

Under ordinary circumstances, on a sunny day, with a packed lunch and convivial company, Levon enjoyed an occasional stroll through the local graveyard. He appreciated them as he did the well-plotted novels of the nineteenth century, with their varied characters, the intermingling of high tragedy (a child's grave) and low comedy *(here lies Ann Mann, Who lived an old maid, But died an old Mann)* and their assured outcomes.

And there was the added factor that the history of a village, medical and social, was often written in the deaths, as well as the lives, of its citizens. What could all these islanders have died from? Cholera and typhoid, perhaps? Drowning, malnutrition, homesickness, hypothermia, stillbirths and dementia? Tetanus poisoning from rusty tailors' needles? From hanging? (One person at least.) Had any died of embarrassment, from fright or of love; with their boots on, with a smile on their faces?

—Where's her grave?

—Over there. I think.

Elias gestured to where the woods bordered the churchyard.

—You *think?*

—It's years since I've been here. Jesus.

—*He* had no problems raising the dead as I recall.

They tramped in silence over grave beds, sheets of snow pulled up over frail elderly bodies that cowered, defenseless, willing the robbers to pass them by.

Eventually, about a mile from the church, Elias halted. His breathing was more labored than their hike warranted, Levon thought, but he held his tongue. A soft clicking signaled the unseen presence nearby of pine trees. The darkness, unmindful of the needles' pricking, had swallowed them whole along with the stars.

—She's here, said Elias blandly.

Levon dropped the sack and caressed his aching muscles.

—I thought you said she was buried in unconsecrated ground.

—She is.

—Here?

—Yes.

—Well, said Levon, the two aren't separated by much, are they?

—One wrong step. That's all it takes on this island.

Elias swished the lantern around. Levon figured he was searching for Hereword's headstone but it soon became apparent that there were none. Instead, numerous objects lay embedded in the snow: baby clothes, a magician's top hat, an original Broadway recording of *Guys and Dolls*, a box of sea shells. An old toaster reflected the lantern's beam.

—That's Arthur Quilley's grave. Kept promising his wife he'd fix the toaster. Fixed the stove instead and gassed himself in it.

—Whose is that?

Levon pointed to a wooden leg carved in the shape of a horse's hindquarter, a hoof painted on the bottom.

—Don't ask.

—Where is Hereword?

—That's her, Elias grunted. Hereword O'Riley Limb.

He trained the lantern on a plain, weatherbeaten wooden box. Taking his cue from Elias's curt nod, Levon knelt in the snow and lifted the lid. Inside the box, wrapped in tissue paper, nestled a pair of white satin shoes.

—Obdulia gave them to Hereword on her last birthday.

Setting down the light, Elias ducked his head inside the sack and like a demonic Santa withdrew from it a pickax, a crowbar, iron hooks and a coil of rope. Lastly, he brought out a Thermos, an item he placed reverentially on the ground beside him.

—Let's get started, he said. What do we do?

Earlier, a decision had been reached that, if the deed must be done, the best thing would be to do it with as much professionalism as possible. During his studies, Levon had researched the methods of grave robbers, or sack-em-ups, or resurrection men. By any name, they brought back the dead: not to life but to the living, to the surgeries of great anatomists like Sir Astley Cooper, the Hunter brothers and, until his unfortunate association with Burke and Hare, Robert Knox. Levon didn't regard himself as an expert but he grasped the rudiments of the procedure, at least. That would have to do.

He gathered up the corners of the canvas, indicating to Elias that he should do the same at the opposite end.

—What's this for?

Taking orders from someone else made Elias even surlier than usual. Wishing to avoid any nasty confrontations, Levon kept his tone conversational, as if discussing a new gardening technique over the backyard fence.

—To catch the dirt. Afterward, we dump it back on the grave, cover it with snow and nobody's the wiser. Theoretically anyway.

—And where did you learn that?

—The school of hard Knox.

Levon slid open the door of the lantern, fussing with it until a skirt of light spread over the grave. As he did, he recited:

> *Up the close and down the stair,*
> *But and ben, wi' Burke and Hare,*
> *Burke's the butcher, Hare's the thief,*
> *Knox the boy that buys the beef.*

Anatomists needed a constant supply of corpses to dissect, Levon explained. People like Burke and Hare provided them.

—Is that who we're like then? Burke and Hare?

—Christ, no. They were murderers. It was a grave robber's job to dig a man out of his grave, not send him to it. Burke and Hare were lazy. They wanted to save themselves the manual labor.

—Speaking of which, said Elias nudging him, you take first go.

—She's your wife. Why do I have to do it?

—Because I say so.

—That's no reason.

—Because right now I'm holding the pickax.

—All right, Levon grumbled. Give it here.

He grabbed the ax and hoisted it over his head. Silently begging Hereword's pardon, Levon shut his eyes and swung. It was a paltry effort that made little inroad into the frozen ground.

—Put your back into it, man, or we'll be here all night.

Elias sat cross-legged beside the grave, unscrewed the cap from the Thermos and swigged from it. Without warning, several crows, irritated perhaps by the presence of these unexpected companions, flew out of the woods, cawing raucously. Both men started at the sound.

—A murder of crows, Levon whispered.

—What are you talking about?

—That's what you call a group of crows. A murder. A skulk of foxes. A tidings of magpies. A murder of crows.

—We'll be jumping at our own shadows next, retorted Elias. Get back to digging.

Levon swung harder, spurred by his irritation at Elias's bravado, and also by his desire to get this hideous business over with. This time the ax lodged deep in the earth's hard white skull, cracking it, spurting chips of icy bone in Elias's direction. With a cry of disgust, he scuttled backward.

—Watch it!

Elias's hands trembled noticeably as he brushed himself off.

—Dogs dig up bones every day of the week, Levon mimicked.

—I'm not scared.

—Of course not.

An accusatory finger was pointed at Levon.

—I'm *not*, Elias insisted. Dead people can't hurt you.

—Can't they? Then it stands to reason they can't help either.

Again the ax descended, the tip of it picking at the earth's scab. A dog, far off, barked once. Elias zipped up the hood of his parka, retreating as far as he could into its furry depths. For nearly half an hour he was silent. However, the pickax, with its dull, repetitive thud, churned up not only the ground but Elias's thoughts as well for when he spoke again, he asked:

—Who did you say wanted these corpses?

—Surgeons, Levon gasped. Anatomists.

—What for?

Levon paused in his digging to unzip and remove his jacket. He was perspiring heavily.

—To study. There was still so much mystery about how the human body worked. By dissecting a corpse, especially one that had died of an unusual ailment, anatomists increased their store of knowledge.

—So, said Elias slyly, the dead were used to help the living?

Recognizing too late the trap that had been laid, Levon shrugged his shoulders in a noncommittal manner.

—I'll take that as a yes, Elias gloated.

—Why not take the ax instead? I can't talk and dig at the same time. Besides, I need a break.

—Already?

—Yes, *already*.

—I thought all prisoners did hard labor.

—I worked in the laundry.

—That's what my taxes are used for? said Elias, outraged.

—Yes, but I'm a reformed man now. I'll never again over-starch a shirt.

While Levon nursed his raw hands, Elias inhaled deeply and swung the ax in a smooth, effortless arc over and over. It was clear that he was showing off but, Levon noted gleefully, the older man's superior physical strength actually served to diminish him in Levon's eyes. Literally. With every powerful heft of the ax, Elias shrank a tiny bit. The grave was swallowing him up.

—What I don't understand, said Elias, is why, if all this dissecting was so helpful, corpses had to be stolen. Why weren't people donating their bodies to science?

—Different attitudes, Levon answered. The bone that held the pen could tell us more about Shakespeare than his autograph ever would but he had such a horror of being excavated that his epitaph placed a curse on any man who moved his bones. To interfere with a body after death was a desecration. Lots of folktales tell of a dead person who's missing a body part—a baby finger, say, or a toe lost in an accident—and is refused eternal rest until they retrieve it and have it buried alongside them. Imagine if they had to scurry around collecting their autopsied livers, hearts and kidneys as well. No, for centuries the only legitimate source of bodies was from prisons. The father of anatomical studies, Andreas Vesalius, was reduced to stealing his first corpse straight off the gibbet, a thief who'd been hanged then roasted for good measure. Do you know the expression, Art is science in the flesh? For anatomists, science was in the art of the flesh. If I'd been caught housebreaking in the eighteenth century, there's a good chance I'd have been hanged, then quartered and drawn by eager medical students.

—Where do the grave robbers come in then?

—They were the black-market suppliers. There weren't enough criminals to go around. Plenty of bodies in a graveyard, though. It was a filthy trade but lucrative if you could stomach it.

—There's money in this?

A familiar light shone in Elias's eyes.

—Was. *Was.*

Levon's foot nudged the Thermos, tipping it over. Righting it, he was heartened to hear a restorative liquid of some kind sloshing about.

—What's in here? he asked.

—Some of Moses Visitor's liquor. He learned the recipe at his grandfather's knee during prohibition. He's refined the process considerably since then, of course. He used to use water from his pond out back. Scooped up a frog once without noticing and added it to the batch.

Elias thought wistfully of Moses's bar where, by this time, last call would have been sounded and then dutifully ignored. He pictured himself settled on his favorite formaldehyde, or was it Naugahyde, stool, chatting companionably with his neighbors. What a story he had to tell them, if only he could.

The contents of the Thermos smelled innocuous enough to Levon. He hadn't touched any liquor in almost three years and hadn't wanted to either; this was purely medicinal, to warm him up. He swallowed, recalling a neophyte grave robber's referring to his first taste of poteen as his *internal baptism*. Levon suspected there were no atheists in either fox holes or grave holes.

He smacked his lips. A faint aftertaste of turpentine about it but not bad otherwise. His next swallow was longer, deeper. Undeniably comforting.

—Go easy, Elias warned. It's more potent than you think.

Shrugging off this admonition as further evidence of Elias's machismo, Levon raised the Thermos once more to his lips. It was at that moment his mouth exploded, igniting a fire that traveled along his throat like a trail of gunpowder. Levon's eyes bugged out from the force of it and his free hand groped blindly in front of him as if to reclaim his jettisoned eyeballs from the snow. Minuscule pickaxes tunneled down to his stomach where the lining was efficiently stripped and brought back up to the surface.

Elias stared impassively.

—That's right, kid. First time's hard on everyone. Bring it all up.

By now, he was knee-deep in the hole they'd dug. *Bring it all up*. The closer Elias came to doing so, the more he fretted. We're all skeletons under the skin, he thought. What possible difference could it make whether Hereword was down there or up here? All of this sentimentality surrounding the dead irked him. As a kid, Obdulia was always on him to get dressed in his finery and carry flowers to Hereword's grave. He wasn't courting her, for God's sake! At least Elias had been spared the expense of providing a headstone, like a bookmark of the dead, letting the reader know where the deceased had left off. He'd had the last word in that argument, for a change.

Jesus, his feet were cold.

—Take over, he said climbing out of the grave. Work the stuff out of your system.

It felt as if the sharp point of a giant corkscrew was burrowing into Levon's skull and the lightest pressure on the mechanism would remove his head from his shoulders with a *whoosh*, followed by a geyser of blood. Nauseated, Levon reclaimed the pickax and lowered himself cautiously into the hole. Down there was the coffin; and in it were the remains of a woman pined for by her daughter. Even if by some miracle, Hereword could be revived, would she recognize the daughter she'd abandoned all those years ago to be shaped by her death and not by her life's example?

And what of Obdulia? On a crowded street, mightn't she pass her mother by without a second glance?

Could Hereword be known in her bones?

—What was she like anyway? he asked Elias.

—Who?

—Who do you think? Hereword.

—Why do you want to know?

The ax's sharp beak pecked at the ground as if searching for worms.

—I'm curious, Levon said.

—Don't *you* start. That's all I heard from Obdulia. Tell me this story, tell me that, tell me about the time when. No, I told her. Don't rehash the past. It's dead, so's your mother. There's an end to it.

—But stories are what keep people alive.

—Hereword didn't want to be alive or she wouldn't have killed herself, would she? And supposing I did tell Obdulia anything about her, what would she gain by it? All she does is brood anyway.

—But it's like re-reading a favorite book, Levon persisted. A story that's familiar. It's a comfort to be in a world you know, with characters you love. Everything is ordered. There aren't any surprises. Events unfold as you expect and want them to.

Elias wiped his runny nose on his sleeve, then held it up to the lantern to admire the slug's trail of snot glistening there.

—There's the difference between us. I want the jolt I get from something new. I'm braced for the unexpected. The challenge of it. Hereword was afraid of life.

But not, he conceded, of death. As he was. That realization had niggled at him for the last ten years. When she did at last kick out with any ferocity, it was against the back of the chair she'd used to stand on, her only support before the world fell away. Elias's legs would have to be cut out from under him before he'd allow himself to be dragged off this earth. Or put into it. To him, death was a contemptible opponent. A certain winner who still needed to cheat by sapping Elias's strength with every passing year, month, *day*.

—My turn, he said.

—No it's not, Levon replied.

—Get out of the goddamned grave.

The lantern was a fragile yellow butterfly, its wings flickering against a thick black curtain, the lamp oil depleting as, over the next two hours, the men spelled each other off, working in silence, each one buried beneath his own thoughts, until a ragged tunnel roughly one third the length of the coffin and eight feet deep had been dug. Levon grasped Elias's outstretched hand to pull him up, but not before he'd performed a brief soft shoe on the wooden surface of his wife's coffin.

—Don't be such a jerk, Levon admonished him. You think dancing on her grave proves how brave you are?

—It was a joke.

—It's not funny.

Leaning on the handle of the ax, Elias bared his teeth, gnawing at the frozen air, tracing the icy trickle of oxygen down his parched throat.

—I always thought grave robbers dug up the whole coffin, he said.

—They didn't need to. The poor were buried in flimsy coffins. All the robbers had to do was cut a hole at the head of the grave, break open the casket, lower the rope and . . .

—And?

Levon placed his hands around his throat.

—Make a noose out of it and drag the corpse up.

—In effect, said Elias, we hang her again.

—Yes.

Elias picked up the rope. He secured two iron hooks to it by tying slip knots.

—What about rich people's graves?

He dangled the hooks, setting his heel in the curve of each, and pulled on the rope to test whether or not they'd hold.

—The rich could afford lead coffins, Levon explained. Iron cages around the grave. Guards. They were better protected.

—The rich always are.

The Bible said the poor were to be resurrected. Elias's father, Seamus, had quoted him that chapter and verse often enough. Camels and needles merged in Elias's mind with an image of his dad's humped back as he sewed late into the night, late into his life. Too poor to retire even after cataracts had blinded him. He remembered Seamus laid out on his deathbed, his cheeks threaded with purplish veins as if he'd sewn himself up in a shroud of his own skin. His tiny yellow teeth were oddly curved, like a bird's claw.

Seamus Limb had been born in Ireland. Four of his siblings were the offspring of his frazzled mother's lawful husband and four were "by the Church." Seamus's father was a Father, a priest. When Seamus was old enough to take communion, the priest, his own father, passed the wafer into his mouth and pressed down on his tongue, as if to say, *Don't speak of this. Accept it.* At fifteen, the rebellious Seamus was shipped from Ireland to stay with relatives in Canada—to the island, where he apprenticed to his uncle, a tailor. His black hair fell as low over his forehead as an Irish sky; he seldom smiled or laughed. All the girls were wary of him, except for one. Elias's mother, Nancy, was a plain girl with a martyr's temperament. Their marriage was not of two people but of nails to a cross. Elias recognized an element of that in his marriage to Hereword: his driving anger, her wooden acquiescence. No redemption for either of them.

He hawked and spat.

—What next?

Levon sighed.

—The trick is to catch the lid of the coffin, he said. The weight of the earth should bear down at the point we want the coffin to break.

Obediently, Elias lowered the rope, manipulating the hooks until he felt them latch onto the coffin's rim. He tensed the rope, satisfied that the hooks were secure.

—OK. We got her. Now, help me pull.

They braced their feet, gripped the rope in their blistered hands, the skin like bubbling water, and tugged. Nothing happened. Elias had reckoned on the coffin, a cheap pine box he'd built himself to save money, splintering at the slightest touch.

—You're not pulling hard enough, he hissed at Levon.

—Yes I am.

—Well it's not working.

—We've just begun, argued Levon.

—Need a hand? said a voice behind them.

Both men stood stock still. Only the rope moved; released from their slackened fingers, it slithered down the hole. Their mouths, too, had slackened but nothing came out. Levon's tongue hung loose as a clapper in a bell, unable to sound.

—It's only *me*, said the voice.

Slowly, Elias and Levon pivoted. There was Simon, swaddled in layers of sweaters and scarves, mittened hand to his mouth, unsuccessfully stifling a giggle.

—Look at you two. Your expressions . . .

—What are you doing here? Levon spat.

—I got bored waiting for you. Frankly, I'd expected you to be done by now.

Elias's teeth were a grindstone against which his tongue sharpened itself.

—We might have been if you'd left us alone. The rope's down there now. One of us will have to go in for it.

—Well, it will have to be Levon. He's the skinniest of us.

—Not really, Levon protested. I'm wearing black. Black's very slimming.

Advancing toward him, Elias ticked off on his fingers:

—Eenie, minie, moe. I'm catching Levon by the toe.

—You left one out. That's not fair.

—And if he hollers, he'll see who the meanie is.

The threat hung in the air, a germ waiting to infect and weaken whoever opened his mouth to argue.

—Get a move on, Levon, Simon urged. I'm freezing to death.

He glanced around at the graves.

—No offense intended.

—I'll lower you down, Elias instructed. The wood should be rotten enough. Jimmy it open with the hook, then bring out the skeleton. Daylight's not that far off.

Elias tapped his watch face to reinforce this.

—Yes, said Simon. Hurry.

Trapped between a rock and a hard place, Levon opted for the path of least resistance. Miserably, he lay on his stomach while Elias knotted the piece of twine, used to tie the canvas sack, around Levon's ankles. He then eased himself headfirst over the lip of the grave.

Pressing his palms against the grave walls, he crept downward. If the stories were anything to go by, there ought to be a guide for this journey of his. Some ancient who could prophesy his future, impart wisdom. Instead, he was all alone. Blind in this darkness, the shades drawn.

He'd lost all sense of time so it might have been hours, or seconds, later when his fingers grazed the rough surface of the coffin. The twine bit into his ankles as he hovered over it, one hand on the lid in an assisted handstand, while the other groped for a hook. There it was: the rope coiled on top, its iron fangs sunk in the wood. He breathed through his mouth in a fruitless effort to evade the noxious odor of decay.

Quickly, he loosened the hook and then probed for a knot hole or loose plank by which he could crack open the wood. Muffled voices filtered down from overhead. He ignored them. They were so far off. How tenuous his connection to the land of the living was after all, amounting to a stranger's grip on his heels, no more than that. Alice and his grandparents were dead, his parents miles away. Who would there be to grieve for him if the string snapped and he was left down here to rot? Obdulia? Not likely, given the circumstances.

His stomach heaved and he swallowed hard. How had he managed to get into this ludicrous position? As a child, he'd felt a similar revulsion when washing the supper dishes. There was the moment toward the end when he had to roll up his sleeve and plunge his hand into a sinkful of fetid water, always fearful of what slimy thing—a potato skin, a soggy heel of bread, cold tongue—his hand might encounter before pulling the plug.

Levon insinuated the hook into a fair-sized knot hole, waggling it until the rotten wood cracked enough for him to tear off strips with his hands. Soon there was an opening the size of a hand mirror at the head of the casket. Peering into it, Levon prepared himself for the sight of a skull, perhaps with bits of flesh like loose plasters still clinging to it, grinning mirthlessly at him.

Instead, what he saw was a foot. Her left foot to be exact. Hereword's limb. There were the dorsal interossei. The lateral, intermediate and medial cuneiform. The peroneus tertius and peroneus brevis. All of it intact.

They'd got hold of the wrong end of the grave.

Gingerly, Levon took hold of her big toe, tugging at it until her entire foot poked out from the hole, as if she'd kicked an opening in the coffin herself. Another yank and the foot detached itself from both the coffin and the rest of the skeleton. Levon didn't know what to do about this. Simon hadn't specified what part of Hereword he wanted, nor even how much of her he wanted. He thought back to his childhood days, mooching around the kitchen as his mother cooked supper. She was always adding a pinch of this or that to her soups, claiming it made all the difference to the flavor. Surely a pinch of Hereword would do then? Holding tight to the foot, Levon yelled up at Elias to reel him in.

Reversing back up the narrow tunnel, the unlikely name of Ignaz Semmelweis sprang to Levon's mind. In the 1840s, Semmelweis, then a fledgling doctor in Vienna, had discovered the cause of post-parturition poisonings by observing that medical students often rushed straight from the dissection rooms to the maternity wards without stopping to wash their hands properly. During a woman's labor, a student would literally insert death into her, delivering the disease that killed her along with her baby.

With Hereword's foot cradled against his chest, Levon felt that he, too, was delivering death into the world.

—What on earth is that? Simon demanded as soon as Levon emerged from the ground.

—Oh I'm fine, said Levon. Thanks for asking.

He handed the foot to Elias and immediately untied the rope from around his ankles, massaging them to encourage the blood to flow again.

—Where's the rest of her? said Elias.

—Down there. And you're welcome to fetch her. That's all of Hereword that I could get.

Simon pulled his toque down around his ears.

—That will have to do. Hand her over, Elias. Or should I say *foot* her over. Elias? *Elias*.

—Hereword was wearing those shoes over there when she hanged herself. One of them must have fallen off when she kicked over the chair. By the time I got there, Obdulia had found her and was trying to cram the shoe back on her mother's foot. Hereword was long dead by that time and her foot was too swollen. Quit it, I told Obdulia. The shoe doesn't fit. She wouldn't listen. Too many fairy tales at bedtime. She believed that shoe would bring her mother back to life.

—That's all very touching, Simon pouted, but we have more important things to worry about now. Give it here and I'll wrap it up.

From his pocket, he produced a crumpled plastic grocery bag that might once have held bananas or a jar of pickled beets.

—No, said Elias.

—What do you mean, no?

—What are you planning to do? said Levon.

Neither man could read Elias's expression. The light made a jigsaw of his features and, given that Levon and Simon each had a different picture of the situation, the line of his mouth might have been interpreted as either a fond smile, or a sneer, depending on how either man put the puzzle together. Ignoring them

both, Elias knelt on the pillow of snow displaced during the digging and produced from the wooden box one of the white shoes,
the left one, that Obdulia had laid on her mother's grave. He
inserted the fleshless foot neatly into the shoe.

—It fits her now, he said.

10

A SPECIAL MEDICINE FOR ONE THAT CANNOT SWALLOW ALTHOUGH NO INWARD MEDICINE CAN BE TAKEN FOR IT

Take the soiling of a Dog that is hard and white, powder it, and mingle it wel with English honey, spread it thick upon a linnen cloth, & hold it to the fire, and lay it all over the Throat down to the Channel bone, use fresh morning and evening, bind it hard to & by God's grace it will help.

D AWN WAS AN HOUR away and Levon, not yet sleepy, decided to keep a vigil over the dying night. Simon and Elias left him in the kitchen with only a curt goodnight before heading up to their beds, Simon bearing with him the bag containing Hereword's bones.

Elias, mindful as ever of the electric bill, turned off the light as he exited the room, having already forgotten about Levon.

He'd been sitting in the dark for a few minutes, his mind dwelling guiltily on that night's activities, when someone flipped the light switch, illuminating a large room, unrenovated since the 1950s, with a larder out back, a pine table and matching chairs, black-and-white linoleum tiles, scuffed from Berthe's bicycle tires, and cupboards painted sky blue.

Levon fully expected it to be Elias, or Simon, returning with last-minute instructions for him, who had turned on the light. Seeing that it was not—that it was, instead, a woman in a white gown, her skin white, her hair wild—Levon yelped and cowered, his face buried in his hands.

—Do I look that bad?

He squinted through his fingers at Obdulia, who stood in the doorway, perplexed.

—Um, no. I was . . . You startled me. What are you doing up?

She yawned and stretched, her flannel nightgown tight across her bosom and hips.

—I'm an early riser. Remember?

She lifted her chin and sniffed the air.

—There's a funny smell in here. Do you notice it?

The grave! Death. Corruption. He stank of it.

—Drains, he said quickly.

—Ah. That's probably it. I was going to make some breakfast. Do you want some?

—Sure, he said. Thanks.

—What are *you* doing up?

—Me? he squeaked. Thinking. That's all. Thinking.

—A penny for them.

Obdulia opened the fridge and removed a plate of butter, cream and a jug of orange juice. She set them on the counter.

—Sorry?

—Your thoughts. You're looking very . . . grave.

Levon almost jumped out of his skin.

—Not at all. I'm . . . um . . .

His fingernail scratched nervously at a globule of dried food stuck to the table. This brought to mind the last meal they had shared and the ugly scene that had ended it.

—I was thinking of, uh, your throat? he asked. How is it?

For an answer, Obdulia leaned over, her hands on the table in front of him. Freckles slid like pebbles down the slope of her cleavage. She opened her mouth wide, her shaggy mane of hair cascading all around her. Her proximity made Levon want to grab his chair and look around for a whip. Back, back, back! he screamed. Silently.

—Open wider, he said. Say Ah.

—Ah.

—Hmmm. It looks sore.

Her epiglottis was a corpse dangling on the gallows of her throat.

Obdulia shut her mouth but remained hovering over him, her lips perilously close to his, enticing him to . . . to . . .

In the center of the table stood a bowl filled with brown farm eggs. Levon picked up three.

—You know, he said chirpily, I used to be able to juggle quite well.

He almost knocked his chair over in his haste to stand up. Obdulia held out her hand for the eggs.

—I don't think you should, she said coolly.

—Please. I can do this.

She crossed her arms over her breasts and watched him, pleased that he wanted to impress her but too annoyed with him to salve his ego if he failed.

—Go on then. Give it a go.

Feet akimbo, he balanced two eggs in his left hand, the remaining egg in his right hand.

—Juggling is not simply a matter of throwing objects up in the air and then catch-as-catch-can, he said. There's a science to it. I have to tabulate height/weight ratios, speed/weight ratios, air denseness.

—The denseness of your audience.

—Huh? he said.

—I'm waiting.

Levon tossed the single egg into the air, followed quickly by the other two. His palms, open and waiting to receive the eggs, remained empty as they fell, with three distinct splats, like gold coins, onto the floor.

—I guess I'm out of practice, he said.

Trying not to laugh, Obdulia retrieved one of the broken eggshells. Flipping it upside down, she set it on his head, the jagged edge of the shell like a crown. Gluey with yolk, it stuck to his hair.

—My prince, she said.

He blushed.

—Just hand me the bowl, will you? Obdulia asked him.

Levon obeyed and she tossed him a dampened dishrag in exchange. He set to work mopping the floor.

—This reminds me of William Harvey's wife. Apparently, she had a parrot she was very fond of. The bird died unexpectedly one afternoon as it was being stroked on her lap. Naturally, Harvey, being Harvey, conducted a postmortem examination to discover the cause of death. He found an almost complete egg in its oviduct, but it was addled.

—And who *was* Harvey when he was being Harvey?

—Who was Harvey? Levon exclaimed, flabbergasted. Who was *Harvey?* He only made the most important medical discovery of all time.

Obdulia turned on the stove.

—Which came first, the parrot or the egg?

—Circulation of the blood! he cried.

—Oh.

She slapped a pat of butter in the frying pan. Outside among the eaves, pigeons swaggered like gangsters, their chests puffed out. There was a constant *phrrrr phrrrr phrrrrr,* as of a gambler riffling a deck of cards.

—It was a *very* important discovery, he assured her.

—I'm sure it was, she said soothingly. It's just . . .

—What?

—You won't be offended?

She swizzled the melting butter around in the pan to coat it.

—How do I know? You haven't said anything yet.

—It's just, said Obdulia, that I find men always have an *explanation* for things, or try to find one, but that doesn't necessarily mean that you *understand* anything.

He'd finished gathering up the mess and was running the cloth under the tap to rinse it.

—And what am I not understanding? he said.

Obdulia paused, egg in hand.

—Never mind, she said.

What *didn't* he understand? Where to start? With the fact that Mrs. Harvey might not have appreciated having her beloved pet slit open like a pea pod? That, perhaps, what she really wanted was for Mr. Harvey to sit down beside her, to draw her head onto his chest, to stroke her arm and kiss her neck. Had he done so, who knows? He might have understood circulation of the blood that much sooner.

Obdulia knocked the egg sharply against the metal rim of the fry pan.

Levon pursed his lips. Now she was cross. How was he supposed to deal with these mood swings, these half-uttered utterances that left him feeling so inadequate? Peevishly, he snatched the crown off his head and tossed it in the rubbish bin.

He would have excused himself and stomped off to bed but for the eggs. Buttery, fluffy. And just at that very second, ready to eat. He rubbed his hands together in anticipation.

—Those eggs are an improvement on Sweeney's, I'd say.

—Thank you. Who's Sweeney? Or should I know him, too?

Using a pot holder she carried the sizzling pan to the table. Levon grabbed two plates and two forks from the sideboard.

—An old friend, he explained.

He took a seat as Obdulia dished out the eggs. She sat down opposite him.

—Nonetheless, the name is familiar.

An anxious wind paced outside the kitchen window, now and then rattling the pane, rattling the trees.

—No, she said, it's gone clear out of my head.

She picked up her fork. Levon did the same. They regarded each other shyly, Levon thinking of William Harvey, Obdulia of Mrs. Harvey.

An egg between them and all of them addled.

In a Hen's egg I shewed the first beginning of the Chick, like a little cloud, by putting an egg off which the shell was taken, into warm water and clear, in the midst of which cloud there was a

point of blood which did beat, so little, that when it was contracted it disappeared, and vanish'd out of our sight, and in its
dillation, shew'd itself again red and small, as the point of a
needle; insomuch as betwixt being seen and not being seen, as it
were betwixt being and not being, it did represent a beating, and
the beginning of life.

11

SIR EDWARD TERTILS SALVE CALLED THE CHIEF OF ALL SALVES

The virtues and use of it

1. *It is good for all Wounds and sores, old or new in any place.*
2. *It cleaneth all Festers in the flesh and heals more in nine days than other salves cure in a moneth.*
3. *It suffers no dead flesh to ingender or abide where it comes.*
4. *It cureth the head ach rubbing the Temples therewith.*
5. *It draweth out rusty iron, Arrowheads, slubs, splints, thorns or whatsoever is fixed in the flesh or wound.*
6. *It cureth the biting of a mad Dogg or pricking of any venomous creature.*
7. It cureth all Felons.

ALTHOUGH IN some respects his life on the island was as regimented as it had been in prison, Levon's world became topsy-turvy, with day traded for night. His shift at the bakery began at midnight and he tumbled, bone-weary, into his bed around noon. He slept until nine or ten at night, woke up, showered, drank a pot of coffee, and read the headlines of the day-old newspaper Obdulia saved for him. Around quarter to twelve, he set off, torch in hand, along a shortcut (Center Road, through the Legacy's field, avoid the bull, climb over the split-rail fence, go around the mulberry bush), arriving for work on the dot of midnight in order to start the process all over again.

His routine varied so little that he was able to chart the passage of time solely by the moon's progress. He watched as it widened from a slit in a black stocking, tantalizing him with a glimpse of white flesh, into a round hole that was soon mended, only to have the seam rip once more.

It was five weeks since he had arrived on the island.

During this time, he feared he was dwindling into a specter, a ghost of his former self. His diminution wasn't physical; *physically,* he was more imposing than ever before. His arm and shoulder muscles had expanded from the effort of hauling giant sacks of flour. His thighs were bulky from kneading slabs of dough with his feet. No, it was Levon's spirit that was wasting away.

His interactions with the living were becoming fewer and fewer. Simon and Elias spent most of their working hours locked in the workshop, seldom speaking to him except to yell out an order. Oliver, Tango and the others continued to ignore him whenever possible. Sometimes, Levon rammed his hip into a table or brought his hand uncomfortably close to the oven on purpose just to reassure himself that he was still alive and sensate to the outside world.

Late in the evenings, before heading to work, and while Berthe and Obdulia slept upstairs, Levon haunted the house. He searched for signs of life—a life from which he was excluded—in various domestic tableaux. He licked a teaspoon left on the counter, a patina of dried coffee tarnishing the bowl. He thumbed the pages of Obdulia's open book, the wings spread like a grounded bird's. He stroked the silken material of her torn blouse, deliberately pricking his finger on the darning needle pinned to the fabric for safekeeping. He spun the record she had been listening to on the phonograph: "Mamma morta," the desolation in Maria Callas's voice maintaining its tremulous pitch, never altering despite countless revolutions.

He listened to the *cric-crac* of wood contracting from the cold.

Alice's death five years ago had turned Levon inside out, trapping him inside the cage of his own bones. Space between the bars was too scant for even a finger to wriggle through and that, he had convinced himself, was how he preferred it. Yes, people continued to twitter at him and yes, Levon repeated their banalities back to them—he couldn't help being polite—but he never allowed anyone to *touch* him. Grief had draped a black cloth over his cage where inside, he could tuck his head down onto his breast and remain hidden from view.

In some respects, prison had been a blessing. His cage there was real. The outside world was banished the second he entered it, and all thoughts of Alice with it. He would not drag her in there with him, not into that grim place. So, he never mentioned her name. He tacked no photos of her to the wall. He did not dream of her.

Until recently.

On his release, there was Alice, waiting outside the prison gates, expecting him to collect her as she had when she was a schoolgirl, her hand clasped in his, trusting in him to keep her safe. He'd failed her the afternoon of the accident and now, even her memory was slipping away from him. His dearest companion, and his confidante.

Or was it simply his grief that was fading? Not all at once, but in bits, like the Cheshire Cat, its taunting grin the last to go.

He couldn't replace Alice in his heart, not ever. And yet, Levon found himself wanting to lift the cloth from his self-imposed cage, even if it was just the teensiest bit, to allow a finger of daylight, delightfully warm, to ease between the bars and coax him into wakefulness. Lately, and he wouldn't say that Obdulia had anything to do with this, but lately, his instinct to, to *flock* had definitely been aroused.

I am lonely, Levon realized, astonished. That's what's the matter with me. I am lonely. I am lonely.

Such were his thoughts as he lay in his bed, watching sunlight creep through the window and, like a thief, assess the value of each item in the room, pausing first in front of his desk, then at his bathrobe draped over a chair, and, lastly, at the trunk of clothes and books his mother had shipped to him.

Levon stretched to take the kinks out of his spine. His bed sagged low in the middle causing his spine to curve like a boomerang. His nose almost touched his knees. His muscles were sore, and he was dizzy too, as if he really had been hurled through the air as he slept, whirling, whirling, until he was returned to this bed in obeisance of a complex law of physics he knew nothing about.

Shifting onto his side, he stared out the window, without blinking, into the sun, then clamped his eyes tight, scaring up a swarm of bees that buzzed, alarmed, inside his lids. Wait. The buzzing was real. He opened his eyes. His alarm clock. But it was only three o'clock. He had meant to set it for 9 P.M.; in his exhausted state, he must have reversed the numbers.

Groaning, he surrendered to his insomnia. He flung his

pajama-clad legs over the bed, inserted his feet into a pair of slippers neatly lined up, waiting for him, and, after donning his bathrobe, wandered into the hall.

His bedroom was on the third floor between a bathroom and a storage room. A trap door led to the attic. Levon referred to it as the servants' quarters and there was a utilitarianism about the decor not evidenced elsewhere in the house. No floral-patterned wallpaper, no rugs, bare bulbs screwed into sockets. Levon had been offered a room off the kitchen; he preferred the third floor because it enabled him to zoom down the ramps Berthe had built for bicycling indoors, an indulgence he associated with the childhood pleasures of sliding down banisters and tobogganing.

The grandfather clock in the alcove below ticked *go go go*, flagging him with its pendulum. Levon spread his bathrobe, balanced for a moment on his toes, then with a running start, launched himself down the ramp. Third floor to second, then a plateau—he lost a bit of momentum here—before reaching the stairs, the final leg, connecting the second level to the ground floor.

He generally preferred not to check his speed until the absolute last second, bouncing along the short carpeted runway between the edge of the ramp and the vestibule door, skittering to a halt right before he was due to slam into it. This time, however, two things happened to alter the normal course of events. First, his bathrobe caught on a loose nail in the banister, jerking him backward for a split second before the fabric ripped and he was released at full throttle, like a slingshot. Next, Obdulia arrived unheralded. She stepped smartly through the door, colliding with Levon at the exact moment he exited the ramp, bursting

with the thrill of his own momentum. He could not stop himself
in time. With a shriek, he knocked them both backward onto the
vestibule floor in a heap, Levon on top and Obdulia, breathless,
underneath.

—Oops-a-daisy, he said.

Levon had not brushed his teeth and his whiskers, like flecks
of loose tea, rubbed against her chin. Even worse, the supple,
lumpen surface under his own triggered memories of his bed
and, to his horror, he felt his body melding to hers where she
dipped in the middle. He scrambled off her.

—What *were* you doing?

Her green eyes appeared to be unspooling across the floor
until he twigged that it was her scarf. Locks of her hair made a
break from their prison of bobby pins. There was a smudge of
dirt on her cheek. Levon bent down and wiped it off with the
sleeve of his robe.

—Running down the ramp, he admitted.

He extended a hand to help her up.

—Oh, she said. I used to do that when I was a *child.*

Stung by her implied criticism, he tightened the sash on his
bathrobe and said:

—Haven't you ever felt like turning back the clock?

Obdulia removed her gloves and beat her coat with them to
remove the dirt.

—I tried that once. Wind a clock backward and it breaks.

She took a step, then halted, grimacing.

—Are you hurt? he asked.

—My ankle. I may have twisted it.

—I'm sorry. Here, let me help you.

—I can manage, she said.

Something about her demeanor disturbed Levon. Testy. Reserved. Knocking her down had been an accident, after all. She wasn't going to hold it against him, was she?

—I'd like to help you, he said.

There it was: a distinct snort. Her nose was out of joint, no question. Manfully, he ignored it, extending his arm so that he could encircle her waist and support her to a chair. She side-stepped him. Quite deliberately! Well, one thing was clear: she wasn't going to allow herself to be held against him.

—Excuse me, she said.

And limped, in a rather more pronounced manner than was necessary, he suspected, down the hall to the kitchen.

Having raced ahead, Levon hastily pulled out a chair for her. Obdulia accepted it grudgingly. Before she could stop him, he went down on his knees to assist her with her boots. *I'm Cinderella in reverse*, she thought. Her cheeks colored. The nail on her big toe, overgrown, ridged and slightly yellowed, had burrowed a tunnel out of her stocking. She'd meant to trim it last night.

—You're not usually home at this hour, he said.

—They're dissecting frogs this afternoon at the school, she said with a shudder. I asked to be excused.

Levon rotated her ankle, which was very slender given the weight it had to bear. Certain parts of the body ought by rights to snap under pressure of their burden more often than they did. He marveled at the construction of the human frame.

—Tell me if you feel any pain.

With a sharp downward thrust, she split open the belly of her sheepskin coat, revealing a red woolen dress underneath.

—And what good would that do? she said.

—If you're hurt then we need to, well, to fix it.

—Hah!

She scowled at him. Her slender eyebrows descended on the furrow in her brow like snakes into a crevice. He rocked back on his heels, perturbed.

—What's the matter?

—I saw you skulking down at the ferry dock, she said.

He chewed his inner cheek.

—You did? When?

—A week ago. Last Monday.

—Oh.

—You were going to leave without even saying goodbye, weren't you?

—Of course not.

—You *were*.

He was.

He had left work after his shift at the bakery in a foul temper. Simon had criticized Levon's batch of *bâtards*. (Sons of *bâtards*, he'd called them.) Elias had sniped at Levon's method of kneading. (What did *he* know about it!) The assistants trod on his toes (*So sorry*, they purred) and pinched his baking powder. And he'd blistered his fingers on the oven to boot. Fed up, Levon had stormed out of the bakery, griping and grumbling. He no longer cared about his parole requirements or about Obdulia or about anything but escaping this blasted island. He didn't belong here. His presence here was a horrendous mistake.

So, instead of heading for Berthe's house, he stomped down to the ferry dock, determined to catch the next boat.

He might have tried leaving sooner except that February's weather had been unusually tempestuous. Storms buffeted the island, layer upon layer of snow dropping over the island like shed petticoats. Conversation on the street became impossible as words were ripped from open mouths and carried away. No ferries ran. Only the elderly enjoyed the gales. Released from gravity, scarves a-fluttering, and with the wind at their backs, they were transformed into veritable Nijinskys, performing *grands jetés* through the air, somersaulting over their grandchildren's heads, rejoicing in their rebellion against decrepitude.

The sky that afternoon was the color of tin. If Levon stretched his hand up and flicked his fingernail at it, he believed he would hear it reverberate throughout the silent village. The street was deserted apart from Georgia Fen, holding a paper sack of groceries under one arm, her sleeping infant under the other. She nodded cheerily as she passed him. He saw the Legacy brothers sitting in the window of Moses's Bar, *The Gazette* split in sections, sports and comics, between them. They waved at him to come in for a drink. He pointed at his watch, saluted them and hurried on.

Of course, Levon hadn't checked the ferry schedule beforehand; he arrived at the dock just in time to see the boat pulling away from it.

Standing there, watching the boat retreat, he heard the frantic giggles of children playing in the nearby schoolyard. *I'm the king of the castle and yer the dirty rascal!* He pictured the tiny hill the kids were so eager to claim for their own, the energetic thrust and parry of attacker and defender. And then he heard another sound, one that caused him to prick up his ears.

Storming up and down beside the children was Obdulia's voice. She was a teacher's assistant and must have been on playground duty that lunch hour. Her voice started off low as she chided them to do up their coats, or to put that stick down, then rose to an almost hysterical pitch as she screamed at them to *stay put*. At the time, he wasn't aware of her watching him; now it seemed that she had been. Perhaps her plea hadn't been directed at the children but at him. It was Levon whom she wanted to stay put.

He sighed and rubbed the bridge of his nose briskly a few times.

—I admit I thought about leaving, he said.

—What stopped you then?

He tweaked her big toe.

—I couldn't figure out when the damned ferry left.

Obdulia chortled.

—Oh it depends on the Captain. He's very idiosyncratic.

—How does anyone ever get across the lake then?

She shrugged.

—Islanders seem to know when it's time, that's all.

—An internal clock, you mean.

—Yes.

—Then, he smiled, I guess it's not time for me to leave yet.

Obdulia gave him back a smile as broad and white as a nun's wimple. She noticed, as Levon's head bent once again over her ankle, that his brown hair swirled and eddied at the crown. How lovely it would be to twirl those long strands around her fingers and trim off the excess, to watch the heaviness vanish and his curls bounce back in a sprightly fashion.

—I hardly see you these days, she said.

—Simon works me pretty hard.

—How is it going? The contest, I mean. He won't tell me a thing.

—I have nothing to do with that.

—But I thought . . .

—I'm a hired hand, that's all, he said firmly.

He wouldn't be the one to tell her. He couldn't risk it. Certain rooms existed in which a person could lose everything. Ordinary rooms most of the time, with curtains and family photos and a comfy armchair. But magicians' tricks were at work. A bank employee, his office no bigger than a broom closet, simply waved his pen and *hey presto!* a pensioner's house disappeared. A young girl was wheeled into an operating room and, *hocus pocus*, she was sawed in half and died. Two teenagers crossed the threshold of a bedroom, shutting the door behind them. When it opened again, *abracadabra*, a mother and a father stepped out.

This kitchen, with its faded linoleum and its lingering smell of cooked porridge, might easily become such a room if Levon told Obdulia that, even as they spoke, the essence of her mother was being distilled and added to dough that, like a human, responded to a person's touch, whose "skin" tasted salty when licked, but who had no heart, no blood, no memory.

Upstairs, on his desk, was Levon's copy of *The Odyssey*, the pages open to Book XI: Odysseus's descent into the underworld. Sunlight, pouring as it did over the rest of his room, had left the book in shadow but Odysseus's words to his mother, oh those words, blazed forth in Levon's memory:

And I, my mind in turmoil, how I longed to embrace my mother's spirit, dead as she was! Three times I rushed towards her, desperate to hold her, three times she fluttered through my fingers, sifting away like a shadow, dissolving like a dream, and each time the grief cut to the heart, sharper, yes and I, I cried out to her, words winging into the darkness: "Mother—why not wait for me? How I long to hold you! So even here, in the House of Death, we can fling our loving arms around each other, take some joy in the tears that numb the heart. Or is this just some wraith that great Persephone sends my way to make me ache with sorrow all the more?"

We can't embrace shadows, Levon wanted to say to Obdulia, but let us fling our arms around each other. In that embrace, he thought, we might find joy.

Afraid of what her response to that might be, all he said was:
—Coffee?
—All right.
—Say please, he admonished her.
—*Please.*
He got to his feet, his knee joints crackling like twigs in a fire.
Berthe's kitchen was well organized and within a minute, he was turning the crank of the old-fashioned coffee grinder, reveling in the sensation of those hard nuggets of caffeine breaking down: the oily, slightly chocolatey scent. He filled the appropriate compartments in the coffee pot and while the liquid bubbled on the stove, *phlp-phlp-phlp*, he unearthed the cream pitcher and sugar bowl. Last of all, he fetched two mugs from the shelf, the handiwork of a local potter, one of several living on the island. Their crafts were displayed in the dim and dusty corner of the general store, next to pyramids of tinned peas and mosquito repellent. The potters, he imagined, had relinquished well-paid

jobs in the city, lured to the island by the rustic setting and dreams of the artisan's life. Their work, though, seemed infected with memories of the daily grind they'd supposedly left behind. The pottery was sturdy, practical stuff, not designed in an artistic sense but merely shaped by two hands throttling the clay as it went around and around on the wheel. The mugs he now filled with coffee were enlivened only by their salmon-pink glaze.

The lit stove had taken the chill off the room. Stifling, Obdulia unwound her scarf and, inevitably, thought of Hereword. She experienced a spasm of irritation at the jerk of grief that continued to yank her off her feet, back to the past, to moments that could not be undone. *My life has been suspended right along with my mother's.* Hypocritical of her, really, to castigate Levon for his fun and games earlier when she worked so hard to preserve the twelve-year-old child she'd been when Hereword died, with all the vividness of that child's pain. There were even times, if she was being honest, that she wasn't sure she even *liked* her mother, a woman who had such fight in her and yet, in the end, when it counted most, had directed it all inward, against herself. Hereword hadn't been able to bear the silly gossip about her marriage, her sense of failure. Plenty of relationships hung by a thread, not all women put it to the horrible use her mother had.

Obdulia watched Levon bustle about the kitchen making coffee (for *her!*). Happiness stunned her.

—Coffee's up.

—Thanks.

She stirred such a quantity of cream into her cup, the black liquid paled almost to white.

—Why don't you like frogs? Levon asked her.

—I do in fairy tales. "The Frog Prince." Stories like that.

—But science is jam-packed with stories.

—Not fairy tales.

—All right, he conceded, the apple that dropped on Newton wasn't poisoned (although the one poor old Turing bit into was) and Galvani didn't exactly kiss his frog . . .

—Who?

—Um, nobody interesting actually.

He scooped three teaspoonfuls of sugar into his coffee and stirred.

—But, he said, have you ever considered how nerve impulses are transmitted?

—Not really.

—Harvey did. In *Exercitationes De Generatione Animalium*, he wrote that certain nerves did not attract like a magnet, or exert a pulling force on muscle, but were "only like pipes and not like reins."

A professorial tone snuck into Levon's voice, like a small boy into his father's shoes.

—And then there was Otto Loewi. In 1921, he had a dream, the identical one, two nights in a row. The first night he made a note of his dream, then fell back asleep. When he woke the next morning, however, he couldn't decipher his handwriting. The second night, when the dream returned, he forced himself awake and scurried off to his laboratory. I'm sure it was a modern affair by 1921 standards but I like to envision a dungeon with flagstones and cobwebs. Bats circling. At any rate, two frogs' hearts were laid out on the table. One had its nerves intact, the other didn't.

He grinned at her.

—The hearts were attached to each other, he said. Not by sentiment, hah hah.

—Hah hah, Obdulia laughed obligingly.

—They were attached by a system of tubes filled with Ringer solution.

—What's that?

The truth was, Levon didn't exactly know what Ringer solution was but he wasn't prepared to admit it.

—Um . . .

She raised one eyebrow.

—Well, he said, *ringer* means double, doesn't it? Ringer solution doubles for, uh, blood. A blood substitute.

—How can you substitute blood?

—You re-create it with chemical components, I guess. That happens with food these days. Even though a package might claim a product is All Natural, what they mean is that the ingredients found in the food naturally are then re-created in the laboratory.

—But that's not the same thing at all.

Levon blushed.

—No, he admitted. Not quite.

—I didn't mean to interrupt, she apologized. You were just at the bloody part.

—Ah, yes. OK. Loewi began the experiment by stimulating the vagus nerve of the first heart, slowing the beats. The Ringer solution transferred to the second heart, the one without nerves, and it slowed down also, just as if its own vagus nerve had been affected. When he accelerated the beat of the first heart, the same thing happened.

—I don't understand.

Levon scratched his head, musing on how best to illustrate a process he was confused about himself. After a moment, he seized hold of her hand. Her arm, encased in its red woolen sleeve, stretched across the table and Levon shoved into her palm his warm, pink-glazed mug.

—Pretend that your arm is the vagus nerve and my coffee cup is the heart. Chemical impulses travel along your arm—the vagus nerve—like so, and then bind with the heart. The heart is the receptor. That's what Loewi discovered. The nerves themselves didn't motivate the heart, it was the particular chemical that was released along the nerve that told it to slow down or beat faster.

—I see.

—It's probably not quite as simple as that. Well, it wouldn't be. I mean, um, the heart. It's a . . . it's complicated, isn't it? But that's the gist of it.

Obdulia, still hanging onto his mug, pressed it against her cheek, savoring the lingering heat. The truth was she'd stopped listening the second he took hold of her hand, distracted utterly by her desire for him. Kiss me, she begged him silently. Lean across this table and kiss me *right this second.*

—Why won't you tell me about your mother? he said.

She frowned.

—I've already told you.

—Not about her death. I know how she died. Tell me the beginning.

—Like, Once upon a time?

—Sure.

She diverted a flow of hair around the bay of her ear, and sighed.

—I'm no good at stories. Really, I'm not.

—I bet you could be if you tried, he said.

—Stories were my mother's department.

At the base of Obdulia's throat was a hollow deep enough for a bird to nest in, the skin white and silken as the membrane of an egg. Levon's finger itched to stroke it, to warm it with his hot breath and hatch from it words of endearment.

—That's a start, he said. She was a good storyteller?

—Yes, but . . .

—But what?

Absently, she patted the scarf that now lay curled up on her lap like a cat.

—Have you ever played the telephone game? she said.

—You mean where a person starts off with a word, whispers it into another's ear and so on?

—Yes. By the time the word has come full circle it's completely unrecognizable from what it was to begin with.

—So?

—I'm afraid of doing that to my mother. Rumors and half-memories are all I really have left of her. What if the person I end up telling you about is someone she never was?

Levon propped his head in his hand. He drummed his fingers on his chin.

—Listen, he said. William Harvey was once called on to pronounce whether five women, condemned as witches, actually were. He proved, scientifically, that they were not and their lives were spared. So, when he heard about an old woman who claimed that she really was, in fact, a witch, he set off to visit her. She lived alone at the edge of a heath, near Newmarket, and regarded this stranger on her doorstep, not surprisingly, with distrust. Thinking fast, Harvey introduced himself to her as a wizard, whereupon the old woman, believing he was one of her kind, invited him in. As soon as they were both safely inside the house, away from prying eyes, she made an odd, guttural sound in her throat, calling forth an old toad from underneath the bed. She explained to Harvey that the toad was a spirit. Her witch's familiar. Anxious to examine the toad more thoroughly, he proposed, as fellow witches, that they ought to take a celebratory drink together and sent the woman off to the tavern for some ale. While she was gone, he quickly set to work killing and dissecting her toad. Apart from its having a stomach full of milk, obviously the toad's supper, Harvey discovered nothing untoward about the innards of it, nothing otherworldly at all. The old woman returned in due course. When she discovered her toad cut up into little pieces, she was *furious*. She flew at Harvey, her claws out, beating at him with her fists. He tried to persuade her that the toad was just a toad, not a familiar. But science was nothing to her.

A sharp intake of breath.

—Are you, said Obdulia, comparing my mother to a toad?

—I'm saying that facts won't necessarily alter a familiar spirit.

Obdulia gazed out the window. Yesterday's snowfall had rethreaded the trees, bobbins of lace spinning out an intricate pattern, yards and yards of it, displayed for a discerning customer to rub between her fingers and test the quality of it.

—Let's go for a walk, she proposed.

Levon's bony knees were almost touching hers, like two generals who have ridden ahead of their troops to negotiate a treaty. Levon had no wish to break off discussions now.

—Your ankle, he spluttered.

—I'll manage. It's not far.

A sparrow landed outside on the windowsill, pecking busily at the crumbs Obdulia left for it each morning.

—All right, he sighed. Where are we going?

Obdulia set the cup, Levon's cup, once more to her lips.

—You'll see, she said.

And drained his heart to the dregs.

A half hour later, his teeth brushed, his hair brushed, his galoshes on, Levon was stumbling behind Obdulia, her long legs easily cutting a path through the papery snow. His life, lately, was a drama in which he had a part but was never certain about his lines, his business or his stage directions.

—Where are we *going?* he said fretfully.

—Not far.

Mist had slipped like a gray stocking over the island, the sun's heel peeking out through a hole in it. They followed the shore-line, the ground rising up and up, through a smattering of trees, until they reached a ridge about two miles from Berthe's house. Below them was an inlet formed from two long fingers of rock, the tips almost joined together to indicate this wide, and no wider. Branches poked out from the crevices in the rock face, some gnarled and thick, others underneath younger and slimmer, all with twiggy fingers extended at the ends of them, like arms waving goodbye through the crack in a train window.

—There's a secret path that leads down to the lake in summer, Obdulia explained.

—That's nice, he croaked. Let's step back a little, shall we?

—Do you want me to tell you this story or don't you?

—Can't you tell it to me *over there?*

He pointed inland.

—Maybe that's our problem, she mused. We step back from the edge when we ought to get closer to it.

Obdulia wiggled her toes farther over the ledge and raised her arms as if to fly. Levon bunched her coattails in both hands to rein her back in, holding on to her for dear life.

—I don't know what you mean by *our* problem, he said. Please come away from there.

—Are you telling me to calm down?

—I'm asking you to *sit* down.

—Oh.

—That is, if you're so all-fired determined to stay here.

A compromise seemed to be in order. Obdulia sat on the edge, her legs dangling down. Having ensured that she wasn't about to topple over, Levon sat down behind her.

—It's a bit awkward, she said. I have to look over my shoulder to see you.

—You could turn around.

—No, she said after a short pause. I want to look forward when I tell you this.

—Ready when you are.

—How do I begin?

A boiled-milk skin covered the frozen lake, inviting the wind to give it a good stir.

—You just do, he said.

—My grandmother, Rose O'Riley, was a midwife. She birthed almost all the children on the island, including the quintuplets who work for Simon. She untangled that skein of arms and legs, drawing those babies out into their proper design, as skillfully as Ariadne might have done.

Rose's red hair was always pulled smooth into a cap. Her jaw jutted forward, sharp enough to cut bread with, people said. All the mothers were grateful to her but also afraid of her. It was well known that Rose's tongue was barbed. Less well known was the reason why. It was to protect what was pastured inside her—a love as defenseless, and blind stupid, as a sheep.

That love was for her husband, Liam. He had a long thin face like a lantern that lit up from inside when he was happy and threw terrible shadows when he wasn't. His feet were splayed as if he couldn't decide which direction to go in. And he obviously couldn't since, more than once, Rose birthed a child that had Liam's nose or mouth. She would snip the umbilical cord and lay this swath of fabric, cut from her husband's cloth, across the new mother's breast. Rose's pride forced her to admire it, sick inside as she was. Liam wasn't a bad man, she knew, only weak. Susceptible to flattery, forgetful of where his bed was after a drink or two. Rose was no fool, only foolish about *him*. Time and again, she swept his infidelities under the carpet, forgetting that, if enough dirt accumulates, the fabric will rot and disintegrate.

Rose was almost forty and still had not conceived. Thinking a child might save her marriage, she tried every remedy she could think of: Mad-dog Scullcap, Flesh and Blood, True Maidenhair, Blueberry Root, Apple of Sodom, Rupturewort, Life Everlasting, Jack-Jump-Up-And-Kiss-Me. She stuffed a clip of Liam's hair in the mattress. Bathed in rain water under a full moon.

Two more years went by, however, and no baby.

Grief over her childlessness turned her like autumn does a

leaf. She grew brittle and frail. Her cheeks lost their high color. She drifted through her days.

Then, one evening, Rose retired to bed early with a crippling headache. She was feverish and her palms left sweaty imprints on the sheets. Had she overdosed herself with some herb? Coneflower, perhaps, which incites the senses? Unable to sleep, she got out of bed and opened her volume of *Culpepper's Herbal,* to a passage that read:

> *But there is a vital spirit in every seed to beget its like; there is a greater heat in the seed than any other part of the plant; and heat is the mother of action.*

Craving a cooling breeze, Rose unlatched the kitchen door and stepped outside into her garden: her seed, her labor. Ordinarily this was her sanctuary but that night, the plants mocked her with their fecundity.

For some reason she was ravenous and she crouched down to dig in the crumbly dirt for some rampion. She used her nightgown to wipe off the clumps of earth and gnawed greedily at the root.

A furnace raged inside her body, stoked by air so dry it almost crackled when she drew it in; stoked, too, by the peppery rampion. She imagined the ground being scorched underneath her bare heels as she hastened out of her garden, through the woods, toward the lake. Pine cones cut her feet, sparks of fiery blood shooting out of her. Branches clawed at her nightdress, slowing her progress, until, impulsively, she tore it off and abandoned it, hanging it on a tree: a ghost, a premonition of her future daughter's fate.

—And then, and then . . . Obdulia faltered.

—Yes? prompted Levon.

—Rose went for a swim in the lake.

Levon poked Obdulia on the shoulder.

—*And?*

—That night my mother was conceived.

—Whoa, he said. I think you skipped an important bit.

She twisted to face him. Red fists of cold boxed her cheeks.

—I *told* you I was no good at stories.

—What's swimming in the lake got to do with getting pregnant?

—A lake is a body.

—Of water.

—A body nonetheless, she stated. Rose told my mother she was a lake child. A water baby.

—That's nonsense!

—It's a *story*, she reminded him. And it's how Rose explained to Hereword why she had no father. Three months before she was born, Liam ran off with one of the Fen girls.

—Oh, said Levon. In that case . . .

—Hereword knew it wasn't the truth but for years, Rose pretended and so did she. They often came here in the evenings to sit, like we're doing now. My mother knew Rose had her reasons but for the longest while, she didn't know what they were. Every night, though, at exactly the same time, Rose's body would tense, straining to catch a certain sound.

—What was it?

—On quiet nights, you can hear the 10:04 freight train whistle clear across the lake. The same train that smashed into Liam's car, killing him and his girlfriend the very night they eloped.

Let's go down there by the train, Rose would say to my mother, and together they'd listen for the whistle. Rose imagined she could hear in it the crunch of metal, the tinkle of glass. Bones cracking. Her world ending. That train circled back to the same spot night after night and so did Rose's fury at being deserted. After a while she stopped living and just relived the evening she came home from a birthing to find a note, a little slip of paper with a few paltry words on it saying sorry, sorry, goodbye.

Levon was uncertain how to respond to this.

—That was a good . . . story, he said.

—Thank you.

She scooted back from the edge and stood up. As if attached by a string, Levon rose to his feet with her. The snow had penetrated Obdulia's coat and her rump was freezing. She rubbed it to get the circulation going. They ought to get going themselves. The mist was evaporating and the moon was out in full, a bully pushing the struggling sun under the lake, holding it there.

—The hour grows late, she said.

—I've never understood how an hour can grow, said Levon. An hour is an hour. Sixty minutes, neither more nor less. It can't grow longer or shorter or bigger or smaller. An hour is not a beanstalk or a . . .

—Oh for heaven's sake, Obdulia shouted at him.

And then she did an extraordinary thing. A marvelous, enchanting thing.

She kissed him.

She flung her arms around him and kissed him.

The heart, consequently, is the beginning of life; the sun of the microcosm, even as the sun in his turn might well be designated the heart of the world; for it is the heart by whose virtue and pulse the blood is moved, perfected, made apt to nourish, and is preserved from corruption and coagulation; it is the household divinity which, discharging its function, nourishes, cherishes, quickens the whole body, and is indeed the foundation of life, the source of all action.

Obdulia's lips puckered into a perfect *o* and Levon's mouth did too. Their lips met, and in that moment, Levon knew that he had finally entered his looking-glass world. Her desire, her need, her fear (yes, he saw it in her eyes) perfectly mirrored his own. And when they parted, shocked and pleased at their mutual boldness, he was aware that this new world *looked* the same—there was the lake, the cliff, the trees. He recognized all of it—but it *felt* utterly different.

Exhaling a sigh, Obdulia's mouth retained the shape of an O. Sweeney's *o*.

I loved a woman who lived on that island once.

This time, Levon kissed *her*. A long, slow, deep kiss that left them both panting for air when at last they parted.

—My goodness, she said.

Levon nodded.

—My goodness, he echoed.

12

PRETIOUS WATER TO REVIVE THE SPIRITS

Four gallons of strong ale, 5 ounces Aniseeds, half pound liquorish, sweet mints, Angelica Barony, Cowslip, Sage, Rosemary flowers, sweet Marjoram of each three handfulls. Distil in a Limbeck—infuse one handful of aforesaid. Cinnamon and Fennel, Juniper berries bruised, red Rosebuds, roasted Apples and Dates sliced and pitted, distil again, sweeten with Sugarcandy, and take Ambergreese, Pearl, Red Coral, Hearts horn powdered and leaf gold put them into a fine Linnen bag, and hang it by a thread.

B ABBITT'S FEAST was three days away. All over the island, pots and kettles seethed on stoves, their leaked odors competing fiercely with one another before the contest had even begun. Normally talkative neighbors fell silent, secretive in their dealings with the greengrocer. Families grew dyspeptic from too many tastings. Occasionally, as Levon strolled through the village, hand in hand with Obdulia, a spoon would be thrust out an open window and down his gullet. The anxious cook, ignoring Levon's coughs and splutters, solicited his opinion as to the saltiness of a broth, the sweetness of a batter. More to Levon's taste were Obdulia's kisses, which he solicited frequently, freely offering his opinion as to their saltiness or sweetness.

Crowds of children rushed to the dock after school, loitering there to gawk at the visitors who arrived daily on the ferry, leading out goats tethered to a string, or bearing haunch-shaped packages wrapped in butcher's paper, birds in cages, a live turtle, a dead hare, boxes stained yellow from turmeric and other exotic spices, hot sauce from Texas, sambals from Indonesia, thick brown apothecary's bottles labeled Secret Ingredient #1 and Secret Ingredient #2, and wicker baskets of pomegranates and bread fruit and passion fruit. An actor dressed as Abiathar Babbitt wandered up and down the main street, handing out lollipops and flyers to advertise the big day. Trestle tables were set up in the community hall, already decked out with swags of dusty red velvet. A podium was raised for use by the Mayor and the guest judge—famed chef Zalman Grant—as well as for Morris Legacy, who would read the same lesson his forebear had ninety years before.

Ovens, in constant use, had raised the temperature of the island to such a degree that snow was melting unnaturally fast. Buds, tricked into thinking it was April, had appeared on the trees within the last week. Grass, too. The air was milder: a light shawl wrapped around the island in place of the heavy winter coat it had worn all season. And with these changes came a giddiness among the islanders, a feeling of hopefulness that a resurrection inevitably inspired. Spring was returning—the rains lately were a sure sign of it, Obdulia assured Levon—and the island opened wide its mouth to receive the proof of it.

In sharp contrast to the rest of the island, Simon's bakery was silent and gloomy as a tomb: no humming mixers, no scrape of knives, no slap of dough on a table. His assistants had been dismissed for the week and unswept flour lay strewn about everywhere, lending a marble whiteness, a sepulchral tone to the place. The only hint of color came as the afternoon sun, moistened by a spit of rain, dabbed at the palette of the bakery's stained-glass window. Berthe disapproved of Jesus's bright pink cheeks and azure robe. The scarlet tint of his lips. Frippery! She pictured biblical scenes in black-and-white, as in the Bible.

—She's ready for baking.

Simon's face, normally so composed, looked hastily drawn— all harsh lines and shadows—as he addressed the assembled company: Elias, Berthe and Levon.

—Let's see it, Berthe said impatiently.

—Yes, Elias concurred less heartily. Let's see her.

Levon noticed that they had all taken to referring to Hereword as *her*, or *she*, or *it*. Never by her name.

—Right, said Elias to Simon, unveil this masterpiece of yours.

They were all jittery, dry-lipped, their eyes fastened on the refectory table in front of them as fiercely as a starving bird's waiting for a worm to show itself.

Pinching the ends of a white cloth between his thumb and forefinger, Simon gently, gently, rolled it back.

Elias crossed his arms over his chest.

Berthe's hands clenched and unclenched, as if working the hand brake on a bicycle.

Levon bit a hangnail on his thumb.

The sun hid behind a cloud.

Simon moaned, unable to contain his disappointment. Last night, all alone, as in a frenzy he applied the finishing touches to his creation, he truly believed he had succeeded. But here, in the dismal light of the dying afternoon, his moment of exaltation gave way to horror at the tangible proof of his failure. He saw it

in the others' faces. He saw it in *her* face. Catastrophe! Here
before him was the thing he'd dreamed of, labored for, had
deprived himself of sleep and health for. And for what? This?
This hideous lump of dough, its jaundiced skin stretched thinly
over molded muscles and well-proportioned limbs, its mouth a
rictus, its eye sockets empty, unseeing, awaiting the glass eyes
that stared at him, accusingly, from a jar on the counter. This
creature was not Hereword!

Where had he gone wrong? He had measured all the ingredients with meticulous care. The recipe was not at fault, it had
worked before. Was it the bones? Too small an amount, perhaps?
Not enough of *her* in this Hereword. A pinch of bone was all he'd
used in the end: her baby toe. Grinding it with his mortar and
pestle had proved tougher than he'd thought. An unexpected
squeamishness had overcome him so that, at first, he made little
progress in pounding the bone to powder. His muscles seized and
cramped. It was so very, very hard. Bones break all the time—his
own foot once, his father's fractured wrist—and yet, this toe had
resisted all his efforts to grind it down. Simon discovered that the
only way he could do it was to recall an unpleasant memory of
Hereword, a muscular hatred that drove his arm on past the
point when it was sore and wanted to quit.

He was a boy again, or as much a boy as he ever was. Ten,
eleven. He had been curled up in his tree cave, alone with his
thoughts; alone, that is, until he heard the crinoline rustle of
dried leaves. Someone was approaching; the tread was too heavy
for an animal's. Had the other boys overcome their fear of the
woods? If so, he was lost. They would poke and pry him out of
his hidey-hole with sticks and run him to ground as if he were a
barn rat. No, it was a girl. She was humming a tune, badly, notes

skimming the melody like stones over water. Girls were even worse than boys. Willful. Capricious. A girl might keep his secret, or she might blab it. You never knew with a girl. Secrets were passwords to gaining entrance with the popular crowd and to be one of them was to be protected against their cruelties. *Fatty fatty, two by four, couldn't get through the kitchen door.* Popularity was its own cave.

Simon pressed himself up against the tree trunk. He willed the girl to pass him without stopping. To leave him be.

No such luck.

She dropped her basket, filled with the dirty cloth caps of toadstools, at the cave's mouth. Then she pivoted, backing her rear end up against the tree trunk and swinging her head down between her legs. Hereword O'Riley! She was about the same age, and almost as unpopular a child at school as he; the kind of girl who brought words like *mendacious* and *cornucopia* into her conversation as if they were old pals she had no intention of introducing to the other kids. Her clothes were always stained with dandelion juice.

Simon tried to speak but his mouth was stoppered by the cork of his knees. Hereword's red hair had flopped down over her head like a hood. Her knee socks bunched around her ankles. She stared back at Simon, blinking owlishly. Then, without a word, she straightened up, reclaimed her basket and departed as quickly as she'd come.

That night, Simon dreamed he was back in his cave, naked, a baby in the womb. He peered out of the forked, mossy opening in the trunk at the world he was about to be born into. Javelins of moonlight struck the ground, quivering, among the trees. An owl demanded to know *who, who, who* dared invade his woods.

A wolf was baying, its jaws unhinged, its sore throat open to swallow the lozenge moon.

Simon cowered. He didn't belong out there. He wouldn't go!

But all at once, the cave began to contract, squeezing him, pushing him out. Stunned by this betrayal, his tiny feet scrabbled to find a toe hold in the cave's moist lining. The tree heaved again, shuddering, propelling him further outward. His newborn's fingers, pliant as candle wax, were of no use. Slivers of bark peeled away in his hands.

—*Mother*, he screamed.

He wasn't ready to leave her.

He felt a biting wind clamp down on his ankles.

Mother.

Where *was* she?

His heart was still too vulnerable to being broken.

Why didn't she *protect* him?

He felt the wind's forceps begin to drag him out. He felt . . . he felt.

He *felt.*

At school the next morning, drained and miserable, Simon sat slumped in his seat across the aisle from Hereword. Had she told? *Had* she? He could scarcely bring himself to acknowledge the possibility. All through morning announcements, he fixed his gaze on his ink-stained desk, the engraved record of previous schoolchildren's lives. *Becky loves Ralph. Fuck math. Ralph loves Sonja.* Finally, unable to stand it a second longer, Simon glanced over at Hereword. She had been sitting at her desk, patiently waiting for him to notice her. Her eyes were blank; it was her hands that told the story. She cupped her fingers around her mouth, forming a cave. Slowly, deliberately, she brought the edges of her fingers together. Her lips were sealed.

She never went near his cave again.

He was grateful to her.

He never forgave her.

Simon sidled past Elias, who was also circling the table, traveling clockwise to his counterclockwise direction: Hereword's face, and time, stopped in the middle. Was that what was wrong with his creation? His monster. Had he ground his own anger into her bones?

Rain tapped, more forcefully now, on the window panes.

Paying no heed to Simon's visible distress, Elias stopped until he was level with Hereword. He placed his hands on his bent knees for support, ignoring the creaking protest in his back. Hereword used to say he was a bull, perpetually jousting with the red flag of encroaching age.

And now there she was, or wasn't. Perhaps if this Mummy could be animated, its muscles and joints galvanized into movement, Elias might recognize this thing Simon had created as Hereword. In life, she had been a nervous person: constantly running her fingers through her hair, jiggling her knee, adjusting her bra strap, dropping things: eggs, plates, tactless comments.

Those were mostly directed at the visitors who streamed through the house. Visitors, always visitors. Come to see her, of course, not him. Female bottoms of all shapes and sizes usurped his favorite armchair while Hereword sat opposite them on a footstool, her head tilted to the side, listening to their tales of woe. After a bit, she sprang up, rapped the women smartly on their knuckles or shins, or plucked a strand of hair from their heads. The visitor would shrink back in her seat, ruing her decision to come, until Hereword patted her shoulder, kindly, saying, *I have just the thing for you*. Elias had no faith in the brews Hereword concocted but those women did. They always left his house optimistic. Restored to life.

If he was being honest with himself, Elias had to admit he was resentful of the time and care Hereword had lavished on those women, most of whom she didn't like any better than she did him. She never said to him, I have just the thing for *you*. He wasn't worth her consideration. Well, he was not the kind of man to fall on his knees, as those women did, and open his heart to her. He hid his pain, his needs, in a maze of emotions. Not that he hadn't dropped plenty of clues; it was simply that Hereword never showed the slightest inclination to follow them. Maybe if she had, he'd never have gone back to Berthe.

Berthe! He glanced over at her, wondering what she thought.

Lengthening shadows fell on the ground like soldiers after a battle. Perhaps it was the dimming light, but Berthe didn't think this inert lump resembled that goose, Hereword O'Riley, one *whit*. Where was her vicious tongue? The sharp claws that had perched on Elias's arm, digging into him, whenever they had passed Berthe on the street? She poked at the bald skull and her finger sank into the soft dough, right up to her wedding ring. She quickly withdrew it, surreptitiously polishing the metal clean against her skirt.

When she had married Elias, his ring was the same one he'd used in his vows to Hereword. It was so tight, they weren't able to remove it without cutting it off; and, since he'd paid good money for it, he kept it on. Berthe, knowing his frugal ways, had lodged no complaint about this. She often fancied she saw, though, imprinted on Elias's ring, Hereword's tarnished ghost, flitting around and around his finger. She had never left him, not really, and never would.

Simon jabbed his finger in the direction of the body.

—What are we going to do? he said.

—About what? Elias asked.

—*Her.* She's hideous. Obdulia will never accept her. It will be a failure and we'll all be laughingstocks.

—I know nothing of the kind.

—I told you it wouldn't work, said Levon.

—Is it too late to start over? Berthe asked.

Her matchstick fingers, the nails polished red, accidentally struck Elias on his arm, igniting his temper.

—And risk the same thing happening again? he raged. Don't be stupid.

—Elias!

—Shut up and let me think.

He placed his fingers against his temples. His expression was so self-consciously thoughtful he seemed a parody of a man thinking. This was true. He had not a single idea in his head but the one he'd started off with.

—We go ahead as planned, he said at last.

Simon flung his arms out, hammocks of flab swinging underneath them.

—Obdulia won't swallow it.

—We go ahead, Elias shouted, as *planned.*

A spring thunderstorm was now well under way. Rain beat against the walls and doors like an angry mob clamoring to get in. There was a crack of thunder and then a blade of lightning sliced the sky, cutting off the electricity.

—Someone flick the lights back on! Simon cried.

Elias, closest to the wall, jiggled the switch. Nothing happened.

—The storm's cut the power, Berthe said.

Even as she said it, she felt like the character in old horror movies who always states the obvious—*The lights have gone out! We're all alone! Look! There's a knife sticking out of his chest!*

—Never mind. Levon, there are candles behind you.

Levon reached behind him until he discovered on the shelf an open box. His fingers closed around the cold, waxen corpse of a candle.

—Who has matches? I don't.

All around him there was a patting sound, like a stunned bird recovering its wings, as everyone checked their pockets.

—Not me.

—Me neither.

—Nope.

—How do I light it, then?

—The oven, said Simon. Use the flame from the oven.

—Can't someone else do it? he asked.

Elias's menacing voice stepped forward out of the shadows.

—No.

—*Please.*

—Go on, Levon, Berthe shooed him.

—Very well.

Reluctantly, he shuffled toward the back of the room, negotiating as well as he could various obstacles in his path, following the sound of the oven's muted roar, lit specially for the purpose of baking Hereword. Levon's job, in lieu of the assistants, was to brush the interior of the oven with a wet broom, cooling it a little, as well as introducing moisture to create steam.

He was meant to have done it earlier and hadn't, loathing the very idea of such proximity to the flames. Now he stretched the cuff of his shirt down over his fingers to protect himself from the heat and unlatched the door. Before he could step aside, a mammoth furry heat bounded out, leaping at his chest, ripping into his lungs. He flung his arm over his face for protection, retreating a couple of paces until, with the oven door ajar, the worst of the heat had slunk away. Levon lowered his arm.

—What are you doing back there? Elias yelled. Get a move on with that light.

Levon stared at the black hole of the oven door and his stomach knotted. The familiar, sour taste of panic flooded his mouth.

—Coming!

Knees trembling, knowing what he would find, Levon stooped and looked inside.

There she sat. The little girl. She hugged her knees to her chest, her cowlicks a flaming halo around her head. A small, infinitely sad smile flickered at the corners of her mouth. She stared back at him as if to say, *Let me out, please let me out. I don't want to be eaten.*

Alice had regarded him with that same sense of trust in his ability to rescue her. And how gladly he would have traded places with her if only he could. But he'd stooped to tie his shoelace, or pull up his socks, he couldn't even remember now, and in that second, that fraction of a second, he'd lost sight of her, and of all the dangers that threatened her.

Levon bowed his head. He had been too late, he was always too late.

He'd failed, or felt as if he had, both Alice and the little girl.

When all things are already in a languishing condition, the heart dying away, there intercedes between these two motions a short time of stillness . . . And while by little and little the heart is dying, you may see after two or three beatings of the auricle, the heart will, being aroused, answer, and very slowly and with difficulty bestir itself and beat once.

And now there was Obdulia.

Oh, the imponderable weight of loving someone. The terrifying responsibility of it. He'd forgotten this bit. His eyes filled with tears.

—I'm sorry, he whispered. Truly, I am.

To his astonishment, the little girl seemed to answer him. In a voice as soft as ash, she whispered, *Somehow you'll manage it. I know you will.*

Two wisps of smoke escaped the oven. Levon saw in them the image of the little girl's parents as, dressed in their gray homespun outfits, they were led out of the house, handcuffed. He had watched as an officer placed his hand, like a priest's, on the man's head to protect it from injury when he stooped to enter the police car. Behind him, the woman waited her turn. She had a pudgy, innocuous face—the sort that was always being mistaken for someone else's—but that afternoon her features were transformed by her state of ecstasy. In her simple, twisted mind, she had triumphed over the monster she believed her daughter to be. She had slain it and was now free. In vanquishing the demons that plagued her, however, the mother had herself become a demon: both to her daughter and to those who had loved her daughter.

A fury overcame Levon then, chasing away all other desires but that of ridding himself and Obdulia of this demon, Hereword, which Simon and Elias had created.

This witch.

The true Hereword lived on elsewhere. Over the last few weeks, at her house in the woods, safe from prying eyes, Obdulia had shared with Levon not only her bed but also what she laughingly called memory-rubbings, her mind passing swiftly back and forth over a faded image until the outline of it, embedded in a charcoal shadow, became better defined: Hereword sashaying around the house, a set of books balanced on her head to improve her posture. Or fetching pails of sand from the beach to build their sand castles indoors when Obdulia had chickenpox. Or reading aloud in the evenings from the *Encyclopaedia Britannica.*

I am Alpha and Omega, the Beginning and the End. Cuddled up to Levon, Obdulia gave birth to her own mother, bringing her into the world through stories of her. She adopted Hereword's voice, her mannerisms and, at times, also her mother's fearfulness and despair. But these moments were less frequent than before, just as Levon's pangs over his loss of Alice had abated too. It was almost as if, far from fading away, Alice was closer to him than ever; as if her spirit had entered into Levon, her exact opposite in temperament, revealing herself in his tenderness toward Obdulia, his selflessness, his newfound contentment. For these had been Alice's qualities, never his, never before.

—Levon! Berthe shouted.

—I'm almost done.

He inserted the candle into the oven, holding it forth almost as a sword, a means to do battle on Obdulia's behalf.

The refrigerated blood returns to the heart, the fountain, the dwelling-house, where by naturall heat, powerfull and vehement, it is melted and is dispens'd again through the body, being fraught with spirits.

Heat. Fraught. Spirits.

The wick ignited.

It was then that the idea came to him.

13

FOR ONE THAT HATH NO
SPEECH IN SICKNESS

*Take the juyce of Sage, or Pimpernel, and put it in the patient's
mouth & by the grace of God it shall make him speak.*

OBDULIA EXTENDED her hands toward the fire, spreading her
fingers so that flames seemed to jump out from between
them. Despite this, she couldn't seem to shake the chill from her
bones. It was as if the old house knew Obdulia was abandoning it.

There would be no warmth in its farewell to her.

A branch of the oak tree lashed the window and rain clip-
clopped against the roof, the drum of hoofbeats accelerating as
the storm worsened. Obdulia imagined she was in the dim
recesses of a carriage, being driven by who-knows-what as she
hurtled toward an unknown destination.

Impatient with herself, she shrugged off these fancies and
returned to her task.

At her feet was a scuffed suitcase, an overnight case of her
grandmother's that she had dragged down from the attic. To
open it, she had to slide two metal bars on either side of the
handle toward each other, until the lock was released. The hinges

were rusty and protested with the prolonged yowl of a cat being rousted from its nap.

Obdulia tossed into the case a balled-up pair of wool socks. She was sorry to be missing Babbitt's Feast and secretly regarded Levon's insistence that they leave the day before as silly. Not that Simon's entry was worth sticking around for. Levon had confessed it at last: a gingerbread house. Honestly! And after all she'd endured of Simon's hints of unveiling something spectacular.

Let's travel light, Levon had said. And when it came right down to it, there was very little she wanted to take with her. *No ghosts*. She smiled to herself. Did Levon really think a ghost could be folded and packed away like a sheet?

She added her nibbled-on copy of *Grimms' Fairy Tales*.

The lining of the case was a burgundy-colored rucked satin with an extra pocket running the width of the lid. For the first time, she noticed an odd bulge in it. Fearful that a mouse or other small creature had crawled in and died, Obdulia grasped the very edge of the fabric and pulled it cautiously toward her, bending over to examine the interior. Something glinted there and her heart played hopscotch, skipping ahead several beats.

It was a mirror. Silver-plated but elegant nonetheless, with the initials *HO* engraved in scrollwork on the back. Holding the mirror up, she recognized it as Hereword's. How often Obdulia had seen her mother's face reflected in that glass, peeking over Hereword's shoulder as she applied her lipstick, or raked her pale cheeks with scratches of blush.

How happy she was to see it again! To see herself in it again. After Hereword's death, Obdulia had spent hours staring into it, conversing with her own image as she dreamily envisioned her mother's face. There was Hereword's smile—everyone said so—

and her hair and her eyes. The mirror was enchanted, Hereword a prisoner inside it. Obdulia had carried it with her everywhere. She took it to school, ate with it beside her plate, kissed it: repeated back to it the bedtime stories her mother had told her, as best as Obdulia could recall them anyway. At night, she tucked the mirror into bed with her, her ear resting against the cool glass, listening to a heartbeat that she convinced herself was Hereword's.

Then, one morning Obdulia awoke to discover the mirror had vanished. She searched among her rumpled bedclothes and under the pillow but couldn't find it. When questioned, Elias remained tight-lipped, disclaiming all knowledge of its where-abouts. She knew he'd taken it, threatened by the presence of her mother's guardian spirit. Shortly after that, he had whisked her away from here, into Berthe's house, into Berthe's life, where any mention of Hereword was unwelcome. Obdulia had learned to swallow her mother's name in order to protect it from her step-mother's withering comments, from her father's cutting anger.

Soon that would all be behind her. Levon was right, the quicker they were gone from here the better. Oh, she enjoyed so much being able to speak of Hereword with him. To say that pre-cious word *mother*. My mother.

She held up the mirror, entranced by the disembodied head of the young woman floating before her. A mother-to-be.

Would Levon notice? No, how could he? There were no signs yet. After all, she'd missed only one period. Still, she was regular as clockwork. Obdulia blushed to recall that her mother, too, had conceived during her first time. She patted her stomach, as if to reassure both of them, mother and child, that each was there. She hoped Levon would be pleased by her news.

After some deliberation, Obdulia returned the mirror to the pocket of the suitcase. *No ghosts*, he'd said and she had agreed. But it was only herself she saw in the glass now. What harm could it do?

Her eye fell on the watch Levon had given her.

Five past five.

Late.

Where *was* he?

14

FOR BURNING OR SCOLDING

Take Alehoof one handful, the yolk of an Egge, and some fair water, stamp them and strain it, and therwith wash the grieved place til the fire be out.

LEVON KNEW in his bones what he had to do.
Cupping the burning wick, he returned to the others gathered around the table. Candlelight threw them into a relief none of them felt. Berthe fiddled with her wedding ring. Simon, normally so ebullient, had buried his face in his hands. Elias, his eyes popping out of his head, snapped his fingers at Levon.

—About time, he said. Bring it here. We've got to get her in the oven.

—Pat her and prick her! Berthe cried out.

—I'm sorry, said Levon firmly. I can't let you do it.

Simon pinched the bridge of his nose and sighed heavily.

—Don't be an idiot, Levon. We've decided.

—*We* never decided anything. Elias did. You said yourself this . . . this . . . whatever it is, is a failure.

—I admit she's not all I hoped for. But what is?

What is? Simon repeated softly to himself.

—For the last time, give me the light, said Elias. You and Simon can carry her to the oven.

Levon was running out of time. He gazed at the figure laid out on her silvery bier of baking sheets. Of course, it would be easy enough to just run away. Leave Elias and Simon to their mad scheme and the consequences be damned. He and Obdulia would be long gone, he'd make certain of it.

I don't want to be eaten.

No. Levon owed it to the little girl, to Alice, to Obdulia. Perhaps even to Hereword. He had to end this once and for all. He had to put to rest those nightmares from childhood in which fairy tales had bled into real life, with real-life consequences for the little girl. Now, he would set things right. It was the witch, and not Gretel, who must go into the oven.

Levon would have his true, happy ending to the story.

—All right, he said. You win.

Pretending to acquiesce to Elias's demand, Levon passed him the candle, deliberately tilting it so that drops of scalding wax splattered Elias's palm.

—Careful with that, you goddamned idiot!

—Poor lamb, Berthe clucked. Let me see it.

Elias gave his burned hand to Berthe to nurse. While she administered to Elias, Levon, still holding the light, saw his chance. Wielding the candle like a sabre, he lunged at Simon, pointing it at his breast. Simon shrieked and backed away from the table. Levon threw the candle at him, extinguishing the flame but freeing his own hands to snatch up Hereword from the table.

She was heavier than he'd anticipated, and more elastic. Her head and legs flopped over his arms like the ears of a Basset hound. She kept elongating, as if she were made of Play-Doh—which, he remembered, she sort of was—and, as he raced toward the oven, praying he wouldn't trip in the darkness, he had to keep rescooping her. Behind him, he heard gasps of bewilderment, then a scramble to follow him.

—Levon! Stop!

—Drop her. *Drop* her.

—Out of my way. Move.

—I *can't.*

—Ouch! What the hell is that?

—*Me,* you oaf.

—Jesus Christ!

Levon paid no attention. He had at last reached the door of the oven, which he'd left open for this very purpose. Wadding the dough up into a tight ball, he lobbed it into the fire.

The others were at his heels.

—Save her, Simon, save her! Elias screamed.

—It's no use. Look.

Simon crouched down and watched, not minding the heat, as the dough charred and blistered. He had to admit that the witch, Hereword, fitted into the oven quite snuggly. Like a cave, really. Her very own cave.

—The Tour de France, Berthe moaned. I'll never get there. Never!

—I'm sorry, Levon stammered. I am.

—Why? Elias whispered hoarsely. Just tell me that.

—I did it for Obdulia, said Levon. I love her.

All three turned to him. His cheeks glowed more brightly than the oven.

—You *what?*

—I love her, he repeated. I do.

Berthe threw up her hands.

—Oh, she said, this just keeps getting better and better.

Levon pointed to the oven.

—Why can't you lay Obdulia's mother to rest? Levon said. She has.

Elias's words struck at Levon with the speed and venom of a rattlesnake.

—Don't you believe it, he said.

—What do you mean?

—She takes after her mother. At least, she'll try to. Mark my words.

A nasty cackle issued from Berthe's throat.

—True, my love, true.

Simon fanned the air. The smoke grew thicker, more acrid. Berthe covered her mouth and turned away.

—No. She's happy, Levon insisted. Now. With me.

—A fairy tale, Simon sneered. But the real dangers for you and for her don't come from the witches and ogres. No, no. Those are just for show.

Simon stepped close to Levon and whispered in his ear.

—The real dangers lie inside of you. Oh yes. That's what trips you up in the end. Greed, excessive curiosity, plain stupidity. You can't fight *those* with magic swords or good-luck charms. No, Hereword will never be laid to rest. She will rise again, just as I promised. Up to the ceiling, no doubt, only—look closely—it will be Obdulia's face gazing back down at you.

Outside the window, a needle of lightning pierced the sky, trailed by a jagged suture to close up the wound. Levon felt sick, exhausted. He wanted to be away from here, far from this room and these people.

At that moment, he heard inside his head a childish refrain. Alice used to chant it as he chased her around the garden, pretending, for her sake, that she was too fast for him to catch; until one day, she was.

Run run as fast as you can. You can't catch me I'm the ginger-bread man!

And Levon did.

He ran out of the bakery.

He ran through the village.

He ran through the woods.

He ran to Obdulia.

15

AN ELECTUARY FOR THE PASSION OF THE HEART

Take Damask Roses half blown, cut off their whites and stamp them very fine, and strain out the juyce very strong, moisten it in the stamping with a little Damask Rose water, then put thereto fine powder Sugar and boyl it gently to a thin syrup: then take the powders of Amber, Pear and Rubies, of each half a dram, Ambergreese one scruple, and mingle them with the said Syrup til it be somewhat thick, and take a little thereof on knife's point morning and evening.

TWO TEACUPS, their insides pearly as the moon, sat side by side on the tray. Obdulia twiddled them so that their handles touched. Obdulia and Levon. Husband and wife. She blushed at her silliness. Her happiness.

Just then, the kettle, plump as an opera singer, began to sing. Because of this, although she'd been waiting for it, she did not hear the front door slam, nor the sound of Levon's footsteps, until she had lifted the kettle off the fire and the shrieking subsided.

—You're here! she cried out.

His face lit up at the sight of her. How she adored that.

—I'm here.

Levon threw himself onto the sofa next to her and kissed her cheek. She stroked his.

—Are you all right?

—Right as rain, he smiled.

He wrung out a sodden sleeve.

—You're late. Was it busy at the bakery?

—Very. Are you packed? he said.

Obdulia pointed to her suitcase. He nodded.

—Good.

She poured steaming water from the kettle into the teapot. Levon could see the join where the spout had been recently mended.

—Well, she said brightly. Here we are. Back where we started.

Levon groaned.

—Oh God, I hope not.

—Now, now, she soothed him. I meant having tea. Do you want some?

—That depends. What's in it?

She frowned, pretending to be hurt.

—It's Earl Grey.

Lovingly, he brushed a strand of hair from her neck.

—All right then. Shall I pour?

Obdulia picked up the teapot. The heat of it was almost more than she could bear.

—No, she said. I'll be mother.

acknowledgments

I WOULD like to acknowledge the affectionate support given to me by my family and friends during the course of writing this book. I could not have done it without them.

Special thanks to Maestro, Rachel Calder, Stephen Dixon, Laine Falk, Lindsay Fleming, Zulfikar Ghose, Steven Heighton, Liesel Litzenberger, Rob Nixon, Rose Richardson and Zal Yanofsky, Maribel Sosa, Bill Swainson and, above all, Heather Wardle.

The writing of this book was aided by generous grants from Ontario Arts Council and Canada Council and by the equally generous grant of time and tranquillity given to me by the Corporation of Yaddo.

about the author

KATE STERNS was born in Toronto in 1961 and grew up in Kingston, Ontario. Her first novel, *Thinking about Magritte*, was published to acclaim in 1992. She now lives in Montreal.